The Bachelor and Spinster Ball

Janet Gover

little
black
dress

First published in 2009 by
LITTLE BLACK DRESS
An imprint of HEADLINE PUBLISHING GROUP

A LITTLE BLACK DRESS paperback

1

Cataloguing in Publication Data is available from the British Library

ISBN 978 0 7553 4716 2

Typeset in Transit511BT by Avon DataSet Ltd,
Bidford-on-Avon, Warwickshire

Printed and bound in Great Britain by
Clays Ltd, St Ives plc

Headline's policy is to use papers that are natural, renewable and
recyclable products and made from wood grown in sustainable forests.
The logging and manufacturing processes are expected to conform to the
environmental regulations of the country of origin.

HEADLINE PUBLISHING GROUP
An Hachette UK Company
338 Euston Road
London NW1 3BH

www.littleblackdressbooks.com
www.headline.co.uk
www.hachette.co.uk

This one is for John,
with love.

Acknowledgements

Volunteer firefighters are amazing people who give their time and effort to help their community. I've seen them in action many times, and am in awe of their dedication and skill. I'd like to thank Dick Irwin of the Queensland Rural Fire Brigades Association for all his help. My thanks also go to Rob and Pam Anderson for information on bushfires and building a cottage.

B&S balls are a regular feature of Australian rural communities. They are the greatest fun, and raise money for very good causes. My thanks go to Michelle Omyla, organiser of the Bull Dust and Bow Ties Ball, for all her advice.

I also want to thank Rachel Summerson for keeping me on the right path, and my brother Kenneth for advice on utes and how to make them explode.

A big thank-you goes to John Hocking for song lyrics, guitars, proofreading and the website.

And, as always, thanks to Catherine Cobain and the team at Little Black Dress for making it happen.

Bec later realised that her argument with her mother probably saved the schoolteacher's life.

It wasn't unusual for Bec and Jean O'Connell to argue. They'd been doing it pretty frequently since Bec came home from the city. As usual, the fight had been over something stupid – what to watch on television. Bec had a passion for romantic old movies. Her mother used to watch them with her, but lately it seemed Jean had developed a dislike of romance and movies; or possibly of her daughter. The upshot of the argument was, of course, that now neither was watching television. Bec was standing on the back landing of their home behind the post office, trying to calm her temper, while her mother had disappeared into the kitchen in a huff.

For a fleeting moment Bec wished she smoked. Like Marlene Dietrich, she could lean elegantly back against the wall and take deep drags of a cigarette through a long ivory holder. She would then stride off confidently to solve her problems and marry Gary Cooper. Instead, she closed her eyes to take a long breath of the warm air. She could smell the eucalyptus and the dry earth, hear the gentle night sounds of the small bush town that she loved. This tiny cluster of wooden buildings in the middle of nowhere might not appeal to everyone, but being here restored her soul. Coming back to Farwell Creek after three years away hadn't been everything she had hoped, but home was still home. She felt her temper begin to ease. She took another deep breath and suddenly she could smell her non-existent cigarette. Smoke?

Bec's eyes flew open. She turned in a circle, sniffing the air, trying to decide where the smoke was coming from. Then she saw the flicker of light.

She opened the door behind her. 'Mum!' she shouted. 'Come here. Quick!'

'What's the matter?' Jean O'Connell was still in the kitchen, easing her mood with a cup of tea and a newspaper.

'The school's on fire.'

The older woman came at a run. The back of their house looked towards the town's tiny school, and the old wooden church beside it. The flickering red light was getting brighter by the second.

'It's not the school, it's the teacher's cottage,' Jean said.

Bec looked at her mother, her eyes widening with shock. They were both thinking the same thing. At almost ten o'clock on a weeknight, there was only one place the town's schoolteacher was likely to be.

'You get Rod,' Bec instructed. 'I'll run over to the pub.'

Jean nodded and headed for the side gate. The police station was next to the post office. Like the O'Connells, the town's only policeman lived in a residence behind his place of work.

Bec sprinted down the side of the house and past the dark post office. The pub was on the opposite side of the town's main road, and through the lighted windows she could see people moving around. It took less than a minute for her to get there.

'There's a fire,' she said as she stepped through the open door.

Conversation stopped. Beer glasses were lowered and all eyes turned to Bec.

'Where?' asked the man on the nearest bar stool.

'The school. It's Miss Mills's cottage.'

'Oh, that's all right then.'

There was a smattering of chuckles, but every man in the place got to his feet. They all ran to the school. There was no need to take cars. Everything in the town of Farwell Creek was within walking distance of the pub.

Jean was there, standing by the schoolyard gate, gazing at the burning building. The fire was already out of control. Flames licked through the open windows and under the eaves. Like most of the buildings in the town, the teacher's house was made of wood long baked tinder dry by the harsh Queensland sun. It was burning like the fires of hell. There was nothing they could do to stop it.

'Where's Rod?' Bec gasped, panting slightly from the run.

Before Jean could answer, Sergeant Rod Tate appeared on the small front veranda of the teacher's cottage. He had some cloth wrapped around his mouth for protection against the smoke. He was half carrying a thin middle-aged woman wearing a cotton nightdress. Miss Mills had one arm around the policeman's shoulder. With the other hand, she was covering her mouth against the smoke pouring through the open doorway behind them. Rod's arm was around the woman's waist as they staggered down the stairs and across the dry yard towards the growing crowd of watchers.

'Are you all right?' Jean moved forward to help.

Miss Mills was racked by a fit of coughing. Jean put her arms around her until the spasm had passed. The schoolteacher drew herself upright, then, becoming aware of the people around her, shrugged off Jean's supporting arm and folded her arms across her chest.

'Rod?' Jean turned her attention to her neighbour.

The policeman wiped the sweat from his face and nodded. He took a few deep breaths of clean air and then looked back at the burning building.

'Has someone called the fire brigade?' Miss Mills asked. Her voice was rough from smoke and coughing, but her accent was still unmistakably English.

Bec almost felt the collective sigh of the townsfolk.

'There isn't a fire brigade to call,' she answered for them all.

'I beg your pardon?' Miss Mills was incredulous. 'No fire brigade?'

Bec shrugged as around her the townsfolk moved subtly away from the criticism in the teacher's voice, all the while watching the fire.

'I should have known.' The teacher shivered despite the heat of the night.

Her house was ablaze from end to end. The flames leaped high into the night sky, dancing to the music of their own crackling roar. The heat was almost painful on Bec's face. One of the windows gave way under the force of the fire, with a harsh crack of shattering glass.

'Shouldn't we do something?' Bec's best friend Hailey Braxton appeared at her side. Hailey's house was the other end of town from the school, but by now, the word was out. The few people who weren't already here soon would be.

'There's not much we can do,' the joker from the pub said.

'There is something we can do,' Rod Tate said in an official voice. 'We can stop it from spreading. There's a lot of dry grass around here. We don't want to lose any more buildings.'

His words were met with a murmur of agreement.

'Girls,' Rod turned to Bec and Hailey, 'we need something to beat the flames out with. Got any empty bags lying around?'

'Chaff bags?' Hailey said. 'We've got lots of them.'

'Great. Get them.' Rod turned to the small crowd of townsfolk. 'We're going to need to wet those bags and beat out the burning grass.'

Bec wasn't listening any more. She and Hailey ran back to the main street towards the big corrugated-iron shed that was Farwell Creek Farm Supplies and Feeds. The sign above the door said *K. and B. Braxton, Props*. But they weren't the proprietors any more. Hailey and Bec now ran the store. Hailey pulled her keys from the pocket of her jeans and let the two of them in. Bec flicked on the lights and they headed towards the back of the building. A large black and white cat blinked sleepily at them from the top of a pile of brown hessian sacks.

'Move, Cat.' Bec unceremoniously pushed the animal out of the way.

'Put them in the back of the ute,' Hailey said. 'I'll see what else we can use.'

Bec hefted an armload of bags into the back of the white Ford work utility parked in the loading dock. She knew the whole town would turn out to help fight the fire. That was the way a small town worked. They would need a lot of bags. She threw in a second bundle. Hailey appeared beside her, clutching an assortment of tools, including shovels and a heavy crowbar that was almost as tall as she was. She tossed them in the back of the ute with a loud clatter and got into the driver's seat. Bec unlocked the big loading-bay doors and pushed them open. A couple of minutes later, they were back at the school, where the cottage was burning even more ferociously than before. The crowd had grown. It seemed the entire population of Farwell Creek was there. All forty-one of them, including the children. The fire was now moving through the long grass, driven by a rising breeze. If it wasn't stopped, it might get as far as the school itself. Bec jumped out of the ute. They had the bags. What they needed was water.

With a hesitant rumble and the rattle that was so common to farm vehicles, a small truck pulled up a couple of metres away. It was very old and very dirty, but the water tank on the back was just what they needed. It wasn't enough to put out the fire, but it would soak the chaff bags. A tall man stepped down from the cab of the truck. His dark hair was cropped short and the skin of his face was tanned deep brown by many hours in the sun. He had shoulders broad enough to hold the weight of the world. Everything about him exuded an aura of calm strength in any situation.

'The cavalry has arrived,' Bec joked, but she was very glad to see him. A crisis was always less scary when Nick Price was with her.

'Good call, Nick,' Hailey said.

Nick had grown up with Bec and Hailey – attending the same school that they were now fighting to save. He stepped close to Hailey's ute, towering over both girls as he effortlessly lifted out the pile of chaff bags. He tossed them to the ground near his truck, then opened a valve on the tank. Water poured out, instantly soaking the bags.

'Thanks, Nick.' Rod Tate joined them. 'Come on, everyone, grab a chaff bag!'

The residents of Farwell Creek didn't need to be told twice. They could see how easily the fire was advancing. Each person grabbed a wet bag and turned towards the school. They spread out in a line in front of the advancing fire, and began beating at the flames with the soaking sacks.

Bec caught her long brown hair into a ponytail, then took her place in the line, Hailey to her right and Nick to her left. There was no time for talk. All she could think about was the relentless march of the flames as she fought them, all the while struggling to find some breathable air under the smoke. They moved slowly backwards as the flames crept forwards, until they found themselves with their backs against the schoolyard fence.

Nick placed a hand on the waist-high wooden rail and vaulted the fence with an ease that Bec envied. He immediately set his boot on the wire mesh below the rail, pushing it towards the earth to open a gap the girls could easily slip through. All along the fence, in the light of the burning cottage, other firefighters were doing much the same thing.

'Are we winning?' Bec asked, panting heavily.

'I'm not sure,' Nick said. 'Let's hope the wind doesn't get any stronger.'

He raised his chaff bag again. Bec was impressed by his stamina. Her own bag felt as if it was made of lead. She raised her aching arms above her head and bent again to her task. The fire had edged four or five metres into the school's playground when the wind gently changed direction. After a moment's hesitation, the flames turned back on themselves and began to die. The school was safe, but the teacher's cottage was lost. With a thunderous crash, the roof collapsed into the centre of the fire, sending bright sparks floating high into the night air. The firefighters ceased their struggle and watched, fascinated by the final destruction of a building that had stood for longer than most of them had been alive.

'Keep your eyes open for new outbreaks,' Rod called to his weary team. 'Spread out downwind.'

Everyone was tired, but still people moved to form a loose ring around the burning building, watching in silence as the flames began to die down. Every few minutes a flurry of activity would break out where a burning ember had ignited a patch of dry grass, but it soon became clear that the worst was past. The heart of the fire was now just a great pile of fallen wood, glowing red as flames licked at the few timbers that remained uncharred. Darkness was returning.

The firefighters, soot-stained and sweating, stood silently catching their breath. The glow of the dwindling blaze reflected in their eyes, giving them an almost demonic touch. The smell of smoke was still thick in the air, but after the roar of the flames, the night seemed suddenly very quiet.

'So, now what?' someone asked.

'We need to keep a watch on this all night,' Rod said.

There was a general murmur of assent. If the wind strengthened, the fire could break out in a new direction.

'There needs to be three or four of us here all the

time,' the policeman continued. 'We'll do a roster, so everyone gets some sleep.'

'We can organise coffee. Food too if anyone wants it,' Jean offered.

'Thanks, Jean,' Rod said.

Bec noticed that even after fighting a fire, Rod had that little extra time and that special smile for her mother. For the umpteenth time, she wondered why Jean had never noticed. Or if she had, why she hadn't done something about it.

'I left a beer on the bar,' one of the pub patrons pointed out. 'I wouldn't mind going back to finish it, if all the work here is done.'

'It's after midnight,' Rod said, 'so technically the pub should be shut. However,' he added before anyone could protest, 'I'm sure the law allows for the publican to serve refreshments to volunteer firefighters. I'll drop by later to talk about the overnight roster – so I'm going to need a few of you to stay sober.'

Bec grinned into the night. There wasn't much Rod didn't understand about policing a small outback town. He knew when the rules should be applied, and when they should be bent.

'Thanks everyone,' the policeman added as people started to move away. 'Good work.'

'I suppose it could have been worse,' someone muttered as they walked off.

'Yeah. We could have lost the school.'

'Even worse – it might have been the pub.'

There was a smattering of tired laughter.

Bec looked around and spotted Miss Mills. She was sitting in the front seat of a parked car. The door was open and the dim interior light showed her drawn and tired face. Very few of the departing townsfolk bothered to speak to her. Bec shook her head. That was unlike her town, where everyone helped everyone else. But the teacher wasn't popular. An unmarried woman in her late forties, she had come from England on a sponsored deal – her passage in exchange for teaching in the outback for a year. She had made it pretty clear from day one that Farwell Creek did not live up to her expectations. It was too small, too far from civilisation, and not at all romantic or adventurous. Nor was Miss Mills quite what the town had expected. She wasn't a bad teacher, which was lucky, because she was all they had, but she and the townsfolk treated each other with distant politeness.

'What about Miss Mills?' Bec said quietly to the small group remaining by the ruins of the cottage. 'She'll need somewhere to spend the night.'

'The pub?' Rod offered.

'You're kidding,' Jean almost snorted.

No one disagreed. Miss Mills disapproved of many things about Farwell Creek, and the pub was very high on her list.

'I can't put her up,' Jean said. 'We've only got two bedrooms.'

There was a slight pause, before Bec spoke up.

'I could sleep at Hailey's tonight, and she can have my bed.'

'All right,' Jean said slowly. 'But just for tonight. Don't go getting any ideas. I'm not having her move in.'

'All right,' Rod said. 'I'd better call this in.'

'Will they send anyone out here tonight?' Nick asked.

'I doubt it. They'll probably send an investigator tomorrow. He can try to figure out how it started.'

'What do you think happened?' Hailey asked.

'I have no idea. They might never find out. I'm just thankful no one was hurt.' Rod wiped the sweat from his soot-stained face. 'Nick. Girls. Can you keep an eye on this until I get back?' he asked.

'Sure,' Nick said.

'I'll come with you and get Miss Mills settled,' Jean said.

The two of them walked to where the schoolteacher was now standing, looking a little lost and alone. They talked for a couple of moments, then the three of them began walking away. Hailey caught Bec's eye and raised her shoulders in a mute question. Bec slowly shook her head. She didn't know why her mother saw Rod as nothing more than the town policeman and a good neighbour. Some women just couldn't see what was right under their own nose.

'I should refill the water tank, just in case.' Nick's voice broke into her thoughts. 'Can I use the bore at your place, Bec?'

'Sure.' There was no need for Nick to drive all the way back to his home on a cattle stud just outside the town. The post office bore would easily fill the small tank on the water truck.

'The two of you will be all right till I get back? I won't be long.'

'We'll keep an eye on things,' Bec said.

'Hit the horn on the ute if you need me,' Nick suggested. He backed his truck away from the fence, and headed towards the post office.

Bec and Hailey leaned against the bonnet of their ute and watched him leave. Nick had always been like that. Thoughtful and responsible. When they were kids, he had also been a lot of fun. He had been the third member of their little gang, joining in their escapades, sharing their adventures and the punishments that sometimes followed.

But there had been a little something extra in the relationship between Nick and Bec. They had shared a first kiss not far from where she was now standing. And they had promised . . . Well, whatever they'd promised, it hadn't come to pass. Bec had left for the city. When she'd returned to Farwell Creek, things had changed. Nick had changed too. She had hoped they might pick up where they had left off, but Nick seemed to have lost his sense of fun. He certainly showed no sign of even remembering what they had once been to each other. Bec wasn't about to remind him. If it was over, it was over. She could accept that. She certainly wouldn't want him, or anyone else, to think she was carrying a torch for him. But it was a shame. He was the best-looking man – and one of the few single ones – within a one-hundred-kilometre radius. She sighed and turned to watch the glowing embers.

'Well, that certainly livened the place up,' she said at last.

Hailey didn't answer.

'I guess they'll have to rebuild it,' Bec continued. 'It's not as if the Creek is overflowing with houses for rent.'

Hailey still didn't reply.

'Hailey? What's wrong?' In the faint glow of the dying fire, Bec thought she saw a glint of tears in her friend's eyes.

'I can't help thinking,' Hailey said in a faint voice, 'that it could have been my house. Or the shop. I would have lost everything that I have left of Mum and Dad.'

Bec slid across the bonnet of the car, and draped an arm around Hailey's shoulders. Older than her friend by several months, Bec had always been the strong one: the leader in all their scrapes and adventures.

'That's not going to happen,' she said firmly.

'The photos. The things in the house. All those memories,' Hailey said, her voice breaking with emotion. 'Or if I lost the shop, all that Dad and Mum worked for would be gone.'

Bec hugged Hailey close. She could feel her friend's grief almost as a tangible thing. A few months ago, a week after Hailey's twenty-third birthday, both her parents had been killed in an accident. Their car had slid off a wet road into a swollen creek, leaving Hailey alone in the world.

Well, not quite alone.

At that time, Bec had been living in Brisbane and hating it. Nothing about the city appealed to her. Nothing about her job as an office manager had appealed either, and she had been looking for a chance to go back to the little bush town that she called home. On hearing of her friend's loss, she had quit her job and come back. It hadn't been quite the homecoming she had imagined. She and her mother were fighting far more than in the past. Then there was Nick, who no longer seemed to want to be part of her life. But no matter how strange her homecoming had been, Bec wasn't about to desert Hailey. She had been at Hailey's side for the funeral, and had held her as she cried and raged against the unfairness of life. Then she stayed to help as Hailey took the reins of her parents' business. The two girls had been running the feed store ever since.

'Nothing's going to happen, Hailey,' Bec said. 'And even if it did, as long as you remember your parents, they're not lost.'

'I suppose,' Hailey muttered in a soft, sad voice.

The two sat in silence for a few minutes. When

Hailey spoke again, her voice was stronger. 'For once, Miss Mills is right. This town does need a fire brigade.'

Bec had to agree.

The sound of an engine heralded Nick's return. Bec watched him pull his truck as close to the glowing embers as he could get. A few minutes later, the first shift of watchers arrived, refreshed by a snack and a beer at the pub. Bec and Hailey said good night to Nick, and headed towards the post office so Bec could collect the things she needed for the night at Hailey's place.

'To be honest,' Bec told her friend, 'I'm glad of the chance to get away from Mum for a night.'

'What was it this time?'

After the events of the past hour, the argument with her mother seemed distant and trivial. 'Nothing important. Ever since I came home,' Bec said, 'we argue at the drop of hat. Over anything. I don't know what's gotten into her. She cries, too.'

The crying was possibly harder to take than the fights. Jean was still quite a young woman. She had been just out of her teens when Bec was born and being a single mother must have been hard. But Bec had almost never seen her cry. Until recently. Something had changed. She didn't know what it was, but it had made her life a whole lot more difficult.

'Well, I'm glad it's you staying with me,' Hailey said as they slipped through the gate into Bec's yard. 'I would hate to have Miss Mills – even for a single night.'

They found Jean and Miss Mills in the kitchen.

'How are you?' Bec felt like a guilty child again. The teacher had that effect on both her and Hailey.

'I'm fine, thank you,' the woman replied.

'That's good. I'm glad you weren't hurt, but I am sorry you lost your things,' Bec offered.

'It's not a major loss,' Miss Mills replied shortly. 'I did not bring anything of value with me when I came to this country.'

Bec had no answer for that.

'I'll just collect some things and then you can settle into my room.'

Jean opened her mouth to speak, but the teacher cut her off.

'There has been a change of plan,' she said. 'There is no point in you moving to Hailey's for just one night. We'd only have to change places in the morning.'

'What do you mean – change places?' Bec asked slowly.

'Well, surely it's obvious,' Miss Mills continued. 'I am going to need somewhere to stay while the house is rebuilt. I don't drive, so it has to be in the town. Hailey has that big house and lives all alone. I shall move in with her.'

There was a moment of silence that seemed to last for hours. Bec saw Hailey fighting for control of her face and her emotions. The last thing Hailey wanted was anyone, least of all the cold and critical teacher, living with her in the house that she had until such a short time ago shared with her parents.

'Well,' said Miss Mills. 'It's all settled then. Hailey, please take me home. I am quite exhausted and would like to rest.'

2

Hailey woke with the sun, as she always did. Her room faced east, and she never quite closed the curtains. As a child, she had loved the early morning light. She loved to hear the kookaburras laughing to greet the day and the sounds of Farwell Creek slowly coming to life. When she was small, she would lie in her bed, watching the curtains move gently as a breeze whispered through the open window. Soon she would hear the sound of someone moving through the house, into the kitchen. There'd be a faint clatter of dishes as her mother started preparing breakfast. Sometimes her mother had sung happily as she cooked. Barbara Braxton had been a big fan of a cooked breakfast: toast, bacon and eggs, even steak sometimes. Hailey had loved those breakfasts. The three of them sitting around the table. Her dad, with his wavy hair that always seemed to need cutting. Her mum, who was always smiling or singing. As she lay in bed, Hailey closed her eyes, remembering the happy times. She could almost hear the movement in the kitchen. The clatter of dishes. The sound of her mother's voice.

A loud crash startled her into full wakefulness.

'Oh, bother!' The voice she heard wasn't her mother's. The accent was unmistakable. Miss Mills was in the kitchen, and it sounded like there had just been another disaster.

Hailey closed her eyes one final time, took a deep breath and slowly got out of bed. For a week now she had been a reluctant hostess to Miss Mills. Hailey was not sure what the woman's first name actually was. It hadn't been offered. The teacher did not invite that sort of intimacy. She knew that Miss Mills was trying to live up to her own idea of what constituted a good guest. She cooked. She cleaned up after herself. She went to bed early and kept the television turned low. Maybe the arrangement was working for her, but it certainly wasn't working for Hailey. She dashed into the bathroom, and a few minutes later walked into the kitchen, a polite smile firmly fixed on her face.

'Ah, good morning, Hailey.' Miss Mills was putting a teapot on to the big wooden table. It had become her habit to make breakfast each morning. Tea and toast. She had suggested making bacon and eggs but Hailey had firmly clamped down on that idea. Not that she needed to watch her weight. She had given up cooked breakfasts when her parents died and she didn't want to reinstate the habit. There were too many painful memories. Even more importantly, she wasn't going to allow Miss Mills to dictate what she ate. The woman was old enough – but she most definitely was not her mother!

'Did I hear something crash?' Hailey asked through gritted teeth.

'Yes. I am afraid I dropped that china bowl. The blue and white one. I am sorry.' Miss Mills paused in the middle of pouring tea into two cups. 'I do hope it wasn't special?'

'No. That's all right.' Hailey muttered. Of course the

bowl was special. It had been her mother's, and like so many other things in the house, it was precious to Hailey. Not that Miss Mills seemed to understand how important a small memory could be. She wasn't the slightest bit concerned at having lost all her personal items in the fire. She'd simply taken the bus to Roma the next day and bought new clothes. The education department would provide new furniture when they rebuilt the cottage. That seemed to be enough for Miss Mills.

Hailey sat down in her place, and reached for her cup of tea. That was something else. Cups and saucers. The Braxtons had always used mugs. It was such a silly thing, Hailey thought, to object to using a cup and saucer. But it was change, and she didn't want change any more than she wanted this woman sleeping in her parents' bedroom. She just didn't know how she could get rid of her. In small bush towns, everybody helped out. That was the rule. Her parents had lived by it, and taught their daughter to do the same. If only there had been some other way she could have helped. Some way that did not involve opening up her house to Miss Mills. Everything the woman did caused some disruption, however small. Things were moved. Dishes were put in the wrong place. The house smelled slightly different, due to Miss Mills's cooking. And the soap in the bathroom was not the type Hailey preferred. They were all stupid little things that bothered Hailey more than they should. She knew why she felt so disturbed. With every little change, she felt as if she was losing another little piece of her parents, and she was trying too hard to hang on to their memory.

'I'm going to work now,' she said, quickly drinking the rest of her tea.

'But you haven't eaten.'

'It's all right, Miss Mills. I'll eat at the shop. I've got things to do there.' Hailey almost ran from the room.

She slipped on her boots and walked down the back stairs. Her house was directly behind the feed store. A low wooden fence with a hinged gate separated the two blocks of land. Hailey closed the gate behind her and walked through the back yard of the shed, past stacks of wooden pallets, molasses drums and assorted bits of machinery.

'Good morning, Cat.'

Hailey patted the animal as she unlocked the store's back door. Cat meowed loudly and rubbed himself against her legs. The slightly chewed body of a dead mouse lay on the concrete slab outside the side door.

'Well done,' Hailey said as she quickly disposed of the body in the small incinerator at the back of the yard.

She and Bec had found the half-grown, half-starved black and white creature in the yard three years before. Bec had named him after Audrey Hepburn's pet in *Breakfast at Tiffany's*, and Cat had moved in. He had grown into a big beast, long and lean, and a prolific mouser. In return for Cat's rodent control, Hailey provided slightly more sanitary cat food and the occasional bowl of milk. As she fulfilled her half of the bargain, Hailey was careful to preserve enough milk for Bec's morning coffee. That first cup of milky coffee was essential to her friend's working day. The electric kettle had just boiled when she heard Bec come in.

'Coffee's on,' she said, without looking up.

'Thanks. You're here early. Is Miss Mills bothering you?'

'Yep. You're early too . . .'

Bec just shrugged. Hailey guessed that meant

another row between her and her mum. Hailey was as confused as Bec was by Jean's moodiness. When Bec and Hailey were kids, the O'Connells and the Braxtons had shared more than the occasional dinner. Hailey's mother had felt sorry for Jean, struggling to raise a daughter alone. Her father had helped out when he could. Jean had grieved with Hailey when they died. But that didn't explain why she and Bec were getting on each other's nerves. Perhaps it was the time they had spent apart, when Bec was in the city. But Hailey didn't think so. Those months hadn't changed Bec; at least not that Hailey could see. She was still the same person she had always been. The city hadn't touched her. It was Jean who had changed, becoming moody and easily angered. Hailey was pretty sure it wasn't Bec's doing, although she certainly bore the brunt of it.

'Don't worry about me and Mum,' Bec said. 'We'll sort it out. We always do. What's on the agenda for today?'

Quickly the girls sorted their day's work. Hailey would stay at the store, doing paperwork, while Bec delivered some supplies to a couple of their customers. As her friend drove away, Hailey marvelled again at Bec's enthusiasm for working at the store. She'd been grateful of the offer of help in those first terrible weeks after the accident, when she'd been struggling to cope with her loss. She never really expected it would become a permanent thing. But it had. In fact, Bec seemed to enjoy the work even more than Hailey did. As she worked, Hailey thought about how things had changed. Bec had been the one who wanted to get away. She had left, only to be drawn back again. Now she seemed to be content to stay. She loved Farwell Creek. Loved working at Hailey's store. Wanted to stay, if only she and her mother could sort out whatever their problem was.

Hailey, on the other hand, was desperately unhappy living and working here. Where once she was the homebody, content to stay with her family in the town she had known all her life, she now wished herself almost anywhere else in the world. The townsfolk were good, decent people, and Hailey was grateful to them for the help they'd given her since her family died. She liked most of them. She loved a few of them. She just wasn't really happy living among them any more. But she was unable to walk away from the store or from the house with its memories; at least those that hadn't been broken by Miss Mills. The crash that had taken her parents also seemed to have robbed Hailey of her self-confidence and her strength. She knew she should be starting to get back on her feet again. But she just couldn't do it. And she couldn't leave the Creek. If she walked away from her past, she would be totally alone in the world, and that would be more than she could bear.

Hailey picked up her guitar and started strumming and singing softly. Like her mother, she loved music. She normally kept her guitar at the house, but the arrival of Miss Mills had changed that. The woman had no time for music. Hailey was still playing when Bec drove into the loading bay at the back of the store. Just a few seconds later, Nick pulled up outside.

'I'm glad you're here Nick,' Bec said as the three of them stood near the front of the store. 'I've had an idea. I want to run it past the two of you and see what you think.'

'What idea?'

'It's a bit complex. There's not really time now. Can

you come back later? Closing time? We can grab a meal at the pub and talk it through.'

'Well . . .' Nick looked uncertain. That was another change. He used to meet them down the pub regularly for dinner and to shoot pool. He seldom came now. But then, his circumstances had changed too, and not for the better.

'Come on, Nick,' Bec said. 'We need you.'

'All right. I've just come for my fencing wire. I'll come back later when you're ready to talk.'

Watching him drive away after collecting his wire, Hailey realised that Nick too had lost the life he had known. The Price family had owned a cattle stud just a few kilometres from the Creek, and Nick had been at school with her and Bec. They had been inseparable. Young and hopeful, with the future just waiting to be claimed. It hadn't work out quite the way they had planned. The drought had broken Nick's father and sent him bankrupt. The bank repossessed the farm and sold it to some rich American cattleman, who almost never visited. The Price family still lived there – but as paid workers and tenants in what had once been their own home. Nick was a proud man. It must still hurt him to think that he would never own the land he had loved and worked since he was old enough to haul himself on to a pony's back. Maybe that explained why he and Bec hadn't gotten back together.

Hailey walked back inside her office. Bec was absently scratching Cat's head as she sat at the computer, searching for something on the internet.

'What are you looking for?' Hailey asked.

Bec just shook her head. 'I'll tell you when I've got a better idea if this can work.'

She maintained her silence on the subject

throughout the rest of that day. Nick returned shortly after five o'clock.

'Right. Let's grab a table at the pub. Before it gets too crowded.' Bec led the way to the front door.

She heard it as soon as she stepped outside – a low throaty rumble from beyond the edge of town.

'What on earth . . . ?' Bec said as the convoy slowly rolled into town, led by a vehicle the likes of which Hailey had never before seen.

Every property and most of the people around the Creek had a ute. They were standard work vehicles: a flat tray back with high sides for carting farm equipment, feed, dogs and even the occasional calf. Hailey had one parked at the back of the feed store. Nick drove one too. But no one they knew had a ute anything like this one. It was the colour of the setting sun at the end of a long, hot summer day – burnt orange, shifting to gold as the light moved across it. The only thing that shone brighter than the paint job was the chrome on the fancy wheels. The bull bar covering the front of the ute was painted a silvery grey, giving it an almost frosted look. On either side, thin CB radio aerials swayed back and forth as the car moved smoothly forward. The top of the cab sported a row of gleaming spotlights, which would illuminate a lot of highway for high-speed travelling. The ute would do some very high-speed travelling. The sound of the engine made that very clear.

'Now that's some ute,' Bec said as it moved past.

'What . . .' Hailey tried, but the words didn't want to come.

'I think it's a Ford,' Nick replied.

'Well it's not like any Ford ute I've ever seen,' Bec said with something very like awe in her voice. 'And as for the driver . . .'

Hailey had also noticed. The car was moving slowly enough for them to catch a glimpse of the man behind the wheel. He was young, blond and big. Big in a very good way. He was wearing a T-shirt, and the brown arm resting in the open window of his door was tanned and muscular. He must have seen them looking at him, because he raised an arm in a casual wave as he drove past. He was gorgeous! They could see that he was grinning.

'What a wanker.' Nick sounded disgruntled.

'You're just jealous because your ute looks like something the dog dragged in,' Bec teased.

The rest of the convoy was passing now. There was a truck loaded with timber. It was followed by another ute. This one was of the working variety, loaded with ladders and other tools. Behind that were two large caravans, hauled by big four-wheel-drive cars.

'This must be the construction crew,' Hailey said at last. 'Miss Mills told me they were due in the next day or two.'

'To rebuild her cottage?'

'Yes, thank God. If she spends too much longer at my place, they won't have to rebuild. We could just bury her.'

'Or you,' Bec offered.

Hailey chuckled, feeling better than she had all day. There was light at the end of the tunnel – or at least at the end of the tunnel that had Miss Mills inside it.

Bec was watching the convoy as it turned at the road leading to the school. 'Do you think one of us should go help them?' she asked. 'I could just run up there and see if he . . . they . . . need anything.'

Hailey chuckled. 'And just what might you be thinking he needs?'

'No way, Bec,' Nick said quickly. 'You said you needed to talk to us. Let's have it.'

'Oh, all right,' Bec said with one last regretful glance down the road. 'I can always go up in the morning.'

The pub was heaving with people when they walked in. It had been unusually busy since the fire, with people from the surrounding area coming to town to look at the ruins and talk over the events of that night. Nothing so exciting had happened for quite a while. The Farwell Creek Hotel had once boasted a shaded veranda along the front of the low wooden building. This had long ago been walled in to form a long, narrow bar. Every one of the tall bar stools was occupied. A door from the bar led into the big main lounge. Many of the tables there were occupied too, and more people were clustered around the pool tables at the back of the room. Men and women alike all wore the bushie's uniform: blue jeans, checked shirts and riding boots. Akubra hats lay on the tables.

Bill Davies, the publican, was behind the bar. His wife, Ruth, would be in the kitchen, cooking steaks. The meals at the Farwell Creek Hotel weren't fancy, but they were big, and for most of the customers that was what mattered. Bill was serving a beer to Matt Johnson. Matt had been a fixture in the town since Hailey was at school. Twice each week he drove a battered old red ute on a long dusty mail run, delivering both mail and small supplies to the farms within a fifty-kilometre radius. He lived with his wife in a converted petrol station on the highway just outside town. On weeknights, he was happy to return home to his wife and a quiet evening in front of the TV, but Friday and Saturday were his pub nights. Knowing his own drinking habits, Matt never drove to the pub. He rode a placid and dependable old brown stock horse, which spent the evening happily munching hay behind the pub until called upon to take his unsteady rider home.

At a nearby table, Hailey noticed her neighbours, Steve and Anne Ryan, already eating their dinner. They owned the town's shop, next door to Hailey's feed and farm supplies store. Between them, Hailey and the Ryans supplied almost anything anyone in the town might need on a day-to-day basis. In a town like the Creek, that meant anything from bread to a branding iron, a saddlebag or a saw chain. Anything really unusual might take a few days, but one or the other would find it. Steve was a quiet man who seemed totally dominated by his loud-voiced wife. Anne was the town gossip. Nothing much happened in the Creek that she didn't know about. She would probably know the name, age, marital status and bank balance of each man in the building team even before they had set up their camp.

A few of the men at the bar greeted Nick with a comment about the weather, or the price of cattle. Nick ordered three drinks, and they found a quiet table at the back of the lounge.

'All right, Bec. Let's have it,' he said as they sat down.

'I think we should form a bush fire brigade,' Bec said.

'We should what?' Hailey said.

'Form a bush fire brigade. I got to thinking the other night. There's nothing we could do if it happened again. Your house. This place.' She spread her arms to indicate the pub. 'We would just have to watch them burn. That's not good enough. We need to organise.'

'But we don't know anything about fighting fires.'

'We could learn.' Bec had always been the leader of

their childhood escapades. She never let anything as insignificant as facts get in the way. 'Nick. You haven't said anything. What do you think?'

Nick's brow creased. 'You know, it's not such a bad idea.'

'Of course,' Bec teased. 'When do I have bad ideas?'

'Well . . .' Hailey and Nick said in unison. 'There was the time . . .'

Bec frowned at both of them, then laughed. The clock rolled back, and once again they were the three musketeers – ready to change the world.

'It's going to take a lot of doing,' Nick said.

'I know,' Bec replied.

'And a lot of money,' Hailey pointed out.

'We'll sort that out somehow.'

Hailey had the feeling that by 'we', Bec actually meant 'Hailey'. That was the way it usually worked.

They were still talking about it when Bec's mother walked into the lounge.

Hailey waved her to join them. 'Jean, what do you think about the town forming a bush fire brigade?' she asked as the older woman sat down.

'A bush fire brigade?' Jean paused to think. 'That's actually a pretty good idea. But can we do it? We don't know anything. We've got no equipment . . . No proper idea how to actually fight a fire.'

'I'm sure we can learn,' Hailey said. 'We can do this. We just need to get enough people on board.'

'We should start with Rod,' Bec said. 'As the town's policeman, he needs to be involved. He might even have some information that can help us.'

'Is he here?' Nick asked.

'I haven't seen him,' Bec said. 'Mum, do you know if he's planning to come over?'

'Now why should I know that?' Jean asked in an exasperated tone.

Hailey hid a smile.

'Do you guys want to order some dinner?' Bill Davies asked as he walked past, his arms laden with dirty glasses. 'Ruth made lasagne. It's good, but there's not much left.'

'In a minute,' Hailey said. 'First, Bill, what do you think about us forming a bush fire brigade?'

'A fire brigade? The four of you?'

'No – the whole town,' Bec retorted.

'Then if this place catches fire, we won't just have to sit and watch it burn,' Hailey said.

'I could always take the insurance money and retire to the coast if it did,' the publican pointed out with a smile.

'Yeah – but you'd hate that,' Bec informed him.

Chuckling, Bill carried on with his work.

Hailey looked at Bec. Her friend was lost in thought, a look of quiet determination on her face. Hailey had seen that look before. When Bec set her mind on something, there was no shaking her. The town might not know it yet, but sometime soon it was going to form a volunteer fire brigade, whether it wanted to or not.

The town meeting was held at the church. It was the only place big enough to hold both the townspeople and those like Nick who lived out of town but were close enough to be a part of it. The school was right next door, and everyone attending the meeting would have to walk past the site of the 'big fire', as it was now being called during late-night sessions at the pub. A dozen years from now, the story would probably have Rod Tate rescuing not just the teacher but also a bunch of kids and the class pet goldfish from a fiery death. That was how small towns acquired their legends.

Nick smiled at the memories the school and the old church brought back. Such good memories. As kids, they had been inseparable – him, Bec and Hailey. Then, as now, the school needed but one teacher, with about twenty kids in her care. The three of them had been the only ones around their age. They had formed their own class, and more than just a class. They had been the Marvel superheroes – fighting for truth, justice and the Australian way! It hadn't worked out like that, of course. The world wasn't that easy to change. People changed far more easily.

He walked through the door into the church. The row of wooden pews faced a raised dais. At the back was what passed for an altar during services, which were held only twice a month. A Catholic priest came to town on the first Sunday of the month for a single service. The Protestant preacher arrived two weeks later. The rest of the time, the church was used for whatever the town needed. And tonight the town needed to talk about Bec's idea.

Bec and Hailey had set up a table on the dais. Rod Tate was with them. Their town was too small to have a mayor, so Rod would chair the meeting. Bec waved to Nick and motioned for him to join them. Nick felt the familiar dull ache in his gut, and thought that, much as things changed, some things stayed the same.

'Hi, Nick,' Bec said as he approached.

'Hi.' He nodded to the others. 'It looks like a good turnout.'

'I think almost everyone from town is going to be here,' said Hailey.

'How are you going to do this?' Nick wanted to know.

'Well,' Bec said, 'I thought we'd just toss the idea out there and see what happens.'

'Sounds like a plan,' Nick said.

'If everyone agrees,' Bec continued, 'we'll have to elect someone to run the show. Do the paperwork. A chairman. Then we'll need someone to do the work – a first officer.'

'Got any ideas who might do those jobs?' Rod asked.

'Yes, I have some ideas.' Bec grinned.

Nick didn't like the way Bec looked when she said that. Or rather, he did like the way she looked. Her amber eyes sparkled with mischief, and the lighter flecks flashed like gold. When they were kids, that smile always meant she was about to get into trouble, and he had always followed her. Not blindly, but willingly, with his eyes wide open – because this was Bec. He needed no other reason. He wished it could still be like that.

'You'd better grab a seat,' Bec said, pointing him in the direction of the front row.

Nick saw a spare seat next to Ed Rutherford. Ed was the town's representative on the regional council. The council was responsible for thousands of square kilometres of country and dozens of towns. Nick didn't imagine they'd get too involved in the goings-on at Farwell Creek. Still, he had a feeling Bec had deliberately placed the councillor in the front row. She was up to something. And if that was the case, why had she so deliberately put him there too? Jean O'Connell soon joined him, and it wasn't long before the room was full. Rod called for order.

'You all know why we're here,' he said. 'You've seen what's left of the teacher's house. In fact, most of you were there the night it happened.'

There was a general murmur of agreement, and a few faint laughs.

'First of all, I want to thank all those who helped out that night,' Rod continued. 'Without everyone mucking in like that, we could have lost the school as well.'

A few heads nodded and there were snatches of muffled discussion. The town had not yet tired of talking about it.

'With that in mind, we're here to discuss a proposal to form a volunteer bush fire brigade.'

The announcement didn't come as any surprise. Since Bec had mentioned it in the pub last Friday, the idea had done the rounds. Small towns were like that, Nick thought. News and gossip and ideas didn't take long to get around.

'Bec and Hailey have been doing some research on

this,' Rod said. 'So I'm going to hand the meeting over to Bec. But before I do, I just want to say that I've seen this done in other towns. It's a great idea – and it can make a huge difference when something like the other night happens. And on that note . . . Bec.'

Bec got to her feet. She had a thick folder on the table in front of her. Nick suspected that much of the detailed research had been done by Hailey. That was how they worked. Hailey was careful and meticulous, but Bec was the persuasive one. She'd make the argument. Nick noted that she didn't open the folder to look at the notes. That too was typically Bec. Once she got her teeth into something, she took it all the way.

'All right,' Bec said. 'It isn't going to be easy. There's a lot to do . . .'

Nick watched Bec as she talked about forming a committee and rounding up volunteer firefighters. He loved to watch her when she had a full head of steam up. She was so strong and passionate and vibrant. To be perfectly honest, he just loved to watch Bec. She seldom wore make-up. She was more at home wearing jeans and elastic-sided riding boots than a dress and high heels. She could toss around a bag of feed or a bale of hay almost as easily as he could. As a teenager, his pubescent dreams had been full of Bec. The way she walked. The way she smiled. He had been devastated when she left town to go to the city for college, and then to live. He'd always known she would come back. Unfortunately, by the time she did, too many other things had changed, and his dreams were gone. His feelings were slower to vanish. He had hoped he could smother them, but so far he hadn't done too well.

'So,' Rod was getting back to his feet, 'questions anyone?'

Not surprisingly, Miss Mills was the first. 'This is all very well,' she said, 'if a bit late from my point of view. But I have to ask – what good is a fire brigade? This town doesn't have a fire engine. And even if it did, what would you attach it to? Farwell Creek doesn't even have a water supply.'

'Yeah.'

'Good point.'

'She's right, you know.'

Nick was surprised to hear people agreeing with the teacher. That hadn't happened often in the six months since her arrival.

'We'll get a truck with a water tank on the back,' Bec jumped in, to forestall further dissent.

'But what do we know about fighting fires?' a voice called from the back,

'We can learn,' Bec said confidently.

'And when will we get the time for that? Some of us have got farms to run, you know.'

'I know you do,' Bec said. 'And if your machinery shed catches fire while you're doing it, or your hay shed burns, what are you going to do then?'

A low murmur of voices suggested that her words were starting to take effect.

'We need a fire brigade,' Bec continued. 'We'll do whatever we have to to make this work. After all, this is the Creek – don't we always make it work?'

A few chuckles suggested that Bec was winning. Before anyone else could change the mood, she called for a vote. The outcome was never in doubt.

'Right,' she said, getting back to her feet. 'The next thing we have to do is form a committee. I would like to propose Councillor Ed Rutherford for chairman.'

That was smart, Nick thought. Ed would get the

regional council on their side. He'd be good at getting people involved.

Beside him, the councillor was getting to his feet. He smiled at the assembled townsfolk and said he would be happy to accept the nomination. From anyone else it might have sounded like a political campaign move, but Nick knew Ed was genuinely interested in helping his community. At fifty, he'd handed over the running of his farm to his sons and was elected to the council. He'd be a good chairman, and Nick confidently joined the rest of the town in electing him unopposed to the job.

'Well, thank you for choosing me,' Ed said as he took a seat with Bec and the others at the head table. 'I'll try to do a good job for you. And I think at this stage the best possible thing I can do is to nominate Bec for secretary. She's organised all this so far with great success, and I can't think of anyone better to keep us on the straight and narrow as we go.'

Ah, thought Nick, Bec's been caught in her own trap. He would bet the secretary's job would be the hardest of all – except perhaps for the chief fire officer himself. Bec accepted the nomination and the vote with good grace. She was always willing to do her share. The new secretary whispered a few words in her chairman's ear, then both looked straight at Nick. Bec grinned and Nick had a sneaking suspicion about what was coming next.

'The next thing we have to do,' Ed said, 'is choose a senior fire officer. Officially, the first officer. I'm a bit old for that sort of thing.' There was a smattering of polite laughter. 'Bec'll have enough to do keeping up the paperwork, so we need someone to actually fight the fires.'

'It doesn't have to be someone in the town,' Bec added, 'but someone close enough to get here quickly.'

Nick waited for her to look at him again. She didn't.

'Whoever is selected will need to have some training and then teach the other members of the team,' she continued. 'So it will need to be someone who can get away for a few days from time to time.'

Bec paused then, as if waiting for someone in the audience to volunteer. There were a few faint mumbles, but no one stepped forward.

'If no one has any objections,' Bec continued after a moment, 'I would like to nominate Nick Price.' She shot him the same grin that had been getting him into trouble since he was about seven years old.

He'd guessed it would be something like that.

A few ragged cheers sounded in the hall. There were no objections. Nor were there any other nominations. Nick had a few seconds to back out – if he wanted to. But he didn't. He believed in his community. He loved this little town. Since his father had been forced to sell the stud, he had felt a little disconnected from the Creek. He wasn't a landowner any more. Maybe becoming the first officer would give him back some of what he had lost. He looked at Bec, who was grinning at him with a look of triumph in her eyes. There was one dream he could never recover. But first officer? That he could do.

'Well then,' said Ed Rutherford, 'as chairman, I hereby declare Nick Price chosen unanimously as our first officer.'

A few people cheered as Nick got to his feet.

'Hey, Nick, you'll look pretty good in a fireman's uniform,' a female voice called from the back of the room.

'If you ladies are going to look after us,' Nick shot back, 'I'm going to be overwhelmed with volunteers.'

The room broke into laughter, and Nick pulled a chair up to the head table.

'What would you have done if I'd said no?' he asked Bec under his breath.

'I knew you wouldn't,' was her swift and confident reply.

Nick had to admit she was right. Everyone was waiting for him to say something. He hurriedly mustered his thoughts.

'You'll need to give me some time to think about all this,' he said. 'But the first thing we need to do is get a list of everyone who is willing to join in. I'd like everyone to put their name and phone number on a sheet before they leave this evening.'

Around the rooms, heads were nodding. That was good.

'And,' he went on quickly, 'I don't just mean the men. I want the women who are willing to help to sign on too.'

'What? So we can make you cups of tea?' another female voice asked.

'So you can help out, just as you did the other night,' Nick said. 'I'd rather have a Farwell Creek woman at my side in a tight spot than a lot of the city blokes I've met.'

'Yeah,' came a predominantly female response.

'This is all well and good,' Bill Davies, the publican, got up, 'and you can count me in. I'll do whatever I can to help. But I have to ask . . . How much will this cost and where is the money coming from?'

That caused a bit of a stir in the room. Nick could see people frowning and talking to their neighbours. He knew what they were thinking. Life on the land wasn't easy, and most of them were hard pushed just to make ends meet. A couple of bad seasons would land many of them in bankruptcy. No one knew that better than Nick.

These were good people, who worked long and hard. They would give as much of their time and effort as the town needed. What they wouldn't give was money – simply because they didn't have it to give.

Nick looked at Bec, but she didn't meet his eyes. She was looking around the room, as if she was hoping by force of her will to make the question go away. Hailey, however, had come prepared.

'There is assistance out there,' she said, getting to her feet. 'Government grants, that sort of thing. But we will need to raise some money ourselves.'

'How much?' someone in the audience asked.

'A lot.'

An awkward silence followed.

'Why don't you hold a B&S?'

The question came from somewhere near the back of the room. In the silence that followed, heads turned, trying to find the speaker.

'Could you stand up and say that again, please.' Ed Rutherford directed his words towards the rear of the room.

A stranger stood up. Strangers were rare enough in the Creek. Especially ones like this. He looked to be in his late twenties, very tall and broad across the shoulders. His hair was sandy blond and too long and too well groomed for a bushman. He looked very fit and tanned. He was wearing jeans, but they weren't the faded workday wear that everyone else was wearing. His shirt was black and had silver studs. Nick thought he looked a bit too much like one of the Hollywood cowboys in Bec's old movies.

'I said, why don't you hold a B&S to raise the money?' The stranger's voice was strong and confident and clear to everyone in the room.

Miss Mills finally broke the silence that followed. 'Just what is a B&S?'

The man moved into the aisle between the pews, where people could see him more easily.

'I'm Terry Gordon,' he told the room. 'I'm foreman of the building team working on rebuilding the school cottage. People call me Gordo.'

He must be the owner of the flashy gold ute, Nick thought. It seemed to fit with the man's image. He was instantly suspicious. He cast a sideways glance at Bec – and he did not like the interest he saw in her face.

'I've already met Miss Mills up at the school,' he said with a nod in her direction. 'And I know she's not local.' He directed his next comments at the schoolteacher, but everyone in the room was listening to every word. 'I guess you don't know. A B&S is a Bachelor and Spinster Ball. It's a great Australian bush tradition. People from all over meet in one town for a weekend. There's music and dancing—'

'And drinking!' someone yelled from the back of the room.

'That too,' Gordo said with a grin. 'There's usually a ute competition as well.'

'And that is?' If anything, Miss Mills's voice had become even more distant.

'A competition for cars. Utilities. Like mine. I don't know if you've noticed it parked by the school. The gold Ford?'

The surge of voices around the room suggested that pretty much everyone had noticed it. The builders had only been in town two days. Most of the locals had not met any of the men, but it was hard to miss that ute! Bec leaned over to whisper something in Hailey's ear. Both girls grinned. Nick had a feeling he wouldn't like what they were thinking.

'It all sounds perfectly dreadful!' Miss Mills said.

'It's a good way to raise funds,' Gordo offered.

'I'm not so sure we want that sort of thing in the Creek.' Jean got to her feet. 'There'll be a lot of drunks wandering around. And I'll bet the rev-heads will start racing those fancy utes.'

'It's called circle work,' Gordo offered. 'Some B&S balls allow circle work. Some don't. You can set your own rules. But either way, there's no harm done.'

'Sounds like fun to me,' a male voice called from somewhere near the front. 'This town could use a bit more fun.'

'How many people might come?' Bec sounded intrigued, although Nick wasn't sure if she was interested in the answer, or the man who was giving it.

'Maybe a few hundred.'

'I don't think we need a lot of strangers coming here,' offered Anne Ryan from the store. 'This is a quiet town.'

'And anyway,' Jean was back on her feet, 'we would never be able to organise something like that.'

'I think,' Gordo broke in, 'the problem is that none of you are really familiar with what goes on at a B&S. How many of you have been to one recently? Ever?'

The shaking heads around the room were all the answer he needed.

'Well, I think some of you should go to one. Get a feel for what goes on. There's one this weekend at Augathella. That's where I'm headed. A couple of you could come with me.'

A low rumble of talk sounded in the room. At the head table, eyebrows were raised.

'I've got my daughter and her family up for the weekend,' Ed said. 'Sorry.'

'I can't leave the store on a Saturday.' That was Hailey. Anne Ryan made a similar excuse about her shop. Bill Davies just shrugged. No one would expect him to leave the pub on a weekend.

'Nick?' Jean looked at him expectantly.

'Sorry.' Nick shook his head. 'I've got buyers coming this weekend to look at some of the young bulls. I can't get away.'

Gordo walked further down the aisle. As Nick watched him approach, he could almost feel his hackles rising. The man walked with a swagger that suggested he had practised in front of the mirror. He exuded a confidence that was close to arrogance, and he was looking at Bec with interest written clearly on his face. He stopped right in front of their desk. Despite the fact that they were sitting on a raised platform, he was still looking down at her. A smile had lifted the corners of his mouth, and his eyes were locked on her face.

'And what about you, Madam Secretary?'

Nick saw that Bec was smiling in a way that would have set his pulse racing – if she had been smiling at him. But she wasn't.

'Why not?' she said slowly, her eyes never leaving Gordo's face. 'Hailey, you don't really need me. This is more important.'

'I guess I can get by,' said Hailey.

'Well then,' Gordo said with a satisfied grin, 'why don't you ride up with me? In my ute. I'll introduce you to a few people. Show you the ropes.'

'That sounds great,' Bec replied, smiling right back at him. All through the exchange, the two of them had not broken eye contact.

Nick saw some movement in the front row. Jean was clearly unimpressed. Her face was tight with annoyance as she watched Gordo charm her daughter. Nick felt something twisting his own gut, and hoped his face didn't betray his emotions.

'That's settled then,' Gordo said to Bec. 'By Monday, you'll no longer be a B&S virgin.'

4

'You can't do this!'

Bec looked at her mother in shock. 'Mum, I'm twenty-four years old. You can't forbid me to go.'

'I'm not forbidding you to go. I'm just saying that you can't seriously be considering going away for the weekend with this Gordo bloke.'

They were standing in the lounge room of their home. At Bec's feet, her overnight bag was brimming with the things she'd need for a weekend away. She was expecting Gordo to appear fairly soon. At least she hoped he would appear soon, to forestall the fight that was brewing. Jean was standing near the door, hands on hips. Bec knew that stance. The last thing she wanted was to fight with her mother, but it didn't seem that she had any choice in the matter.

'I'm not going away with Gordo. I'm going to a B&S. He's taking me so I can find out the stuff we need to know to host our own event.'

'But you don't know anything about him,' Jean argued. 'For goodness' sake, he lives in a caravan on a building site.'

'What's that got to do with anything?' Bec was losing the battle to contain her temper.

'Well . . . He's just not the sort of bloke you should be getting involved with.'

'Getting involved with?' Bec exploded. 'Mum, just what do you think I'm going to be doing this weekend?'

'It's not that I don't trust you . . .'

'Trust me? Do you think I'm planning to sleep with him or something?'

'Bec!'

'Well that's what it sounds like. You don't have to worry. I'm not about to go and get pregnant. I'm not that stupid!' As the words came out of her mouth, Bec saw a flash of real pain in her mother's eyes. Bec knew she had gone too far. She regretted the words, but she was angry. 'If you are that worried about him,' she continued, 'get Rod to check him out on the police computer. Just in case he's an axe murderer or something.'

When Jean didn't reply, Bec knew.

'You already have, haven't you? You asked Rod to check if he had a police record.'

'No!'

'Well then, you were planning to.'

Jean's silence was all the answer she needed.

'How could you?' Bec couldn't keep the disgust from her voice.

'I just want to protect you,' Jean said, her voice quivering with emotion.

'Well I'm a big girl now. I don't need your protection.' Bec pushed past her mother and stormed out the front door.

In the minute and a half it took her to cross the road to Hailey's store, Bec had time to really regret some of the things she had said. Mostly she regretted the comment about getting pregnant. She had no memories of her father. She knew that Jean had been very young when she married and most definitely did not like talking about the husband who had run out on them when Bec was still in nappies. There were no photos in the house. She didn't even know what her father looked like. Growing up, she had cried more times than she knew because she didn't have what Hailey and Nick had – a 'proper' family. Since Hailey's parents had died, Bec had been thinking about her father more often. Wondering who he really was. What sort of a man he was. Was he even still alive? All she really knew about Ken O'Connell was that he was the worst kind of bastard. Worthless and weak. She had always suspected her mother had married him because she was already pregnant. A couple of times she had been tempted to ask, but lacked the courage. Now was not the time. Not the way Jean had been since Bec had come home. Jean was only too ready to argue, or occasionally burst into tears. Bec didn't understand why. There were times she wanted to ask about that too, but hadn't. Perhaps her mother had strong personal reasons to object to Bec's weekend with Gordo. Even so, she had no right to interfere. Bec pushed her guilt aside as she walked into Hailey's office.

'When are you leaving?' Hailey asked, looking up from her accounts as Bec dropped into a chair.

'Soon. I just came over to kill some time. Mum and I . . .' Her voice trailed off.

Hailey leaned over to hit the on switch on their electric kettle. 'She doesn't want you to go with Gordo,' she said as she put coffee into their mugs.

'That's putting it mildly.'

'You know,' Hailey said quietly, 'she might have a point.'

'Not you too?' Bec almost wailed.

'Well, you don't know anything about him,' Hailey continued.

'But it's not about him,' Bec protested. 'It's about the ball. I'm just going along to learn about the ball.'

'Come on, Bec,' Hailey placed the steaming mugs on the desk, 'this is me. I saw the guy, remember. Those big broad shoulders. Green eyes. Fills out a pair of jeans like there's no tomorrow. A killer smile. Don't tell me you didn't notice, because I won't believe you.'

Bec began to smile. 'He looks a lot like Matthew McConaughey, doesn't he?'

Hailey raised an eyebrow.

'Well, all right,' Bec admitted. 'I admit it. He is kinda cute.'

'Cute? Nothing about that man is cute. Gorgeous, yes. Sexy, yes. But never cute. Puppies are cute, and he's no puppy.'

'No,' Bec said slowly, remembering the way Gordo had looked down at her with those startling green eyes. 'He certainly is not.'

'I guess that explains the outfit,' Hailey declared.

Bec looked down at herself. She had forsaken her usual jeans and T-shirt for a short denim skirt and a tight white tank top. Her wide leather belt with its huge silver rodeo buckle emphasised her trim waist.

'And on your feet?' Hailey asked.

Bec lifted her feet and set them on the desk. The Western-style boots were made of hand-carved dark red leather, with high Cuban heels and fringes.

'High-heeled red follow-me-home-and-fuck-me boots!' the girls chorused, as they dissolved into laughter. Bec felt some of the tension leave her.

'Seriously, are you sure you're going to be all right?' Hailey said.

'I'll be fine,' Bec assured her friend, as she sipped the hot milky coffee. 'I really do plan to work this weekend. I'm taking a notebook and pen.'

'Good. Take this too.' Hailey handed Bec a sheet of paper.

Bec ran her eyes down the page.

'Music, food, parking, camping, souvenirs. What is this? A shopping list?'

'Almost. I spent some time looking at B&S websites. That's a list of the sort of things that we need to find out about.'

'But if I spend the weekend working on this, I'll have no time for any fun.'

'Tell your mother that. It might make her feel better,' Hailey said with a wry grin.

Bec took another look at the list. 'You forgot booze.'

'No I didn't. Bill Davies was in here earlier. He said he organised the booze at a B&S a few years ago, before he moved here. He's volunteered to do it again this time.'

'That's generous of him.'

'Well, he plans to make a profit on the weekend. There'll be a lot more visitors to the pub. We'll probably need all the rooms for VIPs. The band. That sort of thing. It'll be good for him.'

'Good for the whole town, I think,' Bec said, getting to her feet. 'And I hope he's not the last person to step forward to help.'

'I'm sure he won't be,' said Hailey. 'Now go home and make up with your mother before you leave.'

'I will.'

'And try to have just a little bit of fun with that gorgeous man while you're away.'

'You'd better believe I'll do my best,' Bec said with a grin.

Her improved mood lasted until she saw the ute parked in front of the post office. It certainly wasn't Gordo's shining dream machine. Underneath a thick layer of red dust, this one was white and a bit battered. There were spotlights on the roof, but only two, and they weren't polished chrome. This ute showed the signs of many years of hard work. She knew it in an instant. It was Nick's. He got out of the cab as she crossed the road.

'I'm glad I caught you before you left.'

'I thought you had buyers coming today?' she said.

'We do. I just wanted to . . .'

'To what?'

Nick took a deep breath. Bec knew what was coming before he even opened his mouth.

'Do you really think you should be going off with this bloke?' Nick said.

'Now don't you start on about this,' Bec said in disgust.

'I just think you should wait until someone else can go with you.'

'Really?' Bec kept her voice light. 'Someone like you?'

If Nick caught the tone of her voice, he ignored it.

'Well, maybe. I could get away next week . . .'

'What is it with everyone around here? I'm not an idiot, I can look after myself.'

'I know that, but you don't know Gordo.' Nick's tone was patient and conciliatory. That only made Bec madder.

'You don't know him either,' she spat back. 'Gordo's trying to help, and God knows we need some help around here. You're all judging him, just because he's new in town and he's not a landowner.'

Bec saw Nick almost flinch as she said the words, but it was too late to take them back. She knew what Nick was thinking. He wasn't a landowner either. Not any more. That might not matter to her, but she knew it did matter to him. It mattered a great deal. She had hurt him, and she never wanted to do that. She was instantly contrite.

'Nick. I'm sorry. I didn't mean . . .'

Before Nick could answer, they heard the unmistakable rumble of a high-powered engine. The sun-gold ute appeared at the crossroads that led to the school.

Hating herself for the look she had put in Nick's eyes, Bec took the coward's way out. 'Tell Gordo I'll be right with him,' she said. 'I'll just get my bag.' She turned on her heel and ran into the house.

Nick watched her go. It hurt to be reminded of the inheritance he had lost, but not half as much as the hurt of knowing what he might be about to lose. He leaned back against the bonnet of his ute, folded his arms and waited for the gold Ford to pull in next to him. Gordo got out and assumed a similar position against his own vehicle. Nick took a long, slow look at the man who would be spending the weekend with Bec. Gordo was wearing blue jeans and a checked shirt. His boots were American in style; dyed snakeskin with Cuban heels. Nick would like to see the man put in a day's work in boots like that, although it was clear from the shine on them that they had never done a day's work. Like the big black Akubra hat, they were all for show. Gordo might look like he'd stepped out of one of the old Western movies that Bec loved so much, but he was no Clint Eastwood. Nick would lay odds that this guy had never been near a horse, other than the ones that purred under the bonnet of his ute. Gordo was probably older than Nick by a year or two. He was tall, but not quite as tall as Nick. He was a bit lighter in build too. The thought leaped unbidden into Nick's mind that he could probably take the man in a fight. The idea surprised him. Nick wasn't a fighter. But there was no doubt he didn't like this Gordo. If he was a blue cattle dog, right now he would be snarling.

'G'day.' Gordo took half a step forward and held out his hand. 'Terry Gordon. Call me Gordo.'

Nick slowly shifted his weight to his feet and returned the handshake. 'Nick Price.'

'I know. You're the new fire chief.'

'The first officer. Yes, I am.'

'That's awesome.'

Nick didn't reply. His eyes were drawn to the Ford. He couldn't help himself. It was impossible to ignore.

'Beaut, isn't she?' Gordo said proudly, his hand stroking the metal as if it was a woman.

'I've never seen anything like it,' Nick answered truthfully.

'There's a 351 Cleveland under the bonnet, with solid lifters and a big cam,' Gordo boasted. 'I've bolted on a toploader gearbox and a nine-inch diff.'

Like most farmers, Nick was a competent mechanic. When you lived somewhere as remote as Farwell Creek, you had to be able to do repairs yourself. He could tinker with a rough-running engine, fix the hydraulics on a tractor and repair a cattle crush with a welder and some scraps of metal. He knew exactly what Gordo was talking about, but didn't understand the fervour in Gordo's voice.

'With her 650 Holley carby, she can pull 400 horses. Goes like a shower of shit.'

Nick could think of no polite reply. It was a car. Didn't the man know there were many, many things in life far more important than cars?

'She should win this weekend at Augathella.'

'Do you go to a lot of B&S Balls?' Nick asked.

'I sure do. They're a real blast. And the ute shows are great. I've won every one I've entered this year.'

The ute shows weren't what Nick was worried about, although he guessed that if Gordo was wrapped up in his ute, he might not—

'Hi, Gordo,' Bec called from the top of the stairs. 'I'll be there in a tick.'

She turned back to say something to her mother. She looked terrific, so alive and expectant and beautiful. Nick saw the look on Gordo's face. He felt an overwhelming urge to punch that smile right off it. But he didn't. He had no right. He might have done once, but that was a long time ago.

Gordo looked at Nick. 'Mate, is there something I should know? About the two of you? Because if there is . . .'

It would have been so easy to say yes. To say that Bec was his and tell Gordo to leave her alone. But it would be a lie, and Nick didn't like lies. Particularly lies about Bec. And if she found out . . .

'She's a friend. A good friend. So you make sure nothing happens to her, because if . . .' He stopped as Bec approached, but he could tell from Gordo's face that his message had been received and understood.

'Hi, Gordo,' Bec said brightly.

'Bec! You look great.' Gordo beamed at her. 'Great boots.'

Nick looked at Bec's feet, his mood darkening. When a man noticed a girl's shoes, he usually noticed other things as well.

'Well, thank you, sir,' Bec replied in a wild American accent as she batted her eyes in an exaggerated fashion.

Gordo laughed at the joke, but Nick didn't think it was the least bit funny.

'Should I toss my bag in the back of the ute?' Bec asked Gordo, oblivious to Nick and his mood.

'Let me.' Gordo took it from her. 'I want to show you something.'

The three of them walked to the back of the ute. The tray was covered with a solid fibreglass lid, with the same shiny paintwork as the body. It was hinged in the middle, creating two separate waterproof compartments. Gordo released a couple of clips and lifted the back part of the lid.

The tray of the ute was as pristine as the rest of the vehicle. Nick could clearly see that no hay bale or fuel drum had ever dented or scratched that surface. But it wasn't just the paintwork that was astonishing.

'Stereo speakers?' Bec said in wonder.

'That's right. Wired into an eight-CD player,' Gordo said proudly. 'I had the sides of the tray thickened and rebuilt to get better sound. You should hear this baby when she gets going. There's ten speakers, not counting those in the cab.'

'Wow.' Bec was seriously impressed.

'So where do you plan to put the bag?' Nick cut in.

'I've got storage built into the front of the tray,' Gordo answered. He unclipped the rest of the fibreglass lid to reveal a storage compartment. It was almost full with what was clearly camping gear.

'Ah,' said Bec. 'I don't have any camping stuff. Not even a sleeping bag.'

'Don't worry,' Gordo reassured her. 'I've got all the gear we'll need. I like to be prepared.'

Prepared for what? Nick wondered.

'Well then, I suppose we should get going.' As Bec spoke, the CB radio on the cab of the ute crackled.

'We should,' Gordo said. 'That call is probably from my mate Mutley. He's coming up the Warrego Highway from Toowoomba. And some other friends are on the Canarvon road. I thought we could all meet up in Roma and head out to Augathella in a convoy.'

'That sounds great,' Bec said.

Nick decided it did too. Having other people there was added protection for Bec. At least he hoped it would be.

'Right.' Gordo stowed Bec's bag and secured the cover over the back of the ute. 'Might see you Sunday, Nick,' he said.

Nick nodded.

'Bye,' Bec said airily.

'Take care,' Nick said.

Bec made her way to the passenger side of the ute. Gordo was waiting with the door open. He laid his hand gently on her back as he guided her into her seat. When he turned the key in the ignition and the big engine sprang to life, Nick took half a step back. It was an almost sexual sound, with the promise of great power and speed once they hit the open road. Gordo slipped the ute into gear and backed away from the kerb. Nick could see Bec's face through the windscreen. She was smiling with eagerness. Then Gordo changed gear and the ute moved away.

Nick watched it go. It took every ounce of strength he had not to hop into his own car and chase the Ford. To grab Bec and drag her back, if that was the only way. Of course, that would only make her mad at him.

'Anyway, my old ute would never catch them,' he muttered to himself as he slid back into his seat.

He was pulling away from the kerb when an idea struck. He spun the wheel and turned away from the main road, towards the school. He could see the caravans of the construction crew camp. At least one had its door open. That meant someone was home. He could drop in and see how things were going. As the fire brigade's first officer, it would make sense for him to have a chat with them. And if the conversation happened to turn toward Gordo and his ute, no one could really accuse him of prying. He drove slowly towards the camp. He could see one of the workers sitting in the sun, a beer in one hand and a cigarette in the other. The guy was barefoot and shirtless, wearing stubbie shorts. A radio sat on a nearby table. He was probably listening to the cricket. He was the sort of guy that people around the Creek tended to avoid, or at best ignore. Not exactly a no-hoper, but not far from it. Itinerant labourers were useful, but you wouldn't want your sister to marry one. Or any woman you loved.

Nick drove on past the school without stopping. He had recognised something in that man at the campsite. He had recognised himself. Why did he think he was any better than an itinerant worker? He had no land and no prospects of ever owning land. He had a job, but that could end tomorrow if his employer so chose. He lived in the stockman's cottage on the farm. Once he had planned to renovate it for Bec and him to share. But that too could be gone in an instant, on another man's whim. What right did he have to think he was good enough for Bec? He had even less to offer her than Gordo did. At least Gordo's ute was in good condition.

J ean wasn't sure which was moving more slowly – the hands on the clock or the sun across the sky. Whichever method of timekeeping she used, the result was still the same. Sunday was passing, and her daughter still wasn't home. She paced around the house, holding a cloth but not actually cleaning anything. She sat in front of a book but didn't read a single word. She even pulled some baking ingredients out of the cupboard, but put them back without so much as cracking an egg.

It wasn't that she was worried. Bec was old enough to look after herself. Her head was screwed on far too tight for the sort of stupid mistakes other girls made. The sort of stupid mistake Jean herself had made. But it wasn't Bec's head Jean was worried about. She'd seen the way Gordo looked at her daughter. Gordo, indeed! What sort of a grown man called himself Gordo?

As she stood near the window, staring up the road, Jean knew she was being overprotective, but she couldn't help herself. It had always been just the two of them. She wondered for the ten thousandth time if she shouldn't tell Bec the truth about her father. When Bec was a child, it had seemed right to make up a story that a child could understand and accept. Then she had gone away to college and found a job in the city. The tragic accident that taken Hailey's parents had brought her back to Farwell Creek. Unfortunately, that same accident had also made it impossible for Jean to tell her daughter the truth. At least, at the time. And since then, she and Bec had been too busy getting on each other's nerves while living under the same roof. There hadn't been the time or the right moment for life-changing revelations.

Jean moved away from the window. Staring up the road would not change the past, nor would it bring her daughter home any sooner. If she spent one more minute in the house, she would simply explode. She needed to get outside. She slipped on her shoes and walked out the kitchen door. The back of her house looked towards the school. She could see the camp that Gordo and the other builders were using as their base while they worked to rebuild the teacher's house. She'd seen Nick's ute head up there yesterday, just after Bec left, and didn't have to try too hard to guess what he'd been doing. She wasn't the only one who worried about her daughter.

Jean noticed someone walking her way from the direction of the school. It was Miss Mills. For a minute she was tempted to duck back inside the house. She was in no mood to talk to the woman. But it was too late. Miss Mills had obviously spotted her and was heading straight for her.

'Mrs O'Connell,' the teacher said as soon as she approached, 'has your daughter returned yet?'

'Not yet,' Jean said. 'How are they going with the rebuilding?' she added in an attempt to change the subject.

'They've barely started.' Miss Mills dismissed the

workers with a sniff. 'And with their foreman racing off like this, it's going to take weeks for the house to be finished.'

'Well, it is the weekend,' Jean said. She didn't like Gordo, but the man was entitled to a day off.

'And I don't like this B&S idea.' Miss Mills wasn't about to be distracted by a bit of common sense. 'It sounds perfectly horrid to me. People getting drunk and racing their cars. Someone suggested that they spit food dye all over each other. There'll probably be no end of goings-on.'

Jean found herself tempted to giggle. Goings-on?

'I'm sure we'll raise a lot of money for the fire brigade,' she pointed out. 'After all, that's what it's for.'

'It's just an excuse for licentiousness,' Miss Mills declared. 'I do hope you're not planning to hold it in the church.'

Jean looked across to the old wooden church sitting next to the school. Miss Mills attended both the Catholic and Protestant services there, telling anyone who would listen that she had no choice given the isolation of the town.

'I don't know, Miss Mills,' she said, a faint smile twitching the corners of her lips. 'In my day, we always held the bush dances in the church.'

In fact, it had been in a church not very much different from the one she was looking at that she and Bec's father had—

'Really!' Miss Mills sniffed. 'In my village, we wouldn't consider such a thing.'

'Ah, but this isn't England, Miss Mills.'

'It most certainly isn't.' The teacher nodded her farewells and continued walking.

Jean felt a wave of sympathy for Hailey. Having that

woman living with her must be a nightmare. Not exactly what she needed when she was still struggling to cope with the loss of her parents. And not doing very well, either. Jean understood the pain the girl was feeling. She was glad that Bec had decided to stay to help her friend with the business. It was such a joy to see the two girls together. They were so alike, and not just their looks. Both were strong, intelligent young women. Recent events had left Hailey a little fragile and frightened, but she'd get past that. She would go back to being the happy, confident girl she had always been. At least she would if nothing else happened to hurt her.

Small towns were usually slow to change, but something seemed to have happened to the Creek. It wasn't just that the schoolteacher's cottage had burned down, although that was more change in one night than the town had seen in a long time. The fire had brought other changes. The bush fire brigade. The B&S ball. Not to mention the construction crew and Gordo. Jean could feel change hovering like a storm on the horizon. She didn't like change. When things changed, old secrets had a habit of coming out. She didn't want that to happen.

Jean looked at her watch. Where was that daughter of hers?

She turned her back on the school and walked along the side of the building that contained both her home and the post office. A fence marked the boundary between the public and private space. The metal gate was hanging from a broken hinge. It was time that was fixed. The garden needed some attention too. In a town with limited water supplies, gardens were hard work. She needed water from her bore to keep her few plants green and healthy. She didn't want to lose them.

Besides, gardening might help, Jean thought. Work out some of the tension of the past twenty-four hours. She headed for her shed to find the necessary tools.

After a few tentative prods at the broken gate, she decided to change direction. She decided her roses needed pruning, and attacked them, slicing through the branches with far more fervour than a mere plant deserved. She hadn't been at it long when she spotted Hailey walking through the door of her store. The feed store normally didn't open on a Sunday. Jean guessed the poor girl was trying to get away from Miss Mills. She didn't blame her in the least.

'Do you need some help with that gate?'

The voice beside her caused Jean to jump.

'Rod,' she said. 'I didn't hear you coming.'

'Sorry,' the policeman said, with a warm smile. 'I saw you working from my window. I've brought my pliers. I thought I could have a go at the gate while you did the roses.'

'I would appreciate a hand. Thanks.'

'You are most welcome.'

Rod turned his attention to the gate, while Jean took another run at the rose bushes.

'By the way,' Rod said, 'I did a quick check of the police bulletins this morning. Apparently the Augathella B&S went off smoothly. A couple of people were pulled up for being a bit too rowdy, but there were no arrests and no injuries.'

As he spoke, Jean felt a weight lift off her shoulders. Not all of it. That wouldn't be gone until Bec was safely home.

'Is it ridiculous for me to worry about her?' she asked quietly. 'She's twenty-four years old and more than capable of looking after herself.'

Rod took her hand in his. His brown eyes were intense as he looked at her. 'Never apologise for loving your daughter.'

Jean looked at his familiar face and nodded. She didn't know if it was his words, or the touch of his hand, but she felt better than she had all morning. Rod squeezed her hand gently then turned back to the gate.

Jean was well aware of her daughter's thoughts on the subject of Rod Tate. She was right in some ways. Rod was a fine man. Hard-working and honest. Handsome too, with those first touches of grey showing in his dark hair. He'd been divorced before he came to the Creek, and to Jean's certain knowledge all the unmarried women in the district, and at least one of the married ones, had tried to work their charms on him – without success. But Rod and she were friends, nothing more. After all, she was forty-three years old. Positively middle-aged. Rod wouldn't be interested in her. Even if he was, nothing was ever going to happen between them. Not the way things were. She had been lying to him since the day they met. Ten years of lying. Nothing she could do would ever put that right. Her chance for love had come a long time ago, and she had messed up. Women like her didn't get a second chance.

Rod stayed with her while she worked, and Jean was glad of his company. The gate was fixed. The roses pruned to a startling degree. The garden beds had been weeded, and Jean was contemplating mowing the lawn when she heard a distant low rumble.

'Thunder?' she asked Rod.

'I don't think so. That sounds like Gordo's ute to me.'

'Same thing,' Jean said bitterly.

Rod raised an eyebrow.

'A warning that there's a storm ahead,' Jean explained.

'Now, Jean,' Rod started gathering the tools, 'I trust you're not going to do anything silly.'

'If you trust me, why are you taking all the sharp implements away?'

Rod smiled and shook his head, but continued to carry the gardening and fencing tools back towards Jean's shed.

'Hi, Mum.' Bec positively bounced out of the ute when Gordo pulled up in front of the house. Her clothes were rumpled. Her hair seemed to have turned green – or at least part of it had. She looked like she hadn't slept since Jean last saw her. She also looked incredibly happy.

'What happened to your hair?' Jean said.

Bec ran her fingers through the wild mess on her head, but quickly gave up trying to restore order. 'Food dye, I guess,' she said.

'And did you have a good time?'

'It was brilliant, Mum. Amazing. And Gordo won best ute of the show.'

'Congratulations.' If nothing else, Jean had her manners.

'Thank you, Mrs O'Connell.' Gordo touched the rim of his hat.

Jean nodded a reply. 'Did you actually manage to get some research done?' she asked Bec.

'I did. I learned so much. We've got to organise a committee meeting,' Bec hurried on. 'As soon as possible. We need to decide on a date, book a band, get a liquor licence. There's so much to do.'

'Maybe it's too much.' Jean didn't expect that argument would hold any weight with Bec.

'No, it's not. We just need to get enough people involved. If everyone pitches in to help, it'll be easy.'

Gordo had retrieved an overnight bag from the back of his ute. 'Here you go, Becca.'

Jean almost fainted. Becca? Her daughter always hated being called Becca. She said it made her sound like a kitchen appliance.

'Thanks, Gordo.' Bec smiled up at the man. 'Thanks for everything. I had a great weekend.'

'It was my pleasure,' Gordo said. 'Maybe we can get together during the week and go through some of those notes you made. Over dinner at the pub, maybe.'

'I'd love to,' Bec gushed.

Jean could hardly believe what she was seeing. The girl was almost simpering. That was so not like Bec.

'I'll talk to you tomorrow.' Gordo flashed his broad smile again. 'Bye, Mrs O'Connell.'

Gripping her manners tightly, Jean said, 'Goodbye.' Nothing on this good earth would make her call him Gordo.

'Mum, we have got to get Gordo on to the committee,' Bec said as they made their way inside. 'He knows all about how to organise a B&S, and he knows all the people we need. The places to hire the stage. The names of bands. Everything.'

'He can't be on the committee,' Jean said firmly. 'This is all about the town, and he's not part of the town.'

'But Mum . . .'

'Besides,' Jean pointed out firmly, 'he's only here to rebuild the teacher's house. He'll be gone in a few weeks.' At least she hoped he would.

Bec's smile faded. 'I guess so.'

'Maybe you should remember that.'

'Yeah. Maybe I should.'

Jean didn't like the way Bec said that.

Gordo wasn't at the committee meeting. Nick was very glad to see the flashy ute at the builders' campsite as he drove past on his way to the pub on Monday evening. He hadn't seen Bec since she'd returned from the B&S yesterday, but already the whole town was buzzing with ideas she'd obviously brought back. Even from his place outside the town itself, Nick had caught the news. He didn't like the way Gordo's name had featured. Just as he parked in front of the pub, Nick saw Hailey walk through the door. Damn, he thought. He had hoped to have a quiet word with Hailey about Bec and her weekend away with Gordo. She would tell him what had happened . . . if anything had. Nick turned off his engine and lights and just sat for a few moments with his hands on the steering wheel. His ute was a battered old white Falcon with mud up the sides and a dent in the tailgate where an angry bull had left its mark. It didn't stack up against Gordo's killer ute with its custom paint job and rows of stereo speakers. Nick got out of the car. He didn't want to think about how he might stack up against Gordo in Bec's eyes. Not that this was a competition. He and Bec could never be more than friends. He just didn't want to see her get hurt. This Gordo was a wanker. Surely she could see that?

When he entered the pub, Nick cast a quick glance around both the bar and the lounge, and as always, his eyes immediately found Bec. She was standing in the lounge, where a corner appeared to have been set up for their committee meeting. She was wearing faded blue jeans that fitted her like a second skin. Her white cotton

T-shirt did a similar favour for her figure. Her hair was loose, and Nick felt a familiar twitch – first in his heart, then somewhere lower.

'Hi, Nick,' Ed Rutherford's voice cut through his thoughts.

'Ed.'

The committee chairman had a tray of drinks in his hands. 'I got one for you too,' he said. 'I think we're all here now. We can get started.'

Nick followed Ed over to the table. Jean and Hailey were talking to Bec. Rod was there, as was Bill Davies. Nick nodded his greetings to the gathered members, then turned to Bec.

'How was Augathella?' He kept his voice carefully neutral.

'Amazing!' Bec said. 'I learned so much that will help us with our B&S.'

'That's great.' Nick watched her face as she spoke. If anything had happened, he'd be able to see it there. Wouldn't he?

'And Gordo was so helpful,' Bec added.

'Let's get down to business.' Ed called the meeting to order.

They took their places around the table.

'I think we should let Bec start,' Ed continued. 'She can tell us what she learned on the weekend.'

'It was awesome,' Bec said. 'There were about six hundred people there.'

'Six hundred?' Nick cut in. 'That's a lot of people. Surely we don't want that many.'

'If we can get them, why not?' Bec asked. 'The more people, the more money we can raise for the fire brigade. Gordo says six hundred is a good number for a ball around here.'

'Rod, will you be able to police that many?' Jean asked.

'I'll get some extra help in for the weekend,' Rod said. 'I'll have to think about how many. Bill, we will need some rooms here at the pub for them.'

'No worries,' the publican replied.

'I've made a list of the things we'll have to organise,' Bec continued. 'We'll need food and drink. Then there's the campsite, the stage, power for lights. Ed, we'll need all sorts of permissions and paperwork from the council.'

'That's fine. I assume that's why you wanted me on the committee,' the councillor said.

Bec had the grace to blush. 'We also need someone to organise the ute show.'

'Ute show?' Nick cut in again. 'We don't want a ute show. That'll just bring yobbos from all over the place to race.'

'Not a race. A show,' Bec said. 'We have to have one. Gordo says that a lot of people won't come if there's no ute show.'

'I don't suppose Gordo's going to organise it for us,' Nick muttered.

'No. But he will help whoever is organising it,' Bec said, ignoring the tone of Nick's voice. 'He'll want to enter the show. He won best ute at Augathella. The second year in a row.'

Nick heard the admiration in Bec's voice. It felt like a kick in the guts.

'Before we get down to that,' Hailey interrupted, 'hadn't we better decide on a date?'

'That's a good idea,' Ed said.

Hailey had prepared a list of other events in the area, and marked on a calendar what weekends might be available for the Farwell Creek B&S. As they discussed the options, Nick had trouble keeping his attention on what was being said. He was too busy watching Bec. Watching the way her eyes sparkled when she talked about the weekend she had spent at Augathella. The weekend with Gordo. He didn't like that one bit.

'That's decided then,' Ed said at last. 'Ten weeks from now.'

There was a murmur of agreement around the table.

'So – what are we going to call it?' Bec said.

'Call it?' Nick was puzzled. 'Isn't it just the Farwell Creek B&S?'

'It can be.' Bec's tone was scathing. 'But that's pretty dull. We need a catchier title. Gordo says a good name can really make a difference to the size of the crowd.'

'What do you consider a good name?' Hailey asked.

'Well,' Bec said, 'look at the other B&S balls. There's the "Plucked Duck", the "Peanut Pullers" and the "Bulldust and Bow Ties".'

Nick snorted derisively.

'Don't laugh,' Bec told him. 'The name is important. You want this to succeed, don't you?'

'Of course I do.' Nick couldn't believe that she even had to ask.

'Than we need a good name.'

'You mean Gordo didn't suggest one?' Nick stood up and moved away from the table. He walked through into the bar and dropped on to a stool.

'Another round for the committee?' Ruth Davies asked pleasantly.

Nick nodded, too annoyed to speak. If he heard Gordo's name one more time, he was going to explode. Or more likely say something he might regret later. He could not believe how bowled over Bec was by that idiot. Couldn't she see that he was all show and nothing underneath? What sort of a man would want to spend his life traipsing around the countryside getting drunk and showing off in his ute? And as for his job . . . you couldn't have a wife and raise a family if you were driving to a different town every few weeks for work. You couldn't even think about a wife unless you had something to offer her. Your own place. A future. All the things Nick used to have, but had lost.

'What's the matter with you?' Bec sat down on the stool next to him.

'Nothing.' Even to himself, Nick sounded like a petulant child, and that only served to make his mood worse.

'Come off it, Nick. This is me, remember. You never could fool me.'

'If you must know,' Nick threw his last vestiges of good judgement to the winds, 'I'm getting pretty tired of hearing about Gordo. Gordo says this. Gordo says that. You should hear yourself.'

'He's helping us,' Bec said. 'Giving advice, and good advice too. Why shouldn't we take his help?'

'And just what is he getting in return?' The words were out before Nick could stop them.

Bec slid off the stool, her face rigid with anger. 'What's that supposed to mean?'

'You don't think he's doing it out of the goodness of his heart, do you? You're not that stupid. He wants something, and I've got a pretty good idea what that might be.'

The anger on Bec's face turned to shock, then to disgust.

Nick couldn't stop himself. 'But maybe that's what you want too.'

'You're wrong, Gordo's not like that. And I don't . . .'

She paused, shaking her head as if in disbelief. 'Anyway, it's none of your business.'

Nick looked into Bec's flashing amber eyes and felt the rock beneath his feet start to tremble. In all the years he had known her, she had never looked at him like that. Even during the worst of their many arguments, he had never seen her look at him with dislike. Not until this moment. Far too late, he wished he could take back the last two minutes.

He searched for the words that would undo the damage, but realised there were none. 'I'm just looking out for you,' he said, hoping that he wasn't making things worse.

'Well I can look after myself, thank you very much.'

'Ah, here you two are.' Ed Rutherford's amiable voice cut through the silence around Nick and Bec. 'I have some more news for you.' He obviously had no idea what he had just walked into the middle of. 'I've been talking to the regional fire board,' he continued innocently. 'There is some training in Roma this week. For all the brigades in this area. Even though ours isn't really official yet, they are willing for you to go and take advantage of the training.'

Bec slowly turned away from Nick. She gave Ed a half-smile. 'I'm sure Nick will enjoy that,' she said shortly.

'No. No. You misunderstand,' Ed responded quickly. 'It's for you too, Bec. I've told them the two of you will drive down tomorrow morning, and will be working together until Friday. I hope that's all right.'

6

Bec picked up the heavy jacket and held it at arm's length while she gave it some intense scrutiny. She was no fashion icon, but even she knew that the jacket was going to be a Disaster – with a capital D. Iridescent orange just wasn't her colour. The shiny silver bands around the sleeves and hem didn't help – and as for the fabric! Sexy was not a word that immediately sprang to mind when she looked at the outfit. Hot might – but not in any way a girl might like.

'It's isn't supposed to look good,' the instructor joked. 'Not even on you.'

'Are you absolutely certain it doesn't come in black?' Bec teased back.

The instructor chuckled and moved towards another trainee, who was hopping around on one leg as he pulled on a pair of protective pants. Bec had a pair of those too. She was having enough trouble with the jacket; she didn't even want to think about the baggy pants with the elastic waistband and braces. She sniffed her jacket cautiously. The thick protective fabric smelled of smoke and sweat. She sighed. Despite the jokes and the smiling face she put on each morning, she wasn't having a good time at all.

The fire brigade training wasn't really bad. It was

hard work but it was also interesting. The trainers had brought a huge red truck from Brisbane and gathered volunteer firefighters from all over the region for this session. The interior of the truck could be turned into rooms of various sizes, with furniture and doors and stairs leading to the outside. To give the trainees some idea of what they might face in an actual fire, the instructors used smoke generators, alarms, flashing lights and even heaters to turn the truck into a very realistic imitation of a burning building. The two instructors were patient and enthusiastic. Bec believed in what she was doing. She should be having a good time. But she wasn't. The reason was standing just a few feet away, looking tall and competent and confident in a fireman's suit, which on him, actually looked pretty good.

She and Nick had travelled here from Farwell Creek in Nick's ute. The journey had taken almost two hours, and in that time they had barely spoken two words to each other. That hadn't happened before in all the years they'd been friends. She was mad at Ed Rutherford for putting her in this position, but mostly she was mad at Nick. Ever since she'd come back to the Creek, he had made it clear he wasn't interested in her. He therefore had no right to care that she had met someone else. Someone who was drop-down-dead gorgeous. Someone who was a lot of fun to be with. Someone who was very, very likeable. It was none of Nick's business. He didn't want her – and he had no right to complain if she decided to be with someone who did!

Bec glanced over to where Nick was standing with some of the other trainees. He looked so at home in his fireman's uniform, like Steve McQueen in *The Towering Inferno*. She looked like a fool, and a dirty, sweaty fool at that. Nick seemed to find the training ridiculously easy. He had barely raised a sweat during the fitness test, running to the top of the fire station tower with ease. He manipulated the fire extinguishers and hoses like he'd been doing it for years. On the very first day he had become the undisputed leader of their group. Not only that, but the only other female trainee was so busy flirting with him, it was a wonder she had time to even think about fighting fires. Sally whatever-her-name-was had blond hair and big blue eyes and somehow managed to look good even in the fireman's gear. She was a tiny thing, far too small to be a decent firefighter, at least in Bec's opinion. And she always seemed to need help. Help that Nick, it appeared, was only too pleased to give her. Not that Bec cared one hoot what Nick did, but how dare he give her a hard time about Gordo, when he was so smitten with little Miss Blue-eyed-and-breathless!

'Rally round, firefighters,' the instructor called from the top of the ramp leading into the big red truck.

Bec joined the others, careful not to even glance at Nick.

'It's time to put some of the things we've been talking about to the test.' The instructor grinned down at them. 'Although you'll mostly be fighting bushfires, there is always a chance you may be called on to help someone get out of a burning building.'

There was an anxious murmur among the assembled trainees.

'That's what this exercise is all about. One of you will be the victim. The other will have to perform the rescue.' The trainer stepped back inside the truck. A few seconds later, smoke began pouring out of the doorway. It wasn't real smoke – that would be dangerous – but it was close enough to the real thing to blind and confuse.

'Right. Sally, you can be our first victim.'

Bec hid a smirk as Sally and the instructor vanished inside the truck. She was keen to see Miss Perfect emerge from this with every blond hair in the right place. The instructor reappeared a few seconds later, and lifted the ramp into position.

'Nick, I want you to be the rescuer. Use the stairs at the far end – and bring her out the same way. Ready?'

'Yep.' Nick stepped briskly to the back of the truck. Bec scowled. Of course he'd be ready to rescue Miss Flashing-eyes-and-simpering-smile.

The instructor banged on the side of the truck, and a terrified scream rang out. Bec jumped, before realising it was simply Sally acting out her role. In two long strides Nick was up the stairs at the back of the truck. He placed his gloved hand on the metal door, feeling for heat. Bec remembered that section of their training. Another moment and he was gone. Inside the truck, Sally continued to scream for help. Her cries were so realistic that the sound started to fray Bec's nerves. It wouldn't be for long, though. Nick would be with her in a few seconds. He would toss her over his shoulder in that caveman style of his, and come striding out of the smoke. He'd be a hero. Any second now . . .

Sally's screams went on and on. A sudden loud thump inside the truck made Bec jump. She looked over at the instructors. Surely it was time they checked to make sure everything was all right? They seemed unconcerned about the time the exercise was taking. Bec was starting to worry. The smoke and flickering light were fake, but that didn't mean the people inside the truck were safe. A person could easily get hurt in such a realistic exercise. There was another loud thump inside the truck. Sally's screams had stopped. Was that a good thing? Bec wasn't sure. She shuffled her feet, fighting down an urge to run to the back of the truck and . . . do something. Anything.

Then the door at the rear of the truck crashed open, and Nick stepped through. Sally's arms were around his neck. His arms circled her small waist and thighs as he carried her down the steps. He laid her gently on the ground, and Bec felt a sudden rush of guilt. If Sally was hurt . . . Nick bent over the prostrate form and began resuscitation.

Bec took a hesitant step forward.

'Well done, Nick. Sally.' The instructors were smiling and nodding. Nick stopped his lifesaving efforts and stood up. He held out his hand and pulled Sally to her feet. They were grinning widely at each other.

'Thanks,' said Sally.

Bec glanced quickly around, hoping no one had noticed her near panic. She had almost made a fool of herself. That was Nick's fault too.

'Okay, that was the easy one. Big rescuer – small victim.' The instructor's grin should have served as a warning to all. 'Now we'll do it the other way. Nick is going to be our victim. Bec, you and Sally have to get him out of there.'

That wasn't quite the scenario Bec would have chosen, if she'd been given a choice. But she hadn't.

'It's about teamwork,' the instructor continued. 'You are far safer working as a team. And you don't know just what you're going to find. So . . . ladies. Are you ready?'

'Yes,' Sally answered cheerfully as she moved towards the rear of the truck.

Bec mumbled something and followed her.

The instructor signalled Nick to follow him into the truck.

'Isn't this fun?' Sally said in Bec's ear.

'I guess.'

'Wow, when Nick carried me out! He is so big and strong.' Sally looked at her. 'I know the two of you came here together, but . . . well . . . it doesn't seem as if . . .'

'No, we're not,' Bec answered, wondering why even relative strangers asked that question. 'We're just friends.' And not even very friendly at the moment, she thought.

'Okay, let's go,' the instructor said as he emerged from the truck in a cloud of smoke. 'Bring him out, girls. Down the stairs.'

Bec took a deep breath and led the way towards the truck. She felt for heat, just as Nick had, then grabbed the handle and swung the door open. The interior of the truck was a haze of smoke and flickering light. She stepped through and flinched as a raucous alarm began sounding close to her head. She looked around. Through the thickening smoke, she could just make out what looked like someone's lounge room. There was furniture, some of it toppled over, but no sign of Nick.

'Where is he?' Sally's voice was muffled inside her mask.

Bec shook her head. She had no idea.

Then she heard a low sound. A faint moan, like that of a person in pain. Nick. She listened intently, trying to locate the source of the noise.

'I can't see him,' Sally yelled over the alarm.

'Shut up! Listen,' Bec snapped back.

There it was again. She could recognise his voice, even when the only sound he could make was a moaning whisper.

She turned slowly. The smoke wasn't real, but it was so thick she could hardly see the other end of the room, and she realised she was panting as if she had run a mile. Nick was here somewhere, and she had to find him.

A big sofa dominated the far end of the room. She stepped to it and looked behind. Nick was lying face down on the carpet, caught between the sofa and the wall. For a second her heart contracted, and she felt a flare of panic.

It's only an exercise, she told herself, but she could hear the tension in her voice as she called Sally to help her.

Bec forced her way between the sofa and the wall. She pushed the sofa and Sally pulled. Gradually the gap grew wider.

'That's enough,' Bec gasped and bent to take hold of Nick. She grabbed a handful of the loose jacket and tugged. His arm moved, but his body was still wedged between the sofa and the wall.

'Shit.'

They could have made it easier for her. Bec dropped to one knee, put her shoulder against the sofa and gave one mighty heave. It slid forward. Sally leaped out of the way, then grabbed the sofa and added her weight to the task. Now Bec's way was clear. She reached under Nick's arms and took a firm hold. She braced her heels against the wall and pulled. He slid a few inches forward. She heaved again, grunting with the effort. He slid a few more inches, then stirred as if regaining consciousness. For a few seconds his arms flailed, and he caught her with a glancing blow on the side of the head.

She almost hit him back.

Sally stepped forward and grabbed Nick's hands. Together the two girls tugged him into the centre of the room.

'We'll have to carry him,' Sally said.

'You have got to be kidding!' Bec knew such a thing was beyond them. 'We'll drag him.'

Both girls renewed their grip on their victim and began dragging him towards the door. It seemed a million miles away, but at last they reached it. Bec grabbed the handle and thrust the door open. Light and sweet fresh air streamed in. She took a deep breath and looked down at Nick. His eyes were tightly closed, but she could almost see the corners of his mouth twitching. She was tempted just to push him head first down the stairs. But that would mean he had won, and she was having none of that.

'Come on,' she told Sally. 'One more effort.'

Side by side, the girls backed down the metal stairs, holding Nick by the shoulders, protecting his head and back, as his feet bounced from stair to stair until they all reached the bottom. Carefully they laid him down. Bec stepped back and straightened her back. She took several long, deep breaths of clear air. Under the heavy protective clothing, she was drenched with sweat. More sweat was running down her face and into her eyes, making them sting. Her hands were shaking so much she hid them behind her body, hoping no one would notice.

'Resuscitation,' the instructor called.

Before Bec could move, Sally had dropped to her knees beside Nick. Her hand was cradling his face and she was . . . well, Bec thought, it was mouth-to-mouth.

A smattering of laughter and applause ended the session.

'Well done, everyone.'

Bec paid no heed to the instructor's words. She stepped back as Nick opened his eyes and lifted himself easily to his feet. He smiled down at Sally.

'I see why they call it the kiss of life,' he said.

Sally blushed, and Nick smiled along with her, sharing the moment.

Bec turned away. She hardly even heard the instructor calling the end to the session. She walked calmly but quickly towards the fire station. Nick would have to run to catch up, and he was showing no signs of doing that. He was still talking to Sally. Bec slammed through the station into the women's locker room. Without so much as pausing for breath, she shed her clothes in an untidy heap in the middle of the floor. She opened her locker and reached for a towel, then stepped through into the shower room. Three open shower stalls lined the wall. She stepped into the nearest one, and turned the tap full on. She shivered with shock as a blast of cold water hit her body. She closed her eyes and forced herself to stand there for the few seconds it took for the water to heat up. As it did, she raised her face to the deluge, eyes closed, and let the water flush away the tension and the sweat and the smell of smoke. Eventually, she reached for the soap.

She was out of the shower, wrapped in a towel and digging in her locker for clean underwear when Sally arrived. The girl's face was a little flushed, and her eyes were sparkling. Bec didn't have to try very hard to figure out why. She could feel her bad mood returning. Just as Sally opened her mouth to speak, Bec's mobile phone rang. Thankful for the excuse to avoid conversation, Bec reached for it.

'Hi, Becca!' The voice down the phone was just what she needed to lift her mood.

'Hey! Gordo.'

Bec saw Sally's brow crease with interest. Well,

maybe she should give Miss Resuscitation Champion something to think about.

'The training's going well,' she said in response to Gordo's query. 'I'm having a great time.'

Sally turned away and started to undress very slowly, placing her dirty clothes in a neat pile on a bench. Bec knew she was listening.

'What about this weekend?' she said.

Sally was avoiding her eyes but Bec could feel her curiosity. She listened to Gordo for a minute then laughed out loud.

'You're right. It is a good idea,' she said into the phone.

She caught Sally's eye and smiled broadly. Sally was naked now, and there was nothing she could do but head for the shower, her curiosity unsatisfied.

Bec felt a small glow of triumph as she said goodbye to Gordo and snapped her phone shut.

The firefighters gathered in the pub on Friday night to celebrate the end of their training. Nick and the rest of the men were there well ahead of the girls. Nick's eyes kept returning to the door as he waited for Bec and Sally to arrive. He'd been watching Bec these last couple of days. Watching how she reacted every time Sally came near him. Whether she was aware of it or not, she was acting like a jealous girlfriend. Nick took some comfort from the thought. It must mean that she and Gordo weren't . . . hadn't . . . It was time, he decided, to clear the air between them. He had nothing to offer her, but maybe she could understand why he felt the way he did about Gordo. Gordo just wasn't right for her. He was a lightweight. All flash and no substance. He couldn't give Bec the future she deserved. Surely she could see that.

A huge cheer went up around the room as Bec and Sally arrived. Sally had dressed up for the evening. She was wearing a dress that clung to her like a second skin. For a short girl, her legs looked remarkably long, which was no doubt due to the high heels she was wearing. While the men around him whistled their appreciation, Nick had eyes only for Bec.

She was wearing black jeans that hugged her figure like an old friend. The jeans were tucked into those red cowboy boots she loved so much. Her red top barely reached her waist, and as she moved, flashes of the soft bare skin on her stomach and lower back seemed to call out for his fingers to stroke it. Her long wavy hair shone like silk. If he buried his face in that hair, he'd be able to smell the crisp, clean, slightly sweet scent of the shampoo she always used. She seldom wore make-up. To Nick's mind she didn't need it. Her skin was tinged golden by the sun and perfect as it was. Tonight she was wearing lipstick, making her lips shine in the most enticing way. All the emotions Nick had felt for her over the years came flooding back. He was a schoolboy again, stealing that first kiss. He was a teenager, lying awake, sweating, on the hot summer nights when she filled his thoughts. He felt again the awakening passion they had shared, before things changed. Before he lost everything – including his hopes for a future with Bec.

Both girls sashayed a little as they made their way to the bar, where half a dozen men vied for the honour of buying their drinks. In the melee, Nick managed to manoeuvre a moment alone with Bec.

'You look great,' he said, hoping she might accept that as a peace offering.

'Thanks.' She was non-committal.

'Look, Bec. I'm sorry. I shouldn't have said what I said back at the Creek.'

'No, you shouldn't.'

'I'm not trying to interfere. Honestly. Surely people who have been friends as long as we have . . .' Nick ran out of things to say. All the fine words he had rehearsed for this moment vanished from his mind.

'It's all right. I guess I was being a bit too prickly.' Bec smiled at him and the world was set to rights.

'Maybe we—'

Nick's words were cut off as the instructors called them together.

'All right everyone!' one of the instructors shouted. 'It's that moment you've all been waiting for. Time to announce the winner of this magnificent trophy.' He held aloft a plastic construction worker's helmet that had been sprayed with gold paint. 'This valuable piece is awarded by us, your beloved leaders, to the trainee who has demonstrated the greatest skill levels – or in the case of you lot, the one who has managed not to kill too many victims, or die too many times.'

Raucous laughter and a few shouts greeted the comments. Nick smiled at Bec and she grinned back, sharing a camaraderie that had been missing earlier in the week.

'And the winner is . . . Farwell Creek's finest, Nick Price.'

A wild cheer went up as Nick stepped forward to claim the trophy. His new mates slapped him on the back as he pushed through the crowd, but Bec's was the only approval he really wanted. She was applauding wildly, and the look on her face was worth every bump and bruise the training had cost him.

'Thank you. Thank you.' Nick took the beer glass

someone thrust into his hand, and raised it in salute. To the cheers of the group, he downed half the pot in a single gulp. When the excitement had died, he looked around for Bec. She wasn't there. He glanced along the bar, and caught the flash of her red top. She was hidden behind some other patrons. He had just begun to walk her way when the crowd moved and he saw that she was in the arms of some other man, who was kissing her in a way that left no doubt as to his feelings.

Gordo!

Nick turned away, all the pleasure from the evening crumbling into dust.

'Well done, Nick.' Sally was in front of him, her eyes shining. 'I knew all along you'd win. You were so good.'

'Thanks, Sally.' Nick bent to allow her to kiss his cheek. As he did, Bec and Gordo appeared at his side.

'G'day, Nick,' Gordo said pleasantly enough.

Nick shook the offered hand.

'Becca tells me congratulations are in order,' Gordo added as he draped his arm around Bec's shoulders. 'Well done.'

'Thanks.'

Nick looked at Bec, but she was too busy smiling up at Gordo to notice. Nick knew that look. He'd seen it on Sally's face just a few moments ago. Well, maybe two could play at the game. He put his arm around Sally's shoulders. The movement caught Bec's eye, and she frowned a little.

'We can't stay,' Gordo carried on cheerfully. 'Becca and I have got a long drive in front of us tonight.'

'A long drive?' Nick looked at Bec.

'We're heading up to Rolleston B&S,' Gordo answered for her. 'There's a big ute show there as well. I'm entered.'

Nick looked at Bec for confirmation. 'So you're not driving home with me tomorrow?'

'Gordo and I only decided to do this yesterday,' Bec said, looking slightly guilty. 'I forgot to tell you. Sorry.'

'No worries.' Nick kept his voice light, but his gut had clenched. 'Have a good time.'

Gordo's arm remained firmly around Bec as they made their way to the door of the pub. Nick let his arm fall from Sally's shoulders as he watched them go.

'Nick, are you coming back to the party?' Sally asked brightly.

Nick looked down at her. She was a very pretty girl, and nice to boot. Why shouldn't he accept the invitation in her eyes? He could rejoin the party, have a few drinks . . .

'No. I'm sorry, Sally,' he said gently. 'I think I might head back to the Creek tonight.'

'Oh,' Her disappointment was clear.

'I'm sure I'll see you around sometime.'

'Maybe at a fire?' Sally joked as she turned away.

Nick walked slowly back to the motel to collect his things. He tossed his trophy carelessly on to the empty passenger seat of his ute. It was getting late, and he faced a lonely two-hour drive back to the Creek. It didn't matter. Whether he was in the car or in his bed, the night ahead loomed lonely and sleepless.

7

A shaft of blinding light sliced through the open doorway and into Hailey's face. The golden rays of the sinking sun were her signal that the working day was done. It was time to close the doors and head home. She clicked on the shutdown icon on the computer, and slowly got to her feet. As the screen darkened, she flicked off the office lights and locked the front door. Pausing to pat the sleeping Cat, she slid the large metal door of the loading bay shut, and clicked the lock into place. When she turned around, she could see the lights in the kitchen window of her home. Slowly she headed towards the fence that separated the store from the house behind it. On the way, she paused to count the wooden pallets stacked ready for shipment. She should do something about those. Which reminded her, she should also send out an order for more feed supplements. Perhaps she should go back and do it now ... She shook her head. That was just an excuse, and no matter how many excuses she came up with, at some point she did have to go home.

She smelled it when she was halfway across the yard. Miss Mills was cooking dinner – again. Hailey guessed it would be another of her endless, interchangeable, tasteless casseroles. Miss Mills believed in a hearty home-cooked dinner. She also believed the evening meal should be hot, despite the fact that the temperature at this time of the year was in the mid thirties. Hailey had told her not to bother, but Miss Mills was determined to be what she called a 'good guest'. And that meant helping out. If only the woman had heard of salads.

Hailey opened the kitchen door and a wave of stifling heat engulfed her. As if the house wasn't already hot enough, Miss Mills had the oven going . . . again. Without even thinking about it, Hailey moved to open the big kitchen window. It wouldn't cool the room much, but it would let out some of the cooking smells. Windows were another of Miss Mills's firm beliefs. They should be closed at five o'clock, whatever the weather or temperature.

'So, Molly, what's it going to be? The money . . . or . . .'

From the lounge room came the urgent yells of some game-show audience. Miss Mills's television habits had come as something of a surprise to Hailey. She had expected the reserved and censorious woman to watch news programmes and documentaries. Instead, she sought out a nightly diet of game shows, reality TV and celebrity gossip. She would sit for hours watching the *Big Brother* housemates bicker. She was fascinated by the lifestyles of the obscenely wealthy, and had once actually shushed Hailey when she dared to speak during the climax of some game show. Miss Mills's secret television addiction should have made her more human and easier to live with. It didn't. Nothing was going to make the woman easy to live with.

'Is that you, Hailey?' a voice called from the lounge

room, where commercials had interrupted Miss Mills's viewing.

'Yes.' As if it could be anyone else.

Miss Mills appeared in the kitchen doorway, an empty teacup and saucer in her hand.

'I've got a nice lamb casserole for dinner,' she said. 'We'll eat at six.'

'I'm afraid I have to go out,' Hailey said. 'I promised Bill Davies I'd play at the pub tonight.'

Miss Mills sniffed her disapproval of pubs, the men who owned them and the young women who entertained patrons in them.

'How are things going with the rebuilding?' Hailey asked brightly, trying to avoid a lecture on what was considered 'proper' behaviour when Miss Mills was her age.

'I don't understand you Australians,' Miss Mills said. 'Why on earth do you insist on showers instead of proper baths? I have asked again and again for a bath, but it appears I will have to suffer showers for the rest of my stay.'

'It's about water usage,' Hailey replied, making a mental note to check the level in her own water tank. 'We use rainwater in our houses, and it doesn't rain all that often out here.'

'No, it certainly doesn't.' Thankfully, at that moment the commercials ended and Miss Mills vanished back in the direction of the television.

Hailey stepped into the bathroom to freshen up. On her way to the pub, she stopped by the store to pick up her guitar. Normally it sat on a stand in the corner of her living room. But not any more. Lately she had taken to keeping it at the store, where she could play without the dark cloud that was Miss Mills's disapproval hanging over her. Hailey thought she had probably inherited her musical talent from her mother, who had possessed a beautiful clear singing voice. She had bought the guitar with money earned working for her father during the school holidays. Playing was her greatest joy. She also loved to sing. She had started writing her own songs, and even sang them at the pub. When she played, she felt close to her parents.

'G'day, Hailey,' one of the patrons greeted her as she walked through the pub door. 'How's the dragon lady?'

'Now, Mick,' she replied firmly, 'Miss Mills is doing a fine job of teaching your daughter. Don't you talk about her like that.'

'So, how is it really?' Bill Davies whispered as he poured Hailey's drink.

'Horrible,' Hailey said softly. 'I know it's only been three weeks, but it feels like for ever.'

'Well, you shouldn't have her much longer,' Bill said. 'The crew were in here for a beer last night. They say the job is more than half done.'

'Thank you, Lord!' Hailey raised her eyes to the heavens.

She took her glass and walked through into the lounge bar, wondering if things would return to normal when the crew left. When Gordo left. Maybe Bec would spend some weekends in the Creek, instead of racing off to whatever B&S and ute show happened to be on. Maybe Nick would stop looking like thunder on the rare occasions she saw him. He seldom came to the pub these days, and when he did, he was unusually quiet. She knew the reason why. Gordo had been a great help in organising the fund-raising B&S. He'd helped them book a band, a stage and a stage crew. He'd found them a caterer and given them a lead on insurance and a liquor licence. He'd found some websites for them to advertise their event, and helped them plan their ute competition. But none of that had made him popular in Nick's eyes . . . or Hailey's own.

'Will you play the bird song, please, Hailey,' asked one of the diners as she walked towards her usual spot at the side of the lounge.

'Sure.' Hailey smiled back.

It meant a lot when the audience asked for the songs she had written. Of course, she still mostly played sing-along tunes by the likes of Neil Diamond and Bob Dylan. A few other requests floated her way as she settled herself on the stool that was kept in the lounge just for her. She placed the guitar on her knee and gently strummed it. As she fiddled with the tuning, she felt the tension drain from her body. This was the one place where she was truly at home. The one thing she could do that brought her total joy. She strummed the opening bars of 'The Pub With No Beer'. Slim Dusty always went down well as the opening track. By the time she finished the song, most of the patrons from the bar had moved through into the lounge, where they could hear her sing. With a nod to the woman who had requested it, Hailey launched into the bird song.

> *'Down by the creek at the break of day,*
> *Kookaburra laughs and he flies away.*
> *So what's the joke?*
> *I wish I knew*
> *Maybe I could fly away too . . .'*

As she sang, Hailey looked across the room and saw a stranger standing in the doorway. He was leaning against the wall, his faded blue jeans and black T-shirt outlining a slender body that looked graceful rather than thin. Wavy blond hair fell to his shoulders. He was gorgeous. The sort of drop-down-dead gorgeous that made her miss a chord. She glanced down at her recalcitrant fingers and began the next verse.

> *'Out on the plain in the noonday sun,*
> *Old Man Emu is on the run*
> *So what's the rush?*
> *I wish I knew*
> *Maybe I could run away too . . .'*

When she looked back up, he was still there, and he was watching her. He hadn't been in the pub before – she most certainly would have noticed. He wasn't one of the school-house construction crew. He didn't look like a builder. He looked too . . . gentle. Not soft, but gentle as in a gentle man. Not only that, he was carrying a guitar case.

> *'Up in a tree, see the sinking sun*
> *Black Crow caws, his day is done*
> *So what's the truth?*
> *I wish I knew*
> *Maybe I could talk to you . . .'*

He wasn't smiling. He wasn't frowning either. He was . . . intense was the only word Hailey could think of. She should have found it disconcerting, but she didn't. She just kept playing, enjoying the feel of the instrument in her hands and the sound of each sweet note. Somehow just knowing that he was watching gave her an added spark that resounded in the music. The applause that greeted the end of the song was even more enthusiastic than usual. Hailey hesitated. The crowd was calling for the next song, individual voices asking for favourites. She barely heard them. Her entire being was focused on the man, who had now moved out of the doorway. He was standing against the wall of the room, still watching her. He caught her look, raised his hands and applauded softly. Now he was smiling, and Hailey felt her heart give just the faintest tremor.

'All right,' she said to him, although the rest of the room thought she was speaking to them. 'I hope you're in the mood for something gentle. Although this was made famous by Simon and Garfunkel, it's actually a very old English folk song.' She started to sing.

'Are you going to Scarborough Fair?
Parsley, sage, rosemary and thyme . . .'

Out of the corner of her eye, she could see the stranger open his guitar case. He slung an acoustic guitar over his shoulder. As he moved closer to her, he began playing, his guitar complementing hers.

'She once was a true love of mine . . .'

He sang in perfect harmony with her. His voice was the sound of waving grass in the wind. It was at once soft and strong, with a rich timbre that sounded almost like an echo. It wove around hers, complementing and enriching her singing, but never once overshadowing her. His long fingers danced across the frets of his guitar like waves across a sandy beach. When he smiled at her, his eyes were green.

When they finished singing, the room was still. Not so much as a foot stirred, until someone somewhere said, 'Wow.'

Then the lounge erupted into applause and cheers.

Hailey felt herself blushing as she bowed slightly to acknowledge the appreciation. Beside her, the stranger smiled and nodded his thanks. The audience was still applauding as Hailey slipped off the stool to signal that she was finished, at least for a few minutes.

'I am really hoping that you're Hailey Braxton.' Even when he spoke, his voice had the rich timbre of a trained singer.

'Why are you hoping that?' Hailey asked.

'Because if you are, then you are the person I've come to see, and I don't have to walk away.'

His eyes really were the most remarkable shade. Not the brilliant green of an emerald, or the blue-green of a gum leaf. This was the rich dark green of young wheat when it first breaks through the soil into the sunlight.

'I'm Hailey,' she said softly.

'And I'm Steve Kelly.' He held out his hand.

Without thinking, Hailey put her hand in his. His fingers closed around her skin like the caress of soft fine leather. He didn't let her go, and she realised that she didn't want him to. Only when the sounds of the room intruded into their space did she think to ask, 'Do I know you?'

'Kelly. The Kelly Gang? You've hired us to play at your B&S.'

She recognised him then. The photos on the band's website hadn't done him justice. He'd looked like any other singer, with his long blond hair and tight blue jeans. In the flesh, he was more handsome. More charismatic. Just so much more!

'Why are you looking for me?'

'I was passing and thought I should stop by. Just to finalise details. Look, can we find a table?'

Hailey finally let go of his hand. 'Of course. Sorry.'

They found an empty table.

'You're good,' Steve said as they leaned their guitars side by side against the wall.

'Thanks.'

'Have you had much formal music training?'

'Not really. A few lessons at school, but that was on the piano. My mother had a guitar. She got me started.' Hailey felt the familiar twinge of sadness in her gut as she said the words.

Steve reached out and took her left hand. Hailey was too startled to protest. His touch was warm and gentle as he turned her hand over and ran his thumb slowly over the tips of her fingers, feeling the calluses formed by many hours' contact with the metal strings of the guitar.

Still holding her hand, he looked at her intently. 'Have you ever thought of playing professionally?'

Had she? It was a dream she had never voiced. Not to Bec. Not to her parents. She had barely allowed herself to think it.

'I'm not good enough.'

He didn't answer right away. Hailey took that to be agreement. 'I like your guitar,' she said, to cover the moment. 'It's a Martin, isn't it?'

'Yes.' He picked it up. 'Have a play; I'll get us something to drink.'

Before she could protest, he had placed the guitar on her lap and was moving towards the bar. She felt she should protest, but the guitar was too much of a temptation. She took a good hold of it and ran her fingers down the neck. It felt good. Better than good. In her wildest dream, she could never think of buying a guitar like this. It must have cost ten times what she had paid for hers. She tested the strings, then played a gentle chord. The sound was so much richer than her guitar. Each note had an extra depth and resonance. Without really thinking about it, she started to strum, singing softly to herself.

'That was good.'

Steve was back, carrying two glasses.

'Thanks.'

'The song you were playing when I came in . . . did you write that?'

'The bird song?' Hailey felt her colour rising. 'Yes. Ages ago.'

'It's pretty good, you know.'

'It's just a silly song.'

'Maybe. But with a bit of work, maybe a keyboard part . . . Do you write much?'

'A bit. There's not much else to do in a place like Farwell Creek.'

When he smiled, his whole face lit up. His eyes sparkled as if they were touched by dew. Hailey felt a curious flutter deep inside her, and a sudden hope that he might take her hand in his again.

He didn't. He lifted his beer to his mouth. 'Tell me about this B&S you're having.'

She told him about the fire in Miss Mills's cottage. She told him about their need to raise funds for a bush fire brigade. She talked about their committee and the difficulties faced by first-timers organising a B&S. 'It's been a lot of hard work,' she said. 'Harder than I thought.'

'But you've had help.'

'Oh yes, a lot of help. In fact, that's how I found

you . . . or rather, your band. Someone recommended you.'

'You must point them out to me some time, so I can thank them.' Steve smiled in such a way that his words seemed to take on an added meaning. 'So, what's it called, this ball of yours?'

'Ah, that's the problem. I have to get posters and things done soon, and I haven't been able to think of a name.'

As they talked, Steve had absently picked up his guitar. He was strumming softly.

'Do you know this one?' he asked as he played.

'Sure. I play it here all the time. The crowd loves it.'

'And this?' He started playing another riff.

'Of course.'

'All right,' Steve chuckled, 'here's the real test.' He started playing another song.

Hailey listened for a few seconds, then smiled. 'That's one of yours,' she said triumphantly.

'Ah, you have our CDs,' Steve said.

Hailey blushed again. 'Not exactly,' she confessed. 'When your band was recommended for the B&S, I had a listen to some of your tracks on your website.'

'That's close enough.' His smile was genuine. 'Did you like it?'

Hailey laughed. 'I liked it enough to want to hire you.'

Steve leaned forward again. His hand moved, as if to take hers, but he stopped before he did. He looked at her intently. 'Did you like it enough to play it?'

'I guess so,' Hailey said. 'I hummed along a bit. I didn't know the words.'

'But you could learn them. And the chords as well.'

'I could. But why?'

This time he did take her hand. He folded his long fingers around hers. 'Because, Cinderella, I'm your fairy godmother, and you are going to play at the ball.'

8

The heavens opened the weekend before the Farwell Creek B&S. Rain fell for about an hour on Saturday afternoon. Eyes were turned towards ceilings as the heavy drops of water splashed on to the dusty tin roofs of the homes, clattering like pebbles. The drops slowly came together to form thin streams of water, which trickled down the iron gutters and into the water tanks. The first splashes of rain darkened the thirsty earth for a few moments, before being absorbed as if they had never been. As the rain became heavier, small puddles formed. In the parched brown paddocks, the young horses kicked up their heels and ran bucking and kicking and squealing with feigned terror. Birds spread their wings and ruffled their feathers to welcome the crystal drops, and the trees seemed to lift their faces to greet the caress of the first rain in months. In the town itself, people scanned the sky anxiously. Televisions were turned to the weather reports, and internet searches displayed weather sites in the committee members' homes. With just six days to go, they were about to begin setting up the B&S site. They needed fine weather.

When the rain stopped and the sun returned, the puddles vanished quickly, soaking into the earth or steaming in the sun. The town heaved a collective sigh of relief. It rained again on Sunday night; a light, rhythmic beat on the roof to lull the townsfolk to sleep.

Monday morning dawned sunny and fine. The grass still bore the remnants of the night rain; the drops of water glistened like diamonds in the early morning light. The kookaburras welcomed the new day with a raucous salute. Their laughter echoed across still paddocks, where the cattle dozed contentedly or nibbled the damp grass. Gradually the town came to life. The sound of an engine broke the stillness. A small stock truck moved slowly along the still deserted main street, past the feed store and the post office. It turned at the crossroads leading to the school, and changed gear as it passed the school and the new teacher's cottage, with its pale blue paint still clean and not yet faded by the sun. Behind the school was a big empty paddock, dotted here and there with slow-moving cattle. The truck stopped at a wire gate leading into that paddock. The driver got out, opened the gate, and then closed it again after taking the truck through. He parked the vehicle and lowered the ramp. A few seconds later, he led a big brown horse down the ramp. It lifted its head and whinnied loudly, the sound echoing across the paddock, to be answered by the startled cry of a crow.

'Settle down, old friend.' Nick stroked the horse's nose. 'There's work to be done.' The animal nuzzled his hand, its breath warm in the chilly air.

Nick swung himself into the saddle and turned his horse's head towards the furthest corner of the paddock. He whistled softly, and a streak of blue-grey flashed from under the truck as his blue cattle dog took its accustomed place at his horse's heels. As he rode, Nick took long, deep breaths of the crisp, cool air, and listened to the small sounds of the bush. This was where he belonged. This was his home. His heart was wedded to the bush. His enjoyment was tinged, as it often was these days, with the sad realisation that he would never again know the pleasure of mustering his own cattle on his own land. His wasn't the only family to have lost their land to the banks in the drought. He was lucky he and his father had been able to stay on to manage the property. But managing someone else's land wasn't the same as owning your own. Ever since the day his father told him what had happened, Nick had been working and saving his money. He wanted nothing else than to buy his own property. He wanted to make a home and teach his children to love the land as he had been taught by his father. But when holdings ran into tens of thousands of acres, you either inherited your land, or you left. Nick didn't want to spend the rest of his life working for some unseen boss. Nor did he want to leave. He would just have to find a way to stay. Maybe when he did, he would also find a way to realise his only other dream. The one that included Bec O'Connell.

Ahead of him, the cattle watched him approach with heads lowered. Slowly they began to move, and he turned his horse to steer them gently in the direction he wanted them to go. They walked though the wet grass, cattle, horse and rider, and dog. The paddock was sparsely covered with trees, and sloped very gently down to the schoolyard fence. At the moment it was covered with tall scrubby grasses, but that was about to change. Bec had convinced the farmer who owned this land to make it available for the B&S. Reluctantly he had agreed, on the condition that his cattle were protected, and the land was not littered or damaged. Nick's job this morning was to take the cattle away to a safe holding area for the next week. He whistled his dog and with a movement of his arm sent it leaping through the grass to turn the leading beasts. A few moments later, the dog was back at his side, tongue lolling as it panted happily. If only it was that easy to make people do what you wanted, Nick thought, as he urged his horse forward around the slow-moving cattle.

Rod Tate decided the rain had been a good thing. He drank his morning coffee and waited for his new constables to arrive. Regional headquarters had given him three uniformed officers for the event, as well as two ambulance teams. The ambulances would not arrive until Friday, but with construction of the site beginning today, the extra police would be needed all week. During the ball itself, he and his men would be on duty twenty-four hours a day. He knew he could rely on some of the locals to help out with crowd control, but there were times when troublemakers needed to see the uniform.

He heard the car just as he finished his coffee, and went to meet his team on the front steps.

'Welcome to Farwell Creek.'

As they shook hands, Rod looked them over carefully. They seemed very young. Their uniforms looked as if they were brand new. Their shoes were so shiny he could almost see his face in them, and their broad-brimmed hats showed no sign of weathering or dust. He reminded himself they were all graduates of the police academy. They'd do just fine.

'I've organised rooms at the pub for you,' he told them. 'That's courtesy of Bill Davies, the publican. I'll take you over in a while so you can get settled. We'll be starting the duty roster from tonight. In the meantime, let's get you some coffee, and I'll fill you in.'

As the constables set about finding the small station's coffee mugs, Rod took a long look at the district map pinned to his wall. The B&S site was outlined in red. The paddock would be a bit soft today, after the rain. But as long as it stayed dry for the rest of the week, they'd be fine. His map showed the gates that would be made in the fences later today to give access to the site. Traffic control would be his problem. His other problem would be stopping the circle work. The ball tickets all clearly stated that circle work was banned, but when you got a bunch of young guys with hot cars together and added liberal amounts of booze, there was no stopping it. At best, he hoped to control it. At least the ground wouldn't be too slippery.

Rod gave a passing thought to Gordo. Although the construction crew had finished rebuilding the school house and moved on, Gordo still appeared regularly in the Creek. On a couple of weekends, he'd taken Bec away to balls and ute shows. Bec seemed rather smitten with the man's good looks and dynamic nature. Jean, on the other hand, wasn't impressed. Rod was keeping an open mind. Maybe the ball would sort things out – one way or the other.

In the big room at the back of the post office, Jean opened the first of the cardboard boxes that had been delivered with the mail bags early that morning. She reached inside and pulled out a T-shirt. It was fluorescent yellow. Or possibly green. Whichever, it wasn't her colour or her style. The word Committee was printed in large letters across the front and the back. The box should contain similar T-shirts for the rest of the committee members, along with a bundle that said 'Steward' for the support team. Not only that, her spare room was filled with boxes of T-shirts. These were souvenirs for the bachelors, spinsters and other assorted revellers who would be coming to the Creek that weekend. As were the boxes of stickers and caps and stubbie holders. Jean had drawn the line at B&S condoms. When she'd been dragged into the committee and put in charge of souvenirs, she hadn't realised just what that job would entail. She did now. She knew more about printing than she had ever expected or wanted to know. She had also spent a lot of money that the committee didn't have. She pulled a sticker from a box and looked at it. There was a cartoon of a canoe on water, with a single occupant who was holding a burning paddle above his head. 'Up The Creek' the sticker proclaimed in large letters. Jean had been against using that as the name of their ball. But Gordo had said it would bring in the punters, and she had been voted down.

She put the sticker back and settled down to sort the mail. There were about a dozen envelopes addressed to the B&S committee. Most would be from people buying tickets. According to Hailey, they had reached the break-even point in ticket sales. That meant the proceeds of the bar, food and souvenir stands would all be profit. Not to mention any on-the-day ticket sales. Jean just hoped it would all prove worthwhile. She hadn't grown up in Farwell Creek. Her home town was a couple of hours' drive further west. She had moved here as a young single mother when Bec was a toddler. But she still considered the Creek to be her town, and she did not want an influx of strangers here. She didn't want a lot of young people making the sort of mistakes she had made. She didn't want Bec making the same mistake. But it was out of her hands now, and that left her feeling very uneasy.

Jean put all the B&S mail into a single pigeonhole, to be collected later by Hailey. The event was shaping up to be a success, which should not have been that much of a surprise, given that Hailey and Bec were organising it. When they set out to get something done, they didn't let anything stand in their way. Jean could understand why a B&S would be attractive to them. They must get bored sometimes, living in this small town. Fridays down the pub were the only real nightlife. It wasn't exactly an exciting existence. Things had certainly become a lot more lively in recent weeks. The fire. The B&S project. Gordo. Jean had very real misgivings, but she'd gone along with what Bec and the others had wanted. No one, least of all her daughter, was going to say she hadn't done her bit.

Hailey sang softly as she checked the 'Up The Creek' B&S website. There were almost a dozen more requests for tickets. The rain obviously hadn't deterred anyone. They'd already sold more than three hundred tickets. And they had almost a hundred entries for the ute show. Hailey allowed herself a small glow of pride. They'd done pretty well for first-timers. The town was developing quite a buzz. The pub was busier than it had ever been, with people meeting there to discuss the latest ball news. Even though she had the house to herself again, Hailey still spent a lot of evenings at the pub, playing her guitar and singing. When people commented on the new songs she was playing, she just smiled and said thank you.

The CD case lay next to the small player Hailey had

installed in her office at the store. She picked it up and looked for the ten thousandth time at the photo on the front cover. It showed the Kelly Gang, resplendent in blue jeans and checked shirts, draped against a stockyard fence. Steve was in the centre, his hat in his hands to let the camera see his handsome face and that mane of beautiful golden hair. The photo inside the CD booklet was even better. It was a close-up. Hailey had always said she would never date someone whose hair was longer than hers . . . but for Steve she would make an exception.

Except, of course, she wasn't dating him. She'd met him only that one time, when they'd played together in the pub. He had sent her a CD of their music, but that was just business. So were the e-mails, even if they did come far more often than business dictated. Steve was just being friendly. And Hailey had convinced herself that he was joking when he'd asked her to play with the band. Still, in the note that accompanied the CD, he had suggested she practise. She had, partly because she liked the songs, but mostly because she liked the sound of Steve's voice. Singing with the CD reminded her of singing with Steve. Brought back memories that put a smile on her face and a warm glow in her heart.

Of course, nothing was going to happen. She wasn't the sort of girl that things like that happened to.

'David Ryan, you'd find those maths problems easier if you looked at the book in front of you rather than out the window!'

'Yes, Miss Mills.'

The boy dragged his eyes away from the window, but Miss Mills knew he'd be looking out there again before long. This was going to be a dreadful week! Why on earth did the committee have to choose a site next to the school for their dratted ball? Her classes would be disrupted all week as they prepared the site, built the stage and whatever else they were going to do. Then, at the weekend, the place would be overrun. She would have to talk to Rod about having someone stationed at the school, to prevent break-ins.

Still, she had to admit the town had rallied very well around the campaign to form a fire brigade. It was all a bit late, of course, after she had lost everything in the fire. Her new cottage, however, was better than the old, with a much nicer kitchen, even if it did have a shower instead of a bath. Those workmen hadn't done too bad a job. The grass had even grown back on the school grounds, so no trace remained of that night. All she had to do now was survive this ball. A Bachelor and Spinster Ball. Really! It all sounded very dubious. Miss Mills had no intention of going. She'd stay at home and lock her doors.

Bec saw Nick's truck going the other way as she approached the ball site. She raised a hand in salute, but didn't see whether or not it was returned. She felt a twinge of sadness. She really missed Nick. Not that either of them had gone anywhere. But the bond between them had. She had first noticed it when she returned to the Creek last year. Losing the property to the bank during the drought had hit him hard. All his life, Nick had known that he would one day inherit the family property. As kids, they had even once joked that they would marry and run it together. They might have grown out of that idea, but in its place, Nick had made real plans; plans that had come crashing down during the drought. Other things had changed too. Hailey's parents were gone. A new teacher lived in a new cottage next to the school. That cottage was the first new building in the town since Bec was a child.

Which brought her to the subject of Gordo. His crew was currently working on some buildings in Charleville, so she hadn't seen much of him for the past three weeks. Not that it mattered. She was too busy with the ball anyway. He'd be here on Saturday. The thought made her smile.

She pulled through the gateway into the now empty paddock behind the school, carefully guiding the trailer that she was towing. The car and trailer bounced slightly as she drove towards the chosen site for the B&S stage. It was the work of just a few minutes to position two ramps against the trailer and drive the small tractor down. Attached to the tractor was a grass slasher. It was time she got to work. She had to cut all the long grass around the ball site and the camp ground.

The stage and the ball compound were fairly close to the back of the schoolyard, with an enclosure behind it for the caravans and tents belonging to the stage crew. They would tap into the power and water at the school, but several generators would arrive during the next day or two to provide light for the camping ground. One area had been marked for the ute show. That would be Gordo's patch. Another part of the site was set aside for food and booze. The portable toilets would no doubt be ... interesting. An outdoor ball would be fun, if it didn't rain. Bec glanced up at the skies. Brilliant blue. She nodded in satisfaction and continued working.

By the end of the day, Bec had cleared a little over half the campsite. The sun was setting as she headed home. Her mother was not in the house. A B&S

committee meeting was scheduled for tonight at the pub. She guessed Jean was already there. She quickly showered and walked to the pub.

The pub was full to overflowing, and the one topic of conversation was the ball. Anne Ryan was there, talking about the recovery breakfast she and the school committee were hosting. Art Miller was accepting the town's thanks for allowing his land to be used for the event. Matt Johnson had broken his habit, riding into town on a Monday to join in the fun, while his horse munched hay in its stable. The pub was so crowded that the committee meeting had to be held outdoors, around a table dragged into the garden, where at least they could hear each other speak. Not that there was much left to talk about. If they'd forgotten anything, it was a bit too late now to act. All that was left was the unexpected, and there was nothing they could do about that.

At last, Ed Rutherford banged his glass on the table and called for order.

'We are now headed into the home straight,' he said. 'As fire brigade chairman, town councillor, B&S committee chairman and whatever other job Bec has seen fit to foist upon me—' His words were interrupted by a ripple of laughter around the table, which Bec joined in. 'As I was saying,' Ed continued, 'it is my duty to toast the bunch of people sitting around this table.'

Most of the group shuffled in their seats.

'I mean it,' Ed continued. 'The purpose of this coming weekend is not to have a good time – at least, not for us to have a good time.'

That brought a few more chuckles.

'We're doing this – you are doing this – to raise

money for the fire brigade. The whole town owes you its thanks. Now I want everyone to raise their glasses and drink to . . . the committee!'

Everyone drank.

'On that subject,' Jean reached for a bag lying by her feet, 'I have here your uniforms for the weekend. Come and get them. They come in two sizes – big and not so big.'

One by one the group collected their shirts. The formal part of the meeting was over, but everyone seemed reluctant to leave. Nick was talking to Rod when Bec brought them both their T-shirts. Rod took his and wandered off to find Jean. Bec and Nick didn't say anything for a while.

'Do you think it's going to be a success?' Bec finally broke the silence.

'I think we'll raise the money we need,' Nick said.

'Good.'

Watching from the doorway, Jean shook her head in disgust. 'Those two need a good slapping,' she said as Rod appeared at her elbow.

Rod knew who she was talking about.

'I assume Gordo will be here this weekend,' he said.

'Barring any accidents,' Jean replied. Her tone suggested that while she would not wish harm on anyone, a minor accident involving Gordo would not necessarily be a bad thing.

'Do you think they'll still be together after the ball?' Rod asked.

'Who? Bec and Gordo or Bec and Nick?'

On the other side of the table, it was Hailey who made the first move to leave. She got slowly to her feet, gathered up her T-shirt and raised a hand in salute. She walked back through the pub, smiling the occasional greeting at her neighbours, but was alone as she stepped out of the front door into the night. Once she moved away from the noise of the pub, the night was very quiet. That would change over the next few days as the stage crew moved in. But tonight, the town was exactly as it had been for every night of her life.

'Miss. Excuse me!'

The shout from the roadway startled Hailey. She spun around to find one of Rod's young constables walking towards her. He was leading a horse.

'Isn't that Matt Johnson's horse?' she asked.

'Yes, miss. It is. I was hoping you would tell me where I could put it for the night.'

Hailey felt a touch of fear. 'What's happened? Is Matt all right?'

'Oh yes, miss, he's not hurt. I've arrested him.'

'You've what?'

'Arrested him. Driving under the influence.'

'Drunk driving?' Hailey's confusion was evident in her voice. 'But he wasn't driving. He was riding that horse.'

'He was still drunk in charge – and on a public road.'

'You're from the city, aren't you?' Jean's voice from behind her forestalled any comment Hailey might make.

'Now, Jean,' Rod said in a placating manner as they approached from the direction of the pub.

'Sir.' The young constable didn't quite snap to attention. 'I asked Miss . . . the lady for help with the horse. I've arrested the rider for drunk in charge.'

'Heaven help us all,' Jean sighed. 'Young man, if you had even the slightest idea of how things worked in the bush, you'd know that by this hour of night, Matt is not the one in charge – the horse is.'

Hailey bit back a giggle, while Rod erupted into a sudden fit of coughing. The young constable looked at his superior with pleading eyes.

'It's all right, Constable,' Rod said. 'I'm sure we can sort this out. Hailey, would you put the horse back in its stall, please.'

Hailey took the animal's reins, while Rod took the constable by the arm and steered him back towards the police station, where no doubt Matt Johnson was already sleeping off his evening's drinking.

'Well,' said Jean to the world in general, 'this is a great start.'

Matt Johnson appeared at the store the next morning to thank Hailey for taking care of his horse. He seemed none the worse for a night at the police station.

'The bed was pretty comfortable,' he told the two girls. 'And I didn't have to put up with the missus' snoring.'

Bec bit back a smile. 'They're not charging you?'

'Not likely, after the ear-bashing your mum gave the sergeant.'

'I would have liked to have been a fly on the wall for that one.'

'Yeah. She was as mad as a cut snake. Scared the willies out of me, I can tell you.'

'She scares me sometimes too,' Bec said. She smiled to make it a joke, but deep down she knew there was some small vestige of truth in the words.

'Will we be seeing you at the ball?' Hailey asked as Matt took his leave.

'Dunno. I thought I might give it a go. Might even bring the missus.' He tipped his hat before walking away.

The girls looked at each other and Bec raised a surprised eyebrow. Matt Johnson never took his wife anywhere. She couldn't remember the last time she had seen the woman. She probably wouldn't recognise her if she bumped into her at the pub. Not that she was likely to.

'Have you seen Cat this morning?' she asked as they loaded supplies into the back of her ute.

'No. There were no bodies on the step this morning,' Hailey answered. Cat was well known for climbing into customers' cars. All the locals knew him, and would bring him back as soon as they could. Hailey got behind the wheel and set out on a delivery run, leaving Bec in charge of the store.

The morning seemed to take an age to pass. Bec kept walking outside to glance up and down the street. It looked much as it did every other day. A few people dropped in to buy something, but mostly they wanted to ask about the ball. What time did the music start on Saturday? When were they scheduled to be stewards? Bec was pleased at the support. Some of the towns-people had been slow accepting the idea of a B&S, but now it was almost upon them, they had all thrown their weight behind it. She could see a lot of comings and goings at the ball site, and was eager for Hailey's return. Bec was due to continue slashing the grass at the camp-site as soon as she was free of her commitments at the store. Back in the office, she was checking the mail for any new ticket sales when she heard a plaintive meow. Cat strolled into the office and went straight to his milk bowl. When he discovered it was empty, he looked up at Bec with accusing eyes.

'Where have you been?' she asked as she reached for the fridge door.

'He came home with me last night.' Nick was standing in the doorway. 'He must have jumped into the back of the ute when I was parked outside the pub.'

'Again? Is there something going on between the two of you?' Bec poured milk into Cat's bowl.

'Us guys have got to stick together. Isn't that right, Cat?' The feline was too busy to answer.

'One of these days he's going to get into the wrong car – and before he knows what's going on, he'll be in Birdsville,' Bec said.

'I reckon he might just find his way back here, though.' Nick smiled fondly at Cat, who was enjoying his breakfast. 'He knows where his home is.'

'I guess he does,' Bec agreed.

Nick stayed leaning against the door and neither of them said anything as they watched Cat drink his milk. The animal finally lifted his head and licked his lips. Then he strolled across the office to the unoccupied chair, jumped on to it and curled himself into a ball. With a contented sigh, he closed his eyes and fell instantly asleep.

'I can offer you a cup of coffee,' Bec said, grinning, 'but it looks like I can't ask you to sit down.'

'I've got to go anyway,' Nick said. 'I was just dropping him back.'

'Are you working up at the site?'

'Yes. We start fencing the various areas today. The stage compound, the campsite and so forth.'

'I'll come up when Hailey gets back.' Bec said. 'I'll get on with cutting the grass.'

Nick nodded. 'See you later.'

The doorway looked very empty when he had gone. Bec slid her chair across the small office, to tickle Cat under the chin. He stretched and purred. Cat always found his way home. It was a talent he had. Bec had thought she'd found her way home too, but now she wasn't so sure. She left the office and walked out into the street. The town looked the same as it always had. The pub and two shops on one side, the post office and her home on the other, next to the police station. The garage at the far end of town had the same faded paint and advertising signs that she remembered from her childhood. Including the school and a handful of houses, Farwell Creek was a cluster of about twenty buildings. It had always been home to Bec. It was only when she left it that she realised how much she loved it. When Hailey's parents died, she had not hesitated for a second. She came back because her friend needed her. She came back because she mourned the loss of two people who were almost family. But most of all, she came back because she knew it was where she wanted to be. It was home.

Change came slowly to small country towns, but it had come to Farwell Creek during the past year. It was more than just the new digital petrol pump at the garage or the new teacher's cottage. People changed too. Hailey's parents were tragically gone. Bec's best friend was struggling with grief and desperate to hold on to their memory and their legacy. The bank had taken Nick's family farm, and taken his future at the same time. Jean had grown short of temper and even shorter of patience. And Bec had changed too. Since Hailey's parents had died, she had been wondering more and more about the father she had never known. Maybe it was time she confronted her mother about Ken O'Connell. Maybe she could find him. Get to know him. Because one day it would be too late, if it wasn't already.

The phone interrupted her thoughts.

'G'day, Becca.' Gordo's energy and enthusiasm seemed to flow down the phone line and wash over her.

'Hi.'

'Are you almost ready for the weekend?'

'I think so. We are starting the set-up today. The stage crew is due to arrive tomorrow. When are you coming?'

'That's why I rang,' Gordo said. 'I won't be able to get away. This job is running over, and we have to finish this week. I'll be stuck here until Friday – then we have to get the gear back to base. I won't get to the Creek until Saturday. Sorry, babe.'

Bec felt a wash of disappointment. Gordo had hoped to finish his job in Charleville earlier in the week, and join Bec for final B&S preparations.

'I'm joining up with Mutley and a few of the others on Saturday morning. We'll get a convoy up and arrive at your doorstep in real style!'

'Great.' Bec tried to sound enthusiastic. It wasn't Gordo's fault, but she still felt as if he had let her down.

'I really am sorry, babe, but I will make it up to you this weekend. I promise.'

'I know you will.'

Bec put the phone down. She was still staring at it when Hailey walked in.

'Are you all right?'

'What?' Bec was so deep in thought, she hadn't heard her coming.

'Are you all right? You're staring at the phone as if you wanted to set fire to it.'

'We've had more than enough fires around here already,' Bec said with a brave attempt at a smile. 'That was Gordo. He's not going to get here until Saturday morning.'

'That's a shame.'

'It's not his fault. Work.'

'I know.'

'But I was hoping . . .' Bec's voice trailed off.

'You were relying on his help. Move, Cat!' Hailey pushed the protesting beast off the chair and sat down. 'Or is it just that you haven't seen him for a couple of weeks?'

'Well . . .'

'Come on, Bec,' Hailey said. 'You haven't been very forthcoming about Gordo. Time to tell all.'

Bec recognised the tone of Hailey's voice. She knew her friend wasn't about to let this go until she had confessed.

'There's not that much to tell.'

'After those weekends away together, there must be something,' Hailey insisted, raising one eyebrow. 'I've seen the guy, remember? I know how gorgeous and sexy he is.'

'I like him. We have a good time together.'

'How much of a good time?' Hailey's tone made it clear just what she was thinking.

'You've got to be kidding!' Bec was shocked. 'In the back of a ute? At a B&S camp site? No way.'

'Are you saying you haven't . . .'

'No.'

'Just how far have you . . .'

'Well, he's gorgeous. We've . . . well . . . a bit. We sleep in the same tent, but with all those people around . . .' Bec knew Hailey wasn't that keen on Gordo. She thought Nick was the one for Bec. She was wrong. 'I like being with him,' she added.

'But?'

'But sometimes I wish he was a little less interested in balls and utes.'

'And a little more interested in you?'

'It's not just that.' Bec searched for the best words. 'Take Han Solo . . .'

'*Star Wars?*'

'He's a rogue and a good-time boy,' Bec continued, ignoring Hailey's raised eyebrows. 'He seems shallow and uncaring, but deep down, he's honourable. We know all along he's going to join the resistance. Not just because he loves Princess Leia, but because it is the right thing to do.'

'And Gordo wouldn't?'

'He might. I don't know.'

'And where is Nick in this little scenario?' Hailey wasn't about to pull her punches. 'Is he supposed to be Luke Skywalker?'

'Well, Luke is Leia's brother.'

'Yes, but Nick isn't your brother. And this isn't a movie.'

Bec didn't answer.

'He's not happy about you and Gordo,' Hailey continued.

'I know.'

'And neither is your mum.'

'After what happened with my father, Mum wouldn't be happy with any man I was involved with.'

'She'd be happy with Nick.'

Later that afternoon, Bec sat on the hard metal seat of the tractor, earphones protecting her from the engine noise as she worked her way back and forth across the ball ground. She was beginning to hate both the tractor and the slasher behind it, but she had now almost finished her job of mowing the entire site. The rain had helped lay the dust, but she still wore a mask to stop herself breathing in the dirt and chaff kicked up by the slasher. Nothing was going to protect her rear from the bumps and bruises that came with driving a tractor that had been built long before suspension was invented.

The campsite was now finished. The lights and generators were in place. So too were the portable toilets. Bec had watched them arrive, and hoped she would not ever need to use one. Nick and a couple of other men were already hard at work with a post-hole digger, putting up thick wooden posts that would be the cornerstones of the fence around the stage and the organisers' compound. The ambulance would be based there, as well as the police and crowd-control teams. The fence itself wouldn't go up until after the stage arrived tomorrow, but there was a pile of fencing equipment already there. Nick had been placed in charge of setting up the site. Bec had not a moment's doubt that it would be done on time and done well. Nick was like that. He never let her down.

Her eye was caught by movement at the school. It was mid afternoon, and classes were breaking up for the day. A boy and a girl darted quickly out from the school building and headed for the big gum tree near the corner of the playground. Bec decided she could use a break. She turned off the tractor and watched the two of them duck behind the tree. She knew that spot. There had been a hole in the fence there when she was a kid. There still was, she guessed as she watched the kids reappear and sprint towards the church. She guessed they must be eleven or twelve years old. In fact, one looked a like Anne Ryan's boy, David. They disappeared behind the building. She could guess what they were doing. The same things she did there when she was their age. That was where she had smoked her first cigarette and was violently ill. When she was not much older than these kids, she'd sampled alcohol for the first time while hiding behind the church. Hailey had smuggled a half-full bottle of wine out of her parents' house. The three of them – Hailey, Bec and Nick – had drunk from the bottle, feeling very adventurous. There had been hell to pay when their parents found out. Hailey's father had taken it fairly well, but Bec's mum was furious.

Cigarettes and alcohol weren't the only things Bec had learned about behind the old church. Her lips curved into a smile as she remembered. How old had she been? Twelve? Thirteen? That first time Nick had grabbed her hand and dragged her through the hole in the fence, leaving Hailey behind. They had run laughing to their hiding place, where Bec had expected Nick to produce another of the cigarettes he sometimes pilfered from his parents. He hadn't. They had leaned back against the wooden wall of the building, breathing hard from their sprint across the school ground. Without warning, Nick had suddenly turned to her and kissed her. Full on the lips. For a few seconds they had both stopped breathing and just looked at each other. Then she had kissed him, a little more slowly this time.

Sitting on the tractor, the sun beating down on her head and her bum aching from the rough going, Bec could remember every detail of that afternoon. That first kiss had been a journey of discovery, for both of them. She could still see the look in Nick's eyes. She could feel the soft warmth of his lips, and the crazy butterflies in her stomach. She could remember the touch of his hands as he put his arms around her. She had been surprised by how soft his lips were. How strong. How good. That day, and in the many months that followed, they had learned all about love. The lessons never went too far, but she could remember them as clearly as if it was yesterday. He had made her feel so alive. Her heart, her body, even her mind. He had touched them all. No one had made her feel like that since. Not the boys she had dated in college, nor the men she met when she lived in the city. Not even Gordo. Nick was the only one who had ever made her feel as if she could reach out and touch the shimmering stars in the night sky. Feel like she must be in love. It might have been puppy love, but it was love. They had never doubted that for one second. Bec suddenly realised that she wanted to feel like that again. The excitement. The eagerness. The yearning. She wanted to be in love again. With Gordo? Or with Nick?

She looked across at the fencing team. Nick was easy to find. He was taller than most men, and years of hard work had made his body muscular and strong. She could still see the boy he had been, in her mind, if not with her eyes. She and Nick had been children then, finding their way, yet the feelings between them had been more real, more exciting and more fulfilling than anything else she had ever known. Things were different now. They had grown into friends – not lovers. At times they were barely friends. But other times, when she looked at him, she wondered what it would be like now they were adults. Maybe that was why she hadn't slept with Gordo. She hadn't exactly lied to Hailey. There had been chances. Gordo had certainly made it clear what he wanted. But did she want to sleep with him? The answer came as a slow ache low in her body. Nick. A part of her still wanted Nick, although she knew their chance was long gone. Maybe Gordo was the one who could help her get over this childhood hang-up. Gordo was gorgeous and sexy and he wanted her. Maybe it was time she said yes.

The town looked exactly as Steve remembered it. The sign saying Farwell Creek. The faded paint on the pub. The main street – the only real street – with its wide gravel verge had a comforting air of familiarity. There were a couple of dusty cars parked in front of the pub, and one near the post office. He guessed that somewhere the B&S site would be humming with activity, but he couldn't see it. If the town was exactly as he remembered it, he hoped Hailey was too. He hoped her fingers really did float across the strings of her guitar with the grace and certainty he remembered. He needed to be sure that her voice truly was the sound of bells on a clear frosty morning. Those songs she wrote . . . were they genuinely as good as he recalled? He tried to concentrate on her music, but all he could think about was that smile. Was it really bright enough to put the sun to shame? She could not possibly be as beautiful as the girl he saw when he closed his eyes and thought of her, which he had been doing constantly since the day they met.

Steve turned his car off the road and parked outside the feed store. For a few moments he just sat and looked through the doorway into the dark interior. He couldn't see anyone, but that wasn't surprising. She was probably doing . . . whatever it was she did in there surrounded by bales of hay and dangerous-looking farm implements. He glanced in the rear-view mirror at the recording equipment that covered the back seat of his Holden Commodore. He had brought all that gear on the remote chance that his memory wasn't playing tricks on him. Hoping he wasn't about to make a terrible fool of himself, he got out of the car.

As he slammed the car door, a figure appeared in the doorway of the feed store. Steve's insides did a fair impression of tumbleweed on a windy day. She was of average height and average shape. Her hair was an average shade of brown. She was wearing faded blue jeans and a T-shirt, and she was even more beautiful than he remembered. His heart leaped at the sight of her. She was everything he remembered and more. The bale of hay, however, was unexpected.

Hailey took two steps, then stopped. 'Steve! I . . . This is a surprise.'

Her voice was birdsong on a spring evening and her smile was brighter than a thousand stage lights.

'Well, I thought I might come out a day early . . .' he mumbled. He might have offered to shake hands, but her right hand was busy balancing the load on her shoulder.

'Oh.' She looked intently at him, and he realised that he had forgotten the gold highlights in her eyes. He wouldn't do that again.

'Yes. I thought we could rehearse a bit before the rest of the band arrive tomorrow.'

She smiled and shifted the weight of the hay.

'Would you like a hand with that?' he asked.

'No thanks,' Hailey said. 'It's not heavy.'

'It looks it.'

'It's all about balance. If you position it just right, then it's easy. I'm taking it next door. Do you want to come?'

'Okay.' At this moment, he would have followed her anywhere, just so that he could keep looking at her.

She turned towards the pub, and he fell into step beside her.

'Do they serve a lot of hay at the pub?' he asked.

'Only on Thursdays,' she said, and they both laughed. 'It's for Matt Johnson's horse.'

'Yes . . .'

'He rides his horse to the pub so he doesn't have to drive when he's drunk,' Hailey explained, 'although things don't always go according to plan.'

They walked into a shed. Part of it had been turned into what Steve imagined was a stable of some sort. The place had a strong, earthy smell of horse and hay and he didn't know what else. He suddenly remembered a dozen songs and jokes about making love on the hay. He looked at Hailey, the way the faded blue jeans and the T-shirt outlined her lithe body. The way she moved. The golden glow of her skin. It caused him such a wave of desire that he felt his hands start to shake. Luckily Hailey didn't notice. She tossed the bale casually into a corner. It landed with a very heavy-sounding thud.

'I must remember never to get you mad at me,' Steve said as they walked back to the feed store.

As they stepped through the office door, Steve heard a familiar sound. He looked down at Hailey. 'You've been listening to the CD I sent.'

'Of course,' she replied. 'It's very good.'

'Well, thank you, ma'am,' Steve drawled in his best cowboy voice. 'I do both kinds of music you know, country and western.'

How he loved to hear her laugh.

'Have you been practising?' he asked.

'Are you really sure you want me to play with you? You're a professional. I just sing at my local pub. I'm not—'

'You *are* good enough,' he interrupted her before she could get the words out. 'You only have to look at the way the crowd responds when you sing.'

'But they're my friends,' she said quietly. 'They'd clap even if I was lousy.'

'Yes, they would,' Steve told her. 'But they wouldn't cheer the way they do. And they wouldn't ask for more. Not night after night. You're good. And I want you to play with us. I want you to play with me.'

He watched her face as he spoke. The thought that she might have changed her mind was almost more than he could stand. Playing with Hailey had been a revelation, and not just musically. The music was good. Better than good, it was great. But the feeling of sharing the song and the emotion with her was better than anything he had ever felt before. That short impromptu concert in the pub had given him more pleasure, more satisfaction than a hundred gigs and a thousand screaming fans. One smile from Hailey was all the approval he needed.

She didn't look at him for a long time, and when she did, he searched her eyes trying to find an answer there. He saw excitement, but also fear and a deep sadness that he didn't understand.

'You don't have to decide now,' he told her. 'Why don't we try a few songs together? Just you and me. Let's see how it feels.'

'I have the store . . .'

'We can do it whenever you want. After work is fine.'

'All right.' She gave in. 'But not at the pub. It's been really busy there this week, and I don't want too many people watching.'

'Wherever you want.' Steve felt a twist of excitement. One chance, that was all he wanted.

'You could come around to my place. I'll make us something to eat and we can play.'

'That would be great. Don't make too much of a fuss about dinner.'

'You've never eaten my cooking,' Hailey said. 'I can just about boil an egg.'

'Then a boiled egg will be fine.' He knew she was joking, but he wasn't. Not really. He would do almost anything to get her to play with him again.

'But I still don't think I'm good enough to play at the ball.'

'Please, just give me a chance,' he said quietly. 'Give yourself a chance.'

The room wasn't exactly rock and roll. There was a couch with a floral pattern. The curtains were floral too. Hailey hadn't realised before how totally into floral furnishings her mother had been. She'd also been into family photographs. They were everywhere. Mostly they featured Hailey and her dad, because her mother had been the one with the camera. There was Hailey as a baby on her dad's knee in this very room. Hailey astride a pony, with her dad firmly holding the reins. A teenaged Hailey behind the wheel of her dad's ute. She still missed both her parents terribly, but it was her father's absence that hurt the most. He was the one she had always turned to for advice. She couldn't help but wonder what he would have said about the man who was at this moment running cables around the Braxton living room. She had a sneaking suspicion they could have been friends.

'I need one more power point,' Steve said.

Hailey dragged an armchair forward to reveal the wall behind, the power point and a very dusty strip of carpet.

'Oops. Sorry. I'm not the world's greatest housekeeper,' she said, a little embarrassed. During her residency, Miss Mills had cleaned the house from top to bottom, or at least it had felt that way to Hailey. It appeared even Miss Mills forgot to clean behind the couch.

Steve didn't seem to notice the dust, or the floral fabrics. He was intent on setting up his gear. When she had agreed to play with him, she had envisioned the two of them with two guitars. She hadn't expected quite so much paraphernalia. There was a microphone on a stand in front of one of her kitchen stools. That was scary enough, without the rest. The recorder was like nothing she'd ever seen before. It had enough knobs and dials and slides to keep an octopus busy. There was an electric guitar too. Hailey had never played an electric guitar. It looked interesting and she wondered if Steve would let her have a try.

'That's it,' Steve said as he plugged in the last cable. 'Sorry it took so long.'

'It is a bit more complex than I expected,' Hailey said.

'This is nothing,' Steve told her. 'I just want to record what we do, so we can play it back and listen.'

'That's all right, I guess.'

'Would you play a couple of your own songs for me?'

'If you like.' Hailey settled herself on a stool, her guitar in her hand. Steve brought the microphone a little closer.

'Now what?' she asked.

'Now you play.'

Nervously she strummed a chord or two, trying to stop her hands from shaking. She was far more nervous playing just for Steve than she had ever been playing for the Saturday night crowd at the pub. She so desperately wanted him to like what she was doing. She opened her mouth to sing the first words, but hardly a sound came out. Steve said nothing. He just sat there and smiled at her, his green eyes alight with anticipation. She tried again, and this time the music took her. She closed her eyes and lost herself in the song, the feel of the guitar, the notes in her ears and the emotions in her heart. She didn't stop when it ended. Her hands flowed on to the next chords, and she began to sing a different song. After three songs she stopped. Her hands stilled and she opened her eyes to look at Steve.

He wasn't smiling. For a moment her heart faltered. If he hated her songs, she would just die. After a moment that seemed to last for a century, his lips moved.

'As I was driving here today, I was afraid you weren't as good as I remembered.' There was a catch in his voice as he spoke. 'I thought maybe it was just wishful thinking. You just couldn't be that beautiful *and* that talented. But I was wrong . . .'

'I'm not—'

'Oh yes you are. I don't think you understand how very good you are. How rare a talent like yours is. That was amazing.'

'Really?' she whispered.

'Oh yeah.' At last he smiled, a grin that grew wider with each passing second. 'It was better than amazing. It was spectacular. Here, listen to yourself.'

He passed her the headphones and she put them on. He did something with his recording device, and suddenly there was music in her ears. Her own music. She listened in wonder. Her eyes sought his face and she knew that in his heart, he heard what she was hearing. Her eyes were wet with tears when she finally removed the headphones. Steve took them from her, then took both her hands in his.

'Do you believe me now?' he said.

'Yes.' There was nothing else for her to say.

Steve nodded and squeezed her hands before letting them go. 'Good. Now, at the risk of being a pushy guest, you did promise me dinner.'

Hailey brushed the tears from her eyes. 'Pushy guest? When it comes to pushy guests, Steve, I have to say you are just not in the race.'

'What . . . ?'

Hailey started laughing, and glad of the distraction, she regaled Steve with stories of Miss Mills's tenancy as she quickly put some pasta on to cook.

'I meant what I said about being a lousy cook,' she said as she pulled a jar of pasta sauce from her cupboard. 'Living out here, pretty much everything comes in a jar or frozen.'

'In my case, it usually comes in a home delivery box.'

'What I don't have,' Hailey said, 'is much to offer you by way of a drink.'

'That's not a problem,' Steve said. He opened a rucksack he'd left on the floor next to his guitar cases and produced two bottles of wine. One white. One red. 'I got these at the pub. I didn't know which you would prefer.'

They talked about music during dinner. And about books and movies. Politics got a brief mention, as did the forthcoming B&S. But mostly, by unspoken agreement, they kept the conversation light. After dinner, Steve sent Hailey back into the lounge room, while he washed the few dishes and made coffee. Hailey picked up his Martin and started playing, with one ear open for sounds of disaster in the kitchen. There were none. Steve was much easier to have in the house than Miss Mills. After a few minutes, Hailey cautiously picked up Steve's electric guitar. She'd often wondered how her songs would sound electric. It shouldn't be much harder than playing her own acoustic guitar. She tentatively tried a couple of chords, slowly finding her way. It didn't seem too difficult. She began playing the bird song, singing softly to herself.

'You've never played electric before, have you?' Steve was watching from the doorway, a steaming mug in each hand.

'It makes the sound very different.'

'It does.' He pulled a chair up next to her, and placed the mugs carefully on the coffee table. Then he took the electric guitar gently from her hands. 'You take the Martin and play with me,' he said.

In his hands, the electric guitar had a magic all of its own. It was her song, but not as she had ever heard it before. He had taken it and added to it to make it more than she could ever have imagined. He caught her eye and nodded. She picked up the Martin.

The coffee got cold as they played. They played Hailey's songs. They played Kelly Gang songs. They played all the different kinds of music they both knew and loved. Hailey had never played better. Steve had unlocked something inside her that made her music more than it had ever been. It flowed around them, the words dancing in the air. Their voices blended in perfect harmony, and as she sang the love songs, Hailey looked into Steve's shining green eyes and realised that, possibly for the first time in her life, she really understood what love songs were all about.

When the last chord had faded, they sat in silence for a while. The only sound in the room was their breathing, a little heavy and fast after the effort of the song. Steve's eyes met hers, and he nodded slowly.

'That was . . . amazing,' he said.

Hailey could only nod. He was right in so many ways. She put her guitar back in its stand and stood up.

'I'll make us some fresh coffee,' she said and dashed into the kitchen.

As she fumbled with the coffee-making, Hailey took several long, slow breaths. She needed a few minutes alone. She had never shared her music like this before. She had played to audiences at the pub, but this was different; more intimate. Now they no longer held the guitar, her hands were shaking. Her heart was pounding as if she'd run a marathon and her emotions were taut and quivering. She tried to calm herself. She mustn't get carried away. It was just a couple of songs. Nothing was going to come of it.

She walked back into the lounge room just as Steve finished rewinding his tape. She had forgotten he was recording their session. He took the coffee mugs from her hands, and set them on the table. Then he guided her to the couch and gently sat her down. He hit the play button, then sat down beside her.

The music was beautiful. Hailey had never heard herself sing like that before. It brought goose bumps to her flesh and tears to her eyes. Somehow her hand found its way into Steve's, and his fingers closed around hers. When the song was done, he leaned forward to turn the machine off. The movement brought him even closer to her.

'So, Hailey Braxton, will you sing with me?'

'At the B&S?'

'Then. And after. Will you?'

Every line of his face told her that this answer was important to him. His eyes were fixed on her face, and his fingers were holding her hand so tightly it almost hurt.

'Yes.' The word was just a whisper.

'Of course,' he responded softly, 'singing is all about passion. And emotion. If we are going to sing together, we have to be careful.'

'Why is that?'

His face moved closer to hers, and she could feel his breath warm on her cheek. 'Because we might get overwhelmed by that emotion. We might let it carry us away.'

Hailey raised one hand to touch his cheek. He had just a hint of five o'clock shadow. She leaned closer to him, inhaling his scent and his warmth.

'Yes, we might,' she said against his lips.

J ean was up early on Saturday morning, but the house was empty. It wasn't yet seven o'clock, but the empty coffee cup on the kitchen bench suggested Bec was already up at the ball site. There must be a million things she had to do. There was certainly more than enough for Jean to be doing, and she didn't linger over her coffee either. Her priority for the day was to get the souvenir stand up and running. The stand was to be set up near the main compound, and had to be ready as soon as the first 'bachelors and spinsters' arrived. Bachelors and spinsters indeed! If Gordo and his ute were an example of the ball regulars, Jean guessed such conservative and old-fashioned terms were not going to apply.

Before heading for the post office storeroom and the many boxes of souvenirs waiting for her, Jean paused at the open door of Bec's room. Bec had never been one for keeping her room tidy. It wasn't exactly a mess . . . but the top of her big chest of drawers was littered with bits and pieces. A hair brush, a bra and several half-used bottles of hand and body lotion. There was a pile of clothes on a chair in the corner, and Bec's favourite red boots sat on the floor near the wardrobe. For a few seconds, Jean was tempted to take a quick look in the drawers. Maybe something there would give her a hint as to how far things had got between her daughter and Gordo. She might find . . . what? Birth control pills?

Jean shook her head. What was she thinking? Bec deserved better than that! Disgusted with herself, Jean stomped out of the room.

She was carrying the first of many boxes to her car when Anne Ryan appeared from the direction of the store.

'It looks like we have great weather for the ball,' Anne said cheerfully.

Jean agreed.

'It's quite something, this ball,' Anne continued. 'Who would have thought a small place like the Creek could do something like this?'

'We haven't done it yet,' Jean reminded her. 'There's a lot of work still to do.'

Anne didn't get the hint. She was one of the few townsfolk not directly involved in the ball. Her argument was that she needed to keep the store open, because the people coming to the ball would certainly need to buy things. Jean couldn't argue with the logic, but it did annoy her that Anne had managed to slide out of doing anything at all while at the same time ensuring she made a profit from the event. The woman wasn't even going to offer to help Jean carry the boxes to the car. Jean ducked back inside for more boxes, hoping that when she returned Anne might be gone. She wasn't.

'Isn't it interesting, all the new people in town now?' Anne said in a slightly conspiratorial tone.

Here it comes, Jean thought. Anne was obviously dying to impart some nugget of gossip. There was no other reason for her to be looking for someone to talk to this early in the morning.

'Why, I notice that young singer is back. The one with the long blond hair.'

'Of course he is,' Jean said shortly. 'He's playing tonight.'

'But he came yesterday,' Anne said. 'And he didn't stay at the pub last night.' She grinned smugly.

Jean didn't like what the woman was insinuating – but at the same time she was startled. Would Hailey . . . ? Anne was obviously waiting for Jean to ask. Jean wasn't going to give her that satisfaction, and instead picked up another box to stack in the car.

'He spent the night with Hailey!' Anne announced triumphantly.

Jean was very glad that her back was to Anne as she spoke. The look of stunned surprise on her face would have given the woman ample reward for that piece of juicy gossip. Jean's mind raced, but she made no comment and continued arranging the boxes in the back of the car as she regained control of her features. When she was certain her shock no longer showed, she turned back for the next box. Anne had an expectant look on her face.

'I knew it was him,' the woman continued when Jean said nothing. 'I recognised the car from last time he was here. But last time he stayed at the pub. This time he was at Hailey's. I haven't seen either of them yet this morning, despite the fact that everyone else in town is up and about.'

Jean was lost for words. She wasn't quite sure what shocked her more, Anne's pleasure in spreading such vicious gossip, or the thought that Hailey had invited a man she hardly knew into her bed. Coming so soon after her own doubts about Bec, it was almost more than she could handle. Still unable to respond, she saw, to her great relief, Rod approaching from the direction of the police station.

'Good morning, ladies,' he said, touching one finger to the broad brim of his police hat.

'Rod, have you got a minute to give me a hand with these boxes?' Jean almost pleaded.

'Of course.' His eyebrows rose slightly, but he followed Jean into the post office storeroom without another word.

'Ooh! That woman!' Jean exploded as soon as she was inside. 'There are times when I just want to—'

'Let me guess,' Rod said, a smile twitching the corner of his lips. 'I'll bet she just couldn't wait to tell you about Hailey.'

Jean blinked in surprise. 'And how did you know?'

'Jean, I had a constable on patrol all night. He reported a strange vehicle at Hailey's place.'

'This would be the same constable who arrested Matt Johnson's horse?' Jean was not one to easily forgive.

'He's a good kid,' Rod said. 'Just a bit over-eager.'

Jean managed not to sniff at the mere thought. 'I hope Hailey will be all right,' she said. 'I mean, I'm no prude, but a travelling musician? And she's been a bit . . . vulnerable since her parents died.'

'I'm sure she knows what she's doing.'

They thought the same about me once; Jean didn't say it out loud. Then she pushed the thought aside. This wasn't the day for difficult memories.

'So, how are things looking for the souvenir stall?' Rod continued. 'Planning on making a fortune?'

Jean flicked open one of the boxes, to display plastic and foam stubbie holders with the words 'Up The Creek' printed on the side. 'It amazes me that people are willing to spend good money on junk like this,' she said. 'But if they are, I'll happily take their cash.'

'It's all for a good cause. Is Bec about? I wanted to ask her about the ute show.'

'She'll be over at the site,' Jean said through pursed lips, 'waiting for Gordo to arrive.'

'Now, Jean, let her be,' Rod told her. 'She's old enough to make up her own mind.'

'I know. I just don't want her doing something she might regret.'

'We all do things we regret,' Rod said softly. 'The trick is not to let them take over the rest of our lives.'

Jean bit back an expression of surprise. It was unlike Rod to make such a personal comment. Before she could respond, he had turned away and was looking out the door.

'Anne's gone,' he said. 'She's probably looking for someone else to tell. Let's get the rest of these boxes out there.' He stacked the two biggest boxes, one on top of the other, easily lifted both and set off towards the car.

Jean picked up the last box and followed, wondering if everyone in town, including Rod, had come down with some sort of ball madness.

He pushed the last box into place and shut the tailgate of Jean's car. 'You'll be over at the ballroom later?' he asked.

That was the name they had given the fenced-off dancing area. With its wire fence and dirt floor, it didn't look like any ballroom Jean had ever seen. Not that she'd ever seen a real ballroom, just the ones in Bec's old films.

'I guess so,' she replied.

'I don't suppose you'd save a dance for a man in uniform?' His tone was light-hearted, but his eyes held a more thoughtful message as he waited for an answer.

'I don't know . . . I wasn't planning on getting in the middle of that lot.'

'Tell me you'll save me a dance, and let me worry about that lot,' Rod said.

'All right.' She wasn't convinced, but the twitch of his lips made it impossible for her to say so.

'Great. Thank you, madam. I'll see you later this evening.' Rod touched his hat, made an exaggerated bow and, smiling, turned away.

Jean had no idea what he was on about, but that didn't matter. Rod would never do anything to cause her grief. She slid behind the wheel of her car. She would take the boxes up now, although she didn't expect the first of the ball guests would arrive for quite some time yet.

Nick was about a kilometre out of the Creek when the convoy passed him. He'd seen them coming in his rear-view mirror, all big chrome bull bars and CB aerials. He heard them too, as they passed, expensive sound systems blaring through open windows, the thumping of the music drowning the low, throaty rumble of the powerful engines. He recognised the leading ute. It was Gordo, of course, on his way to find Bec. Nick's fists closed tightly around the steering wheel as one by one the flashy vehicles passed him. He was driving the old farm truck with the water tank on the back; the same one he'd taken to the fire at the school when this had started all those weeks ago. As the Farwell Creek Fire Brigade first officer, he'd decided they should have some sort of firefighting ability at the B&S. It wasn't that he was expecting trouble – well, maybe a bit. He just wanted to be prepared. All those city blokes with their flash utes wouldn't understand how easy it was to start a bushfire, and how difficult it was to put one out.

As he drove down the main street, he saw the convoy had pulled over near Bec's house. That figured. Gordo was probably knocking on her door right now. Nick kept driving past. One of the new constables was standing by the gate into the B&S site. Nick pulled up in the gateway.

'Hi!'

'Mr Price.' The constable nodded. 'We've got a good day for it.'

Nick glanced up at the clear blue sky. 'We sure do. Anybody arrived yet?'

'No, sir. That lot behind you look to be the first of the visitors.'

Nick glanced in his mirror. The convoy, with Gordo still in the lead, was just approaching the gate. It was hard to see, but he thought Gordo was alone in the cab of his ute. Nick suppressed a smile.

'How did things go last night?' he asked.

'No worries, sir.'

'Good. I suppose all of you will be on duty tonight?'

Nick didn't need to see the constable's eyes flick towards the road. He could see in his mirror that the convoy was lined up behind him, waiting to drive on to the campsite.

'Ah, yes. We'll all be around.'

Nick nodded. 'Well, here's hoping things stay quiet.'

The constable nodded, and opened his mouth.

'Do you know where the sergeant is?' Nick asked before he could speak.

'He's still at the station, sir.'

Nick heard the not-so-gentle revving of an engine behind him. That would be Gordo.

'Fine. If you see him, could you tell him that I need to speak to him.'

'Ah. Yes. Sir . . .'

'It's about fire safety during the event tonight,' Nick said, trying not to laugh at the look of almost panic in the constable's eyes. 'I'm sure you'll agree that we need to make sure everything is in order.'

'Yes, of course. Ahh . . .'

Nick smiled. 'Yes, Constable?'

'Perhaps you could move on through the gate, please. The vehicles behind you . . .'

Nick could almost feel the frustration, if not actual anger, behind him. He decided he had delayed as long as he could without giving the poor young policeman a heart attack.

'Oh, of course. Sorry. I didn't mean to cause a traffic jam.'

He dropped the truck into gear and moved forward, as slowly as he possibly could. He was still chuckling as he pulled up at the stage compound. He knew it was childish to take delight in baiting Gordo, but damn it – he was entitled!

He saw Bec immediately. She was walking towards him from the school grounds, wearing the same bright committee T-shirt that he was. On her it looked good. She had tucked it into a pair of tight jeans that emphasised the way she walked; with long, free strides that reminded him of a young thoroughbred filly. Her hair, which had suddenly seemed to be very long, was loose, and bounced on her shoulders as she walked.

Nick felt something inside him tighten. He stepped down from the cab of the truck. As he slammed the door, Bec looked up and smiled. She had never looked happier, or more beautiful. Nick was about to step forward when he realised there was someone else alighting from a vehicle next to him.

'Hey, Gordo!' Bec called as she raised her hand.

'Bec. It's good to see you.' Gordo stepped past Nick without so much as a sideward glance. In a couple of strides he reached Bec, and kissed her full on the lips. It wasn't a passionate kiss, just one that lingered a moment, as if to say there was more to come later. As he turned, he dropped an arm around her shoulders, and then he looked at Nick. He was smiling the sort of smile that made Nick's blood boil. Nick wondered how good it would feel to slam his fist into that smiling mouth.

'Hi, Bec,' he said instead.

She didn't answer for a moment. She was frowning, and seemed lost in her thoughts, but before Nick could really wonder what that was about, she smiled.

'It's going to be a great day, guys, I just know it!'

'It is indeed,' Gordo said, moving a little closer to her. 'I've been looking forward to this for ages.'

Bec glanced up at Gordo as he said that, and Nick felt an icy shaft slice through his gut. She had looked at him like that once, years ago, when they were little more than children. He'd been too young then to know what it meant, or to really appreciate what a gift it was.

'Are you looking forward to judging the ute show?' He thought that was probably the best way to get Gordo's thoughts away from Bec.

'Judging?' Gordo shook his head. 'I'm not judging, man. I'm competing. I've won every ute show this year. I'm on a roll!'

'Wait a minute.' Bec pulled away from Gordo and looked up at him. 'I thought you were going to judge this for us.'

'I never said anything about judging.'

'But . . . there's no one else.' Bec sounded confused, and a little desperate.

'Why don't you do it?' Gordo offered. 'Anyone can judge. There aren't any real rules about it. A good-looking chick is always an acceptable judge.'

'And with Bec as judge, you might just have a bit of an advantage?' Nick offered.

'I don't need an advantage.' Gordo's hackles were up at the mere thought. 'I'm going to win this whoever judges.'

'Gordo!' Bec was starting to sound annoyed. 'I can't judge the ute show. I have too many other things to do.' She glared at both men, as if they were to blame for all her problems.

Nick had a lightbulb moment. 'Didn't the Ford dealer from Roma donate the trophies for the show?'

'Yes . . .'

'I know he is coming. Get him to judge it.'

'That not a bad idea,' Bec said thoughtfully.

'As chairman, Ed can help him out,' Nick added. 'And you could have a popular vote for best ute of the show.' He was on a roll. 'And announce it from the stage when the ball starts.'

'That's even better,' Bec said.

'We'll need some way to cast votes,' Nick said before Gordo could get involved. 'I'll find an old drum and cut a slot in it. It won't take five minutes. Can you lay your hands on paper and some pens?'

'Miss Mills must have something at the school we can use,' Bec said. 'I'll go now and find her. Maybe we can get her to help count the votes or something. Surely she wouldn't disapprove of that.'

'I wouldn't be so sure.' Both Nick and Bec chuckled,

leaving Gordo outside the joke. Nick felt good about that too.

Bec suddenly seemed to remember Gordo. 'I'll talk to you later,' she said shortly. 'I've got to do this now.'

'No worries.' Gordo hid his disappointment well. 'I'll just head down to the ute site. If you like, I can make sure things get started properly there.'

Bec seemed to have a sudden change of mood. She put her hand on Gordo's arm and treated him to a smile. 'Thanks, Gordo. I'll come down soon. It's just that today I'm going to be pretty busy . . .'

'I know. Don't worry about it. Just make sure you've got time to dance with me tonight.'

'You bet!'

As he turned to leave, Gordo looked at Nick. His lip curled in a smile. Nick understood exactly what he was saying. He hoped Gordo understood his unspoken reply.

'Come on.' Bec started walking towards the school.

They had barely taken two steps when a bus appeared on the track leading to the stage compound. It was very big, with tinted windows that hid the occupants from the inquisitive looks of those outside. The paint job was really something. Bright red and blue and yellow, it declared in no uncertain terms that the Kelly Gang had arrived. It bounced slowly over the track towards them.

'I guess that's the band,' Nick said. He was about to step forward, to direct them to their allotted parking area, when the driver turned of his own accord. That was curious.

'I wonder if Hailey knows they are here,' said Bec. 'She's supposed to be looking after them.'

The bus had parked in its allocated space, almost as

if the driver had known exactly where to go. The door opened and a man got out. He was a big man. Not tall, but big, and it was all muscle. Every square centimetre of his skin was covered with tattoos, including his bald head. He looked a little rumpled, as if he'd been travelling all night. The next man to alight was tall and good looking, with long blond hair. He was wearing blue jeans and a shirt that did not look like it had been slept in.

'They look like . . .'

Nick never heard what Bec thought. Her voice trailed off and her eyes widened in surprise as she watched Hailey alight from the bus, and entwine her fingers in those of the tall blond man.

12

Hailey had never looked happier. Even from a distance, she seemed to glow. As she approached, the blond man whispered something in her ear, and she laughed with such joy that watching her, Bec's heart ached. She assumed the man was the band leader. He certainly fitted the description. Blond and drop-down-dead gorgeous. Hailey had told her about that unexpected meeting in the pub, and of course the whole committee knew the band was booked to play at the ball. Apparently there was a lot Hailey hadn't said. There was no doubt in Bec's mind what had happened, and part of her was glad for her friend. Another small part of her was a little worried. Hailey had never done anything like this before. She had barely dated, let alone fallen into bed with a man she hardly knew. What would happen tomorrow when the band moved on? And in one tiny, tiny corner of Bec's heart, she felt a twinge of sheer jealousy, because the man she was dating just didn't make her feel like that.

'Hi, Bec,' Hailey said. 'This is Steve Kelly.'

'Hi, Steve,' Bec said. 'You're the band.'

'Well, part of it.' He turned to indicate the rest of the men alighting from the bus. 'That's Blue, the drummer. Don't be scared by the tattoos, he's a pussycat really.

The tall, skinny guy is Ash. He plays bass . . .'

Bec didn't pay much attention to the introductions, Hailey was grinning at her like a cat that had sampled more than a little cream. She had to know what was going on.

'Nick,' Bec said, 'could you take the guys over to the stage. Introduce them to the crew so they can set up.'

For a second, Nick looked a little put out by the request, but then the light of comprehension dawned in his eyes. He nodded in a knowing fashion. 'Sure. This way, guys.'

'You're coming too?' When Steve looked at Hailey, it was as if the two of them were alone in their own universe.

'I'll be there in a minute,' Hailey said.

As soon as the men were out of earshot, Bec turned to Hailey. 'Well?'

Hailey dragged her eyes away from Steve's departing back. She threw her arms around her friend in a bear hug that left Bec gasping for air. When she let her go, she was almost jumping up and down on the spot.

'He wants me to play with them tonight,' Hailey said.

'At the ball? That's great! But that's not what I meant, and you know it.'

Hailey blushed. She looked in the direction Steve had taken, and then she smiled, a slow, sweet, reminiscent smile that gave Bec her answer.

'How . . . when . . .' Bec wanted to know. She would never have expected Hailey to . . . well, not so quickly.

'Last night. At my place. We played.' Hailey's eyes softened with emotion. 'He's such a wonderful musician. We even played a couple of my songs. And when he sings . . . it was just . . . There was just so much connection when we sang. So much we shared. It just happened.'

'And you're happy about that?'

Hailey nodded, everything about her exuding excitement and happiness. 'He's just wonderful,' she said. 'He's gorgeous and so sexy. He's kind. He makes me laugh and he's . . .'

'Wonderful?'

They both laughed. Bec reached out to hug her friend. For the first time since her parents' death, Hailey was genuinely happy. Bec fought down the tiny twinge of jealousy. Hailey deserved this. She only wished Gordo made her feel the same. He didn't even come close. The closest she had felt was when she was just a kid. When she and Nick . . . she bit back the memory and hugged Hailey even tighter.

'When we first met, Steve said he wanted me to play with him. I didn't tell anyone in case it didn't work out. But it is going to happen!' Hailey started walking towards the stage. 'Bec, I'm so excited. Nervous too. What if I blow it?'

'You won't,' Bec assured her. 'It'll be just like Judy Garland in *A Star is Born*.'

'I do hope not,' Hailey said. 'I seem to remember that had an unhappy ending.'

'Well . . .'

'You'll be there for me, won't you?' Hailey stopped in her tracks and grabbed both Bec's hands.

'Just try and keep me away,' Bec said, feeling the tension in Hailey's grip. 'We'll all be there for you.'

By the time they reached the stage, the band had most of the equipment out of the bus. The stage was about the same height as the back of a big truck. About the same size too, with a high canvas roof in case of rain.

A couple of iron beams supported a dozen or more lights. A black curtain formed a backdrop, while at the front, a low barrier was designed to keep the crowd at a safe distance. A set of stairs at the back led through the curtains and into the staging area, where a large marquee served as dressing room, bar and café for the stage crew and the performers. There were a few minutes of general chaos as electricians and members of the stage crew started setting things up. It didn't take long. Soon short blasts of music echoed across the site as the band got ready to play.

'You just wait,' Hailey said to Bec and Nick as they watched. 'They're great.'

'Hailey, come on up here,' Steve called.

'Aren't you guys going to play first?'

'No need. We play together all the time. We need to rehearse with you – come on.' Steve walked to the edge of the stage, bent over and held out his hand.

Without the slightest hesitation, Hailey walked to the edge of the stage. Blue came forward and also held out his hand. Hailey reached for the two outstretched hands, and in one swift, smooth motion, the men lifted her to the stage.

Nick stepped to Bec's side. 'Are they . . . ?'

'Yes.'

She look up at Nick. He loved Hailey like a sister, and on more than one occasion when they were kids, he'd stepped up to protect her. Bec had a sudden clear memory of a time when they were all about fifteen. Some boy had joined their class. He was the son of an itinerant worker and had taken a fancy to Hailey. When she hadn't returned his feelings, he had pushed just a little bit too hard and earned a black eye for his trouble. Bec could see the concern in Nick's eyes now, and knew that some things didn't change with time. Nick would still protect Hailey, and if that meant using his fists, he'd do that too.

'It's all right, Nick,' she said.

'But tomorrow he'll leave.'

'She knows that.'

'I just don't want to see her get hurt.' Nick looked back towards the stage, where Steve was adjusting Hailey's microphone.

'Sometimes it's worth the risk of getting hurt,' Bec said softly, hoping that Nick might understand what she was trying to say. She waited for him to reply. He didn't and when she looked up at him, his eyes were still on the stage, where the band was now ready to play.

The music started gently, but began building quickly as the band got into their rhythm. At first Hailey stood a little to one side, her face a mask of uncertainty. Although her hands were moving, her guitar was lost in the strong and confident sound of the band. After a few bars, Steve waved her closer to a microphone. He sang the opening line of the song alone, then gestured for Hailey to join in. At first Bec couldn't hear anything, but as the look of sheer terror slowly faded from Hailey's face, her voice began to rise above the music. Steve stepped closer to her. Hailey's eyes never left his face as they sang the chorus together. Then he stepped back to give her centre stage, and she sang as Bec had never heard her sing before.

It was pure magic. With two male voices on backing vocals, and the counterpoint of Steve's electric guitar, Hailey's voice blossomed. The music waltzed across the dusty ground and danced among the gum trees. The song seemed to take wing and soared above the small knot of people, each note as pure as sunlight. As the last chord faded away, Bec looked around. Hailey had an audience. The stage crew and the people setting up the bar and souvenir stand had all stopped work and been drawn to the stage to listen.

'I never knew she was that good,' Nick said in a hushed voice.

'Neither did I,' Bec agreed.

The song ended, but the music didn't. The band played on into the next, a slow, sexy song about love and sex and pain. Bec's hips started swaying. On the stage, Hailey and Steve stepped closer together as they sang. The two voices merged into a sensual harmony as their bodies picked up the rhythm of the music. The whole stage seemed alight with sexual tension. Watching them, Bec felt a small ache somewhere deep inside her. She was very aware of Nick standing close to her, his body moving gently in time with her as he too felt the music take hold. She turned towards him. He wasn't looking at the stage. He was looking at her. His eyes caught and held hers. Their bodies began to move in unison, slowly drawing closer together. Something was happening to Bec, something was building inside her that she hadn't felt in such a long time. It was just as it was when they were young, learning the facts of life behind the old church. But it was different now. They weren't children any longer.

'Wow, Hailey's pretty good, isn't she?' The voice crashed down on Bec and Nick like a thousand cutting hailstones.

'Gordo!' Bec felt a huge ache of loss as Nick stepped a little away from her. 'She's just great.' She struggled to cover her confusion.

'Yes. Very catchy song.' Gordo moved closer to her

and dropped his arm around her shoulders.

She wanted to shrug him off. She felt, rather than saw, Nick draw away.

On stage, the song ended. The band crowded around Hailey, hugging her and patting her back as in front of the stage the small audience burst into applause.

'Onya, Hailey,' Gordo shouted.

As the applause died down, Bec looked around for Nick, but he wasn't there. She wanted to go and find him, but before she could move, Hailey had jumped down off the stage.

'What did you think?' she asked, her face brimming with excitement.

'You were great,' Bec replied, suddenly aware that Gordo's arm was once more around her shoulders.

'Wasn't she?' Steve was at Hailey's side. 'You just wait until tonight, Hailey. You are going to knock 'em dead.'

They looked at each other with such shared pride and exultation that Bec felt tears prick at the back of her eyes. She could almost touch the emotion the two of them shared. She couldn't stop the surge of jealousy in the corner of her heart. Nor could she stop herself from wishing that Gordo had not chosen that very moment to appear at her side. Not when she and Nick were ... were what? She had been back in the Creek almost a year and nothing had happened. What made her think that now would be any different? He'd just been moved by the music, while she ... she was too caught up in memories.

All the band members were now off the stage, crowded around and talking wildly. Bec didn't hear a word of it. She felt as if she was being swamped.

'Bec!' Another committee member suddenly appeared.

'I've got the hog roast people at the gate. They want to know where to dig their pit.'

Pit? What was the woman talking about? Bec looked around, then saw the question for what it was – a chance to escape.

'I'd better go sort this out,' she told the group.

'Are you coming down to the ute ring?' Gordo asked, holding her hand to stop her walking away. 'I think everything is ready. But you should check it.'

'I will.' Bec pulled her hand away a little more roughly than she intended. 'I'll get there as soon as I can. I've got to do this first.'

She turned and almost ran away.

Hailey watched Bec walk swiftly away, wondering what had just happened. But she didn't wonder for long. She had too much happening around her. The band members were talking loudly about the music. The stage crew wanted instructions about lights and sound. A few townsfolk who'd been in the audience wanted to tell her how great she was. She felt as if she was lost – or she would have, had not Steve been right by her side. Each time she felt as if her life was spinning out of control, she just had to look at his smiling eyes and know that everything was all right. In fact, everything was better than all right. Her whole body was tingling. She felt more alive than she ever had before. In part it was due to the thrill of singing, but mostly it was due to the man who still held her hand as if he would never let her go.

'Okay, guys!' Steve said now, raising his voice slightly to be heard above the general hubbub. 'The crowds are going to start rolling up soon, so we had best clear out. We don't want to give them too much of a preview of what's in store for tonight.'

The band members nodded their agreement. 'We could use some sleep,' Blue said, running a hand over the Celtic symbols tattooed on his bald pate. 'We drove through the night to get here early enough to rehearse.'

'There are rooms booked for you at the pub,' Hailey said. 'I can take you down there.'

As the band members collected their things, Steve gave Hailey a quick hug. 'You were just great,' he said softly in her ear.

Hailey felt his warm breath against her skin. She looked up at him, and for a long time the world held its breath.

'Come on, you two.' Blue was back, smiling at Hailey in a manner totally at odds with his intimidating appearance.

The group set out for the short walk to the pub. While the rest of the band settled into their rooms, Steve and Hailey turned back towards her house. Once inside, with the door safely shut behind them, he pulled her into his arms and kissed her.

'My God, you are marvellous,' he said as his lips gently caressed her cheek and traced a slow, sensuous line along her neck.

Hailey locked her arms around his neck as she swayed against him, her whole being aching for his touch. She pressed against his strong body, hearing him moan slightly as she ran her fingertips through his hair. All the passion that the music had unleashed surged through them both. Steve kissed her again, long and slow and deep, then slowly reached up to take her hands and with a long, shuddering breath stepped away from her.

'I should go to the pub too,' he said, his voice low and

rough. 'I didn't get much sleep last night either.'

His eyes sparkled with mischief, and Hailey felt herself blush as she remembered. She lifted one hand to stroke the side of his face, then ran a fingertip gently over his lips. He seemed to stop breathing as her fingers found their way to the open neck of his shirt, to feel the pulse pounding beneath the warm skin of his throat.

'And I have a hundred things I have to do for the ball,' Hailey whispered.

Steve took her hand from his flesh, and gently kissed her fingers.

'I hate to go, but I think I have to.'

Hailey sighed. 'I know.'

'It's ball day,' he said. 'Everything you have worked so hard for all these weeks. You don't want to miss a moment of it.'

'You're right. I don't. But . . .'

'If you keep looking at me like that, I'll never leave.' Reluctantly Steve let go of her hand, and began gathering up the bits and pieces of equipment he'd left there last night, when their singing together had given way to something else.

Hailey took a long, deep breath to get her emotions back under control. 'So. This evening?'

'We'll come over to the site late in the afternoon for final checks. We'll have a set list by then, and don't worry – you know all the songs.'

Hailey nodded. 'All right. Now get out of here before I change my mind.'

'About what?' Steve said as he kissed her briefly and headed for the door.

Hailey watched him walk out the door and close it behind him. She felt his absence like a physical contraction in her chest. She dropped into a chair. What was she doing? As if the prospect of playing in front of a huge audience wasn't terrifying enough, now she was getting involved with Steve. Getting involved? She had a feeling the tense was all wrong. She was involved, and there was no turning back. She lifted her eyes. On the far side of the room, a photograph of her parents looked back at her. She suddenly felt their loss more keenly than ever. If they were here, what would they say? Her mother, she knew, would urge caution, but her father? His face smiled back at her from the frame. He would tell her to listen to her heart, and right now, her heart was telling her that these few days of happiness were worth whatever might follow.

'Have you got that in extra large?'

'What?' Jean tried to focus on just one sound in the cacophony that surrounded her.

'I want the blue singlet. Extra large. Plus a stubbie holder. No. Two stubbie holders.'

Jean did the maths in her head. 'That'll be twenty-five dollars.'

Her customer dug into his hip pocket for the cash, while being careful not to spill the contents of his beer can.

'Here you go.'

Jean added the notes to the thick bundle in the bum bag strapped to her waist. She was amazed at how quickly the souvenirs were vanishing. And at the most ridiculous prices, considering the quality of the merchandise. All were stamped with the words 'Up The Creek', and the cartoon of the canoeist clutching his burning paddle. Gordo had organised the artwork through a friend who was an artist. Jean wasn't impressed with it, but she had to admit, most people seemed to find it funny. More importantly, she was raking in the cash, and that was what this was all about.

'How much for the T-shirts?' a male voice off to one side asked.

'Twenty dollars,' she replied without thinking.

'Black, please. Large.'

When the crowd thinned a bit, Jean decided it was time for a break. Leaving one of the mothers from the school committee in charge of the stall, she slipped away to the relative quiet of the backstage area. The security barriers here kept the crowds at bay, and it was too early yet for the band to be getting ready. Jean guessed they would all be having lunch at the pub. Lunch wasn't such a bad idea. She'd been on the go now for several hours. She thought briefly about slipping home for a peaceful half-hour and a sandwich. Attractive as that sounded, she decided against it. Despite all her initial objections to the ball, now that it was underway, she was curious to see how things were going in other parts of the site.

Strolling across the ball site, she looked at the faces around her. Most of the bachelors and spinsters seemed to be in their twenties. A few were older. Most were wearing blue jeans and T-shirts. Many of the T-shirts boasted artwork not too dissimilar to the drawing on the Farwell Creek shirts. Most of the crowd, it seemed, were B&S regulars. A lot of the girls were wearing shorts. A couple had denim skirts, but Jean couldn't help but wonder at the dress code. Formal, it said on the posters and the tickets. No entry without shoes and a bow tie. She doubted many of these people owned dinner jackets or long frocks. Of course, her idea of formal might be a bit different from the average B&S dress code.

As she made her way towards the barbecue area, Jean spotted Bill Davies, barely visible behind the crowd packed five and six deep around the bar. She guessed some people had brought their own supplies to the event, but even so, there'd be a lot of money spent at the bar before the weekend was over. Jean was pleased, but at the same time had just a niggling concern. It was barely lunchtime, and already there were more than a few revellers looking a bit the worse for wear. God knew what they'd be like by nightfall!

She tried to guess at the number of people already on the site, but gave up trying. Several hundred at least. Perhaps more, if you included the workers. Certainly the population of Farewell Creek had multiplied many times over during the past few hours. And they were still coming. Every few minutes another vehicle would appear at the gate. In some cases, they came in convoys, particularly the utes. She could see the glint of sun on a chrome bull bar now as another one made its way across the paddock. The ute show part of the site was heaving with people and cars. Loud music was pumping from at least one of the vehicles, adding to the noise of the official sound system at the stage compound, from which Emmylou Harris was playing at a deafening level. Jean guessed that Bec would be down among the utes somewhere. With Gordo.

The food stall was almost as popular as the bar. Being a bachelor or a spinster was obviously hungry work. Jean slipped around the back. Ruth Davies and a couple of mothers from the school were serving burgers to the crowd as fast as they could cook them.

'I do hope I've ordered enough food,' Ruth said as she tossed some more burgers on the sizzling barbecue plate. 'I've sold a lot already.'

'There's that hog roast coming tonight,' Jean reminded her.

'Oh, they're here already,' Ruth said, pushing the hair out of her eyes with the back of her hand. 'I heard them asking Bec earlier where they could dig their pit.'

'Pit?'

'Apparently that's where they roast the hog.' Ruth shrugged. 'In a pit.'

'Did she get them sorted out?'

'I imagine so. Are you hungry?' Ruth asked.

'Yes, I am. That smells pretty good.'

'Here. Take this one.' Ruth handed her the burger she had been cooking. 'That lot can wait,' she added, nodding in the direction of the hungry crowd waiting in line.

'Do you need more help?' Jean asked.

'I do, but I don't know where you'll find anyone.'

Jean took the offered burger, nodded her thanks and backed out of the stall. Ruth and her ladies needed a clear run. Munching the burger, which wasn't too bad, Jean thought about where she might find extra hands. The whole town had pitched in to help. Everybody was doing their bit – rostered to work as a steward, or to serve beer or food. Others would join in the clean-up detail on Monday – a job Jean wasn't looking forward to one bit. Even Anne Ryan, who had insisted on keeping her store open all weekend, would probably help out then. That was the way towns like Farwell Creek worked. Everyone did their bit. Well – almost everyone. Jean stopped walking. There was one person who wasn't on any of the rosters. Who hadn't lifted one finger to help, despite all the help she had received before this started. Jean tossed the wrapper of her burger into a bin, and wiping her hands on a paper napkin, set off in the direction of the schoolteacher's cottage.

'Miss Mills, it's Jean O'Connell!' she called when her knock on the front door wasn't answered.

After a few moments, the door opened.

'Hello, Jean,' Miss Mills said.

'How are you?' Jean smiled. 'I thought you might be out enjoying the spectacle.'

'I don't think so,' Miss Mills replied primly. 'As you know, I was against this idea from the start. My opinion hasn't changed.'

'Well, it is for the good of the town,' Jean said, a smile firmly fixed on her face. 'It all started here. Remember? The whole town turned out when your cottage caught fire.'

'Of course I remember,' Miss Mills said.

'And you'll also remember how everyone helped. Hailey put you up. Other people donated things you needed.'

'What is your point?' Miss Mills asked testily.

'Well, the whole town has also pitched in to help this weekend.' Jean deliberately kept her tone light. 'And we are still a bit short-handed. I was hoping you might be able to help out. The food stall is in particular need of an extra pair of hands.' She braced herself for a curt refusal. She wasn't giving up without a fight. She had all her arguments ready, and if that didn't work, she might just physically drag Miss Mills to the barbecue.

'Well . . .' Miss Mills looked thoughtful. Then her lips curved into an uncharacteristic smile. 'I imagine I could help for a short time.'

'You . . . you will?' Jean couldn't hide her amazement.

'Why do you look so surprised? I always do my part. I like to be a good neighbour.'

'Yes, yes. Of course.' Jean could feel herself mentally correcting her own grammar and pronunciation as she spoke. Miss Mills had that effect on people. It must be because she was a teacher.

'But I do not want to be out there after dark,' Miss

Mills added. 'I will not be forced to listen to that terrible music. Nor do I wish to be around the sort of drunken behaviour I expect will occur this evening.'

'Of course not. Well . . . I . . . Thank you, Miss Mills,' was all Jean could say.

'And for goodness' sake, my name is Eudora.'

The teacher left a dumbfounded Jean on her step and disappeared back inside the cottage. She emerged a few moments later wearing stout shoes under her long cotton skirt, and a broad-brimmed straw hat on her head.

'Come along; show me where I'm needed.'

'Yes . . . Eudora.' Jean followed meekly in her wake.

Jean's shock at Eudora Mills's agreement was mirrored at the barbecue stall. Ruth Davies raised an eyebrow, but was too busy to say anything. She managed to thank Eudora for her help, bravely keeping a straight face and not even hesitating over using the woman's first name. Then she set her to work taking orders.

'One burger, burned to buggery,' an obviously drunk patron ordered, waving his money around.

Eudora swept the note away in one deft movement. 'One burger, well done, please,' she asked the cooks, her smooth English accent not the slightest bit disturbed by her surroundings.

Ruth Davies' face was a picture as she struggled to hold back her laughter.

Jean walked away, and laughed out loud when she was far enough away not to cause offence. After a success like that, she might as well go and see what was happening at the ute show. If Bec was there, she'd get a laugh out of knowing that the terrifying Miss Mills was slinging burgers.

She approached the ute show area with faint feelings of trepidation. More than a hundred vehicles were lined up on display. Shining with hours of loving care, they were every colour of the rainbow. Blue and green and yellow, the hazy purple of the setting sun. There was even a bright pink one that Jean soon discovered had won 'Best Chick's Ute'. There were brand-new utes and reconditioned old utes. At one end of the line, Jean found utes that looked more like the ones she saw every day around the Creek. They were mostly white, a bit battered and dirty, with water bags hung from the bull bars. Most were almost wallpapered with stickers advertising B&S balls around the country. Some dated back several years. The Farwell Creek stickers already in place were easy to spot – they weren't yet faded and dusty. The shabby utes were the entries in the 'Feral Ute' section, although she wasn't exactly sure what was meant by feral. They looked like ordinary work utes to her.

People were walking around, examining the utes as if they were fine works of art, while proud owners stood protectively by. Jean wondered what would happen if someone accidentally scratched the paintwork, or even left a dirty hand mark on a gleaming door. She shook her head at the thought of the amount of money that had been poured into some of the cars. That was all they were – cars – but it was obvious that some had soaked up very large sums. As a single mother with a growing daughter to feed and clothe, Jean had never had much spare cash. When she did, it was used carefully or wisely saved. To spend thousands of dollars painting a car with ornamental lightning bolts was just beyond her comprehension.

Equally incomprehensible was the cacophony of

music assaulting her ears. She'd seen the speakers in the back of Gordo's ute, and she imagined many of the others would be the same. But why must they all play at the same time? On full volume. With different music on each. It seemed a waste of time and battery power. Or maybe she was just too old for this sort of thing. The reason for the noise quickly became clear. The competition being judged was for the best sound system . . . in a ute, of course.

Jean joined the crowd of spectators. The judges were conferring in a huddle. Jean recognised the car dealer from Roma who was sponsoring the event, and the committee chairman, Ed Rutherford. Ed's teenaged granddaughter had joined them, which Jean guessed was a good idea, as she was very pretty and seemed to be getting a lot of attention from competitors and spectators alike. At last a decision was reached. Ed's granddaughter held a small gold trophy aloft and walked down the line of utes, clearly enjoying holding centre stage. At last she turned and, with a flourish presented the trophy to Gordo. As a ragged cheer went up, Gordo grabbed the girl, lifted her in the air and planted a big kiss on her cheek as he put her back down. The crowd was still cheering that effort when he did the same to Bec, who was standing at his side. Only this time the kiss wasn't on the cheek. Nor was it quick. Jean watched her daughter's face as Gordo put her back down. She was laughing and seemed happy, but there was something missing. The sort of something Jean would expect to see on a girl's face when she looked up at her man. Was there something going on there – or rather *not* going on there – that she didn't know about? Perhaps she didn't need to be worried after all.

*

Bec stepped slightly away from Gordo as he turned to accept more applause from the people around them. She was pleased for him. He liked to win. He looked so happy as raised the trophy above his head, accepting the congratulations of his friends and the admiration of his competitors. Such a lot of fuss for a very small, cheap fake gold trophy. And just what was he celebrating? It wasn't as if he had built the sound system himself. Someone else had done the work; Gordo had simply paid for it. In her mind, she couldn't help but draw a comparison to the night Nick had won the firefighter's trophy. He had worked and sweated on that course. Not to win, but to learn the skills that might one day save a life. The trophy had been a tribute from his peers, which he had accepted with self-deprecation and good grace.

Bec shook her head. It was time she stopped comparing Nick and Gordo. They were two totally different men. And it wasn't as if she had to choose between them. Both had made their feelings very clear. Gordo wanted her. Nick did not.

Someone nearby spoke to her, and as she turned to answer, she saw her mother watching from the edge of the crowd. She was surprised to see Jean in the middle of the ute show. She had no illusions about her mother's opinion of Gordo. It was just one more wedge among the many that had come between them in the past few months. Perhaps Jean had become caught up in the excitement of the day. Perhaps this would be a good time to mend some fences.

'Hi, Mum. Gordo just won his second prize of the show.'

'So I saw,' Jean said.

'G'day, Mrs O'Connell.' Gordo left his admirers to tip his hat to Bec's mum.

'Congratulations,' Jean answered grudgingly.

'Thank you, ma'am.'

'I reckon Gordo is going to win best of show,' Bec added proudly. 'There's nothing here to touch him.'

'Now, Becca, let's just wait and see,' Gordo said, shaking his head, but Bec knew it was all an act. He was going to win. There was no doubt in anyone's mind of that, including Gordo's.

'How much longer will this go on?' Jean asked, indicating the ute show.

'A while,' Bec said. 'There are a couple more classes to go, and we need to keep the voting for best ute open for as long as possible.'

'And you're going to be here till then? I just ask because there are other things to do, and you are part of the committee.'

'Mum!' Bec protested. 'I am supposed to be in charge of this.'

'Fine, just don't forget you're supposed to be helping Hailey get ready for her performance tonight.'

'As if I'd forget that!' Bec was affronted. 'I said I'll be there for her – and I will.'

Her mother opened her mouth as if to say something else, but didn't. She just nodded and abruptly turned and walked away.

'Damn it!' Bec said. 'Why does she have to do that? All the time. She doesn't trust me.'

'Now, Becca.' Gordo put his arm around her to soothe her. 'I'm sure she just worries. That's all.'

'No. It's more than that,' Bec said. 'Ever since I came back from the city she's been like this, and I don't know why.'

'Have you talked to her about it?'

'I just can't seem to find the right time,' Bec said,

realising as she said it that she wasn't being strictly truthful. She might have found the right time if she had tried a little harder.

'Hey, don't worry about it now.' Gordo smiled his dazzling smile. 'Forget about it and let's just enjoy ourselves.'

Bec felt a flash of annoyance. Gordo always avoided difficult conversations and decisions. His way was to live each day without thought for the one before – or the one after. That was all very well, but some things were too important to shrug off quite that easily. This time, however, he was probably right. She should relax and enjoy herself.

The sun was starting to sink low in the west by the time the last of the ute classes had been judged. Bec was tired. She needed a few minutes of peace and quiet before launching into the main event – the ball. She and Hailey had agreed to meet at her place to dress for the evening. A cup of coffee and a bit of girl time would be the perfect antidote to the overdose of ute-fuelled testosterone she'd experienced during the past few hours.

'Hey, Bec, is it too late to cast my vote for best ute?' a voice asked close to her elbow.

'Almost,' Bec said. At her feet sat a box with a slot in the lid. A sign on the side proclaimed this to be the ballot box for choosing the best ute of the show. Two more voting slips slid through the slot. Bec picked the box up. 'That's it, folks,' she declared. 'I'm taking this back to the stewards' compound. Results will be announced tonight at the ball.'

A couple of people cheered. Someone slapped Gordo on the back with a knowing wink. Bec smiled bravely, but all she wanted was to be around people whose world did not revolve around utes.

'Bec.' Gordo was at her elbow. 'Have you got a minute?'

'Sure.'

He took her hand and led her away from the ute lines, back towards the campsite. Tents were everywhere. Some people were camping in groups. Others had set up next to their cars. People were already lounging around the campsite. A few were resting before the big event. Others were already well into party mode. Looking at the growing piles of empty beer cans, Bec thought some of them might not even make it down to the stage. Gordo didn't go to the main camping area, but turned slightly up the hill, towards a small stand of trees somewhat removed from the rest of the event. His blue tent was pitched there, in a spot as private as any was likely to be on a B&S campsite. There was a stone-ringed fireplace, set and ready for lighting, and through the open tent flap Bec could see a double air mattress, with a blue blanket tossed over it.

'I know you live here,' Gordo said as he moved closer to her, 'but I thought that after the ball tonight we could come back here. Just the two of us. Celebrate. I have champagne in the esky. What do you think?' The words he didn't say hung in the air between them.

Bec looked at the tent and the air bed. She listened to the music and engine noise and voices that they could not escape. She thought about the chance that someone would just stumble into the tent. It wasn't at all what she had imagined. She had envisaged something more romantic. Candles and dinner, perhaps. A room with a real bed and a proper bathroom. But this was Gordo. He didn't put much store by that sort of thing. He had made a special effort to create this private campsite that he thought was special. For her. Bec looked at his smiling face. He was gorgeous, even though his clothes were covered with dust and he smelt of car polish and motor oil. This was what she wanted, wasn't it? Her mother's voice sounded for a moment in her ear, but she pushed it firmly away and turned to look up at Gordo. He must have seen the answer he wanted in her face. He put his arms around her and pulled her close, his kiss full of promise for the night ahead.

Hailey was standing in the O'Connells' kitchen, wearing nothing but a large towel, when someone knocked on the door. She looked around for Bec, but her friend was still in the shower and even less prepared to receive a visitor. Hailey put down the coffee she was making, and peeped cautiously through the curtains. Steve was standing on the step. Hailey's heart gave a little bounce. He looked gorgeous. He was obviously dressed for the show, in tight black jeans and a black Western shirt that was unbuttoned at the top to reveal the line of his throat and the light smattering of golden hairs on his chest. He was wearing a black hat, tilted back so as not to hide his face or those expressive green eyes, which at this moment were looking at the gap in the curtains where she was hiding.

Hailey ducked back and pulled the curtains shut. He knocked again.

'Hailey? Is that you?'

How she loved his voice. It was like chocolate wrapped in fine velvet.

'Are you going to open the door?'

She couldn't let him in! Not dressed like this. Or rather, undressed like this! Cautiously, she opened the door a crack and peeped through. His face lit up when he saw her, and all her scruples vanished. After all, he had seen her wearing far less than a towel.

'Come on in.' She opened the door for him to slip through, then shut it quickly behind him. She turned to find Steve looking at her with appreciation.

'I hope you don't normally answer the door dressed like that?' he said with a wicked grin, as he placed his hat and a couple of carrier bags on the kitchen table.

'You'd be surprised.' Hailey tossed her head, but the flirtatious gesture went awry as drops from her wet hair flew across the room, spattering Steve's face and shirt.

'Sorry.' She stepped forward to brush the drops away.

'Don't be. I'm not,' Steve growled softly. His arms snaked around her, pulling her to him. He kissed her long and slow, oblivious of the water staining his shirt. His hands caressed the bare skin of her shoulders, sliding down to feel for the edges of the towel.

Hailey grabbed his hands and reluctantly broke the embrace. 'No. No. No.' If she repeated the denial, she might believe it. 'Bec's just in the shower. Her mother might come home any minute. And besides, we have a show to get ready for.'

'Damn!' Steve took a couple of deep breaths. 'You're right. In fact, I'm here about the show.' He retrieved the two shopping bags. 'These are for you.'

Hailey took the offered bags. 'What are they?'

'I wanted to make sure you felt like part of the band.' Steve sounded a little hesitant. 'So I bought your costume.'

Intrigued, Hailey opened the first bag and removed a black Akubra hat, almost identical to Steve's.

'Try it on,' he said. 'I had to guess the size.'

Hailey placed the hat carefully on her wet hair. 'It's close enough.' She grinned at him.

'All the band wear one at the start of the show,' he said, a huge grin spreading across his face, 'but I have to say, Blue doesn't look half as cute in it as you do.'

Hailey took a playful swipe at him, which nearly resulted in a towel moment. She dropped the hat back on the table, then clutched the towel with both hands, wriggling to set it more firmly in place.

'If you do that again, I won't be responsible for my actions,' Steve said, his voice a sensual caress against her heart. Hailey felt an answering call deep inside her own body. For a few seconds they stood just outside each other's reach, and their eyes touched and caressed and held.

'You'd better look in the other bag,' Steve said, his voice low and husky.

Hailey dragged her eyes and her thoughts away from Steve and opened the bag. She carefully removed a piece of fabric, which sparkled as it caught the light. She gently shook it out. It was just gorgeous; every girl's fantasy in black silk liberally sprinkled with sparkling diamantes and sequins. It was more Hollywood than Farwell Creek.

'Wow!'

'I thought it would look pretty good on stage,' Steve said. 'On you.'

Hailey held the dress at arm's length. 'Steve. It's . . . wonderful.'

'I hope it fits.'

'Something this beautiful . . . I'll make it fit,' Hailey said. 'Ah . . . I do get to wear something underneath it, don't I?'

Steve grinned wickedly. 'On stage – most definitely. But later . . .' The words hung in the air.

'Thank you. Thank you. Thank you.' Hailey hugged him vigorously with one hand, while still clutching her towel with the other. She deftly slid away when he made a not very subtle grab for the towel.

'Out!' she ordered, laughing. 'Now . . . or the band will have to go on without either of us.'

'All right.' Steve was laughing too as he gently kissed her goodbye. 'I'll see you backstage.'

Hailey shut the door firmly. When she turned around, Bec was standing in the hallway. For a moment, Hailey thought she looked terribly sad, but then she grinned and winked.

'Sorry, I didn't mean to interrupt,' she said.

Hailey blushed. 'Look what he brought me . . . for tonight.' She dropped the hat on her head and held up the dress.

'That's great,' Bec said. 'You'll look just great.'

She turned away and resumed making the coffee that Hailey had abandoned when Steve knocked on the door, but Hailey knew her too well. She recognised the set of her shoulders. 'Bec? What's wrong?' she asked.

'I wasn't eavesdropping, honestly, but I couldn't help seeing the two of you together.'

'And?'

Bec handed Hailey a mug of coffee and sat down at the table. 'I just think . . . well, you've only known him for a couple of days.'

'Well, we did meet a few weeks ago, remember, when he dropped in to talk about playing tonight.'

'That hardly counts.'

'And we've been e-mailing a lot. And talking on the phone,' Hailey hurried on.

'That's exactly what I mean,' Bec said. 'It's all happened so fast. I just don't want you to get hurt.'

Hailey reached out to squeeze her hand. 'I know,' she said. 'But this is what I want.'

'But what's going to happen when the ball is over?'

'I don't know,' Hailey said. 'But that doesn't matter. During these last few months, I have felt so alone. Barely alive. This morning, I woke up happy. The day was beautiful. Life was beautiful and worth living again. That feeling was worth anything that might happen in the future.'

Bec looked at her for a few moments, then slowly nodded. 'All right then. If you're sure.'

'I'm sure.'

'Well then, we'd better start getting you ready.' Bec got to her feet, and the two girls repaired to her bedroom.

It took Hailey just a few minutes to dry her short wavy hair till it formed a cloud around her head. At times like this, she wished she was tall and blonde. That would give her more confidence as she stepped on to the stage. Then she looked in the mirror and saw the black sequinned dress hanging on the door. That was a vote of confidence if ever there was one.

She put down the hairdryer and went to put it on. The fabric wrapped around her body like a second skin. She tied the straps at the back and tuned to look in the mirror. God – she was sexy! She had never thought of herself as sexy before. She was just – herself. The girl who ran a feed and farm supplies shop and sometimes played a bit of guitar. The black silk had turned a figure made taut by hard physical work into something more suited to a movie star. The low-cut top gave her cleavage. The slinky fabric emphasised her waist. And . . . her bum did not look big!

'Who is that gorgeous creature?' Bec emerged from

the bathroom behind her. 'Surely she's some Nashville star come to grace us all with her presence.'

Hailey tossed her discarded towel at her.

'Are you going to wear it like that?' Bec asked as she disentangled herself. 'It's short, but you could get away with it. You've got the legs for it.'

'I think it'd look better with jeans under,' Hailey said. 'More in keeping with the rest of the band.'

'That's true. I've seen Blue. He's hardly the sequins type.' Bec grinned. 'Do you want to borrow my red boots?'

Hailey shook her head. 'No thanks. I've got . . .' She didn't go on. Instead she reached into the bag of things she'd brought from home earlier that day. 'I thought I'd wear these.'

She was holding a pair of black embossed Western boots, with high Cuban heels.

'Wow!' Bec said, coming over for a closer look. 'I've never seen them before. Are they new?'

'Not exactly.' Hailey took a deep breath. 'Mum and Dad bought them for me. Just before the crash. I've never worn them.'

To forestall any sympathetic comments from Bec, Hailey grabbed a pair of her friend's socks, then slipped the boots on.

'What do you think?'

'You know, your folks would be very proud of you tonight.'

'I know.' Hailey felt a lump form in her throat.

'Right. Now it's my turn.' Bec leaped in to break the silence.

'What are you wearing?' Hailey said.

'Well, since no man saw fit to buy me a fabulous outfit, I had to buy my own.' Bec turned and reached into the wardrobe. 'Ta-daaa . . .' She produced the dress with a flourish.

'Where on earth did you get that?'

The dress was pale yellow satin, with a generous helping of frills and a bow on each shoulder.

'In the op shop last time I was in Roma,' Bec said. 'I think it must have been a bridesmaid's dress.'

'Maybe in 1980,' Hailey offered.

'Well, it's all right for you, you'll be up there on that stage being adored from afar. I'm going to be surrounded by beer-swilling, dye-spitting drunks. I'm not wearing anything I'll ever want to wear again.'

'I'm not sure I'd want to wear it the first time,' Hailey said.

'I just wanted to . . . you know . . . feel like a girl.' Bec felt her heart sink. Hailey was right, of course. The dress was a disaster. She had wanted to look feminine and attractive. Instead she would look like a fool. She tossed the dress on to the floor and sank down on the bed.

'Is this about Gordo or Nick?' Hailey asked.

Bec sighed.

'Come on, Rebecca.'

There was no getting around it now. When Hailey called her Rebecca, she wasn't about to let go.

'Gordo has made a special effort tonight. A campsite away from all the rest. So we can . . . be alone . . .' Bec's voice trailed off.

'And this would be the first time?'

Bec nodded.

'You don't seem exactly thrilled at the thought.'

Bec didn't answer.

Hailey picked up the pile of crumpled yellow fabric from the floor. She held the dress up at arm's length for a few seconds and studied it. 'All right. Get me some scissors,' she ordered, 'then tell me why not.'

Bec did as she was told. 'You know, we've spent four weekends together. We've driven a million kilometres in that damn ute of his. Just the two of us. We get on really well.'

'But?' Hailey asked between snips.

'Well, he's gorgeous and sexy and all that, but . . .' Bec grappled for the right words. 'It's not how it should be.'

'In what way?' Hailey let the scissors and dress fall into her lap.

Bec paused. 'Think about *From Here to Eternity*. Burt Lancaster and Deborah Kerr making love on the beach as the waves crash around them.'

Hailey tossed another bow on to a growing pile of yellow satin on the floor. 'There's no beach in the Creek.'

'You know what I mean. The passion. The excitement. The earth moves.'

'Can you find me a needle and some cotton?' Hailey said.

'I guess I'm just a bit jealous of you,' Bec said when she was back sitting on the bed.

'Of me? Why?'

'Because of the way Steve looks at you. And the way you look at him. After just one day. I don't think I'll ever feel like that about Gordo.'

'And where does Nick fit into all this?' Hailey asked as she stitched. 'Didn't Debroah Kerr have a husband?'

'Yes, she did,' Bec said. 'But Nick's a friend. He's not interested in me like that.'

'He was once, I seem to remember.'

Bec nodded. The memories were never that far away. 'Yes, he was. But we were kids. Things are different now.'

'Are they?' Hailey looked at her intently.

'Yes. They are,' Bec said firmly. 'And now there's Gordo. And he's fun and gorgeous and sexy and he wants me. And I want him.'

'Well then,' said Hailey. 'If that's the case, you'd better look spectacular. What do you think?' She held up the yellow satin dress, now considerably altered.

'Wow. That was fast,' Bec said as she took it. She slipped it on, and wriggled as Hailey pulled up the zip.

'That's better,' Hailey said.

Now it was Bec's turn to look surprised as she regarded her reflection in the mirror. Hailey had stripped all the frills off the dress, leaving behind a soft sheath that caressed Bec's body like a lover. The bodice was tight, revealing curves that for most of the time were hidden beneath a loose cotton work shirt. The fabric slipped gracefully over her hips, flaring slightly as it fell to mid calf.

'Well, with this dress, there might be fireworks after all.'

'We're not quite there,' Hailey said thoughtfully. 'I think you could show a bit more leg.' She brandished the scissors.

A few seconds later, Bec was showing almost enough leg to get arrested. Hailey nodded. 'Better. Now – shoes?'

'I was going to wear my red boots,' Bec said. 'They're all I've got.'

'They'll work,' Hailey said, 'but you're going to need a bit of red up top – just to set it off.'

'I can wear some lipstick,' Bec suggested.

'You most certainly will,' Hailey said. 'But that's not enough.'

She started rummaging around in the big chest of

drawers that stood next to Bec's wardrobe. 'I need something red. Or reddish. Maroon? Burgundy?'

'I've got it,' Bec said. 'Hang on a minute.'

She vanished only to reappear with a cardboard box under her arm. 'I picked this up in Roma the other day. Eudora Mills had arranged for a lot of old scrap fabrics from one of the shops there. They're for the kids to use in art classes or something. There might be something here . . .' She upended the box on to her bed.

'Ah-ha.' Hailey pounced on something soft and sheer and the colour of fine red wine.

'Be careful,' Bec begged as Hailey started wielding a needle and thread far too close to her skin for comfort.

She was finished in just a few minutes and stepped back to admire her handiwork. 'Move over, Karl Lagerfeld,' she said triumphantly.

The scrap of dark red fabric was twisted around Bec's waist like a belt, emphasising her trim figure and setting off to perfection the colour of her boots.

'That'll do,' Hailey said. 'I had to sew it on, so you're going to have a bit of trouble getting that dress off. You'll have to break the thread – or get someone else to break it for you.' She raised one eyebrow.

'Are we done?' Bec asked, ignoring her. Even as a child, she had never been one for dressing up. A denim skirt was about as girlie as she ever got. She might have wanted to feel a bit special this evening, but patience had never been her strong suit.

'Just about. Just our faces to go.'

Hailey once more took charge as she rifled through Bec's limited make-up supplies and her own slightly more extensive cosmetics bag.

'Now we're done!'

The two girls stood side by side and looked into the mirror.

Bec almost didn't recognise the women staring back at her. Her dress wasn't exactly haute couture, but it was just the thing for a B&S – girlie and totally disposable. As for Hailey – the glamorous creature standing beside her was obviously a star. She couldn't be nervous about performing. She would just walk on stage and wow them.

'We look pretty good,' Hailey said, a grin slowly spreading across her face.

'We look fabulous, sister.' Bec struck a dramatic pose. 'And any man who doesn't think so is an idiot!'

15

They are all idiots, Nick thought as he leaned against a tree, watching the activity in front of him. The sun was sinking, but at this time of the year, the evenings were long, and there was plenty of daylight left to illuminate the scene. About ten utes, with a collection of drivers and hangers-on, had moved away from the main ball site, around a slight rise and gathered near a patch of open ground, out of sight. At least, so they thought. Nick had seen them go, and had a fair idea of what was coming next. He'd sent one of the other stewards looking for Rod Tate and then followed the utes. He was on foot, but he guessed they weren't going far. It didn't take long to catch up with them.

The sudden roar of a high-powered engine shattered the air around him. One of the utes leaped forward. Its wheels were spinning in ground made soft by the rain. In a haze of exhaust smoke, the ute turned and began to describe a circle. Louder and louder the engine screamed as the back of the ute broke out, and in a moment the whole car was sliding sideways. The cheers of the onlookers were lost in the mechanical roar as another ute moved forward, its engine screaming like a tormented soul.

Nick bit back the urge to go down there and break a few heads. He had to wait for Rod.

Another couple of utes had joined the fun, and four vehicles were now circling the bare dirt, engines roaring, tyres spinning, as a cloud of dust and engine smoke drifted slowly away on the light breeze. Nick could smell the fuel and burning rubber. Someone turned on their stereo, and a blast of electric guitar lifted the sound to an even more impossible level. Nick winced as two of the sliding utes passed within a hair's breadth of each other. The latest driver to join the fray had some friends with him. Standing in the back of the ute, two men and a girl clutched the row of spotlights on the roof the cab as they fought to keep their balance. If there was a collision . . . Nick could understand a bit of fun, but this was getting dangerous.

'I was wondering when this would start,' Rod said as he appeared at Nick's side.

'They really are idiots,' Nick said.

'Maybe,' said Rod.

The two men watched in silence for a few more seconds.

'Are you going to stop them?' Nick asked.

'If I can,' Rod said. 'Some of the balls allow circle work. Done properly, with a bit of control and common sense, it can be a lot of fun. But this is an accident waiting to happen. My guess is those guys have already had a few too many beers for anyone's good. Come on.'

Nick followed Rod as he stepped out of the tree line and walked towards the utes that were still parked, while their drivers waited for their chance to join the fun. They had almost reached the nearest ute when someone spotted them.

'Shit! The pigs!'

Technically Rod was the only one wearing a uniform, but Nick guessed his steward's T-shirt put him in the same category.

'Hi, guys.' Rod pushed his hat back a bit, and took position a few feet in front of the group of drivers. Nick stood beside him, content just to be seen. At this point, his size was the most useful contribution he could make.

'We weren't doing any harm,' one of the drivers muttered.

'Of course you weren't,' Rod said. 'You were just having a bit of fun. Right?'

'Yeah. That's right.' The slightly belligerent voice belonged to a youth who didn't look old enough to legally drink the beer that was in his hand.

Nick watched as Rod gave the youth a long, slow look. The teenager shuffled his feet in the dirt, his bravado quickly slipping away.

'Who owns that?' Rod asked, indicating the ute with the powerful sound system.

A blond man with a can of beer in one hand leaned through the ute's open door and hit a switch. The blaring music was abruptly silent, making the engines of the circling utes seem even louder.

'I'll be right back,' Rod told Nick.

Nick watched with surprise as Rod stepped away from the line of parked utes and towards the area of earth already laid bare by the circle work. But Rod knew exactly what he was doing. The drivers spotted him in seconds. One of the cars turned tail and immediately headed back to the main campsite. The others pulled over and the drivers stepped from behind their wheels. Nick cast his eyes along the assembled group of drivers. He half expected to see Gordo with them. But he wasn't.

The utes were all rough workhorses, covered in stickers and dust. There was no way Gordo would risk getting his precious show ute dusty doing circle work. Not to mention the risk of scratching the immaculate paint. The man was, Nick had long suspected, all show and no substance.

Nick brought his attention back to the situation at hand. Rod was having a quiet chat to the drivers, his face friendly, his words calm but his tone making it very clear he was not a man to be trifled with.

'So, guys, on the tickets it clearly says no circle work.' He smiled. 'Maybe you just didn't see that bit.'

Nick almost choked. Not see that bit? The words were printed in big letters across both the top and bottom of the ticket.

'No. No. We didn't, Sergeant.' One of the drivers leaped at the offered escape.

'That's not a problem. We all know now, don't we?' Rod cast his eye around the assembled group. All were nodding vigorously. 'Fine. So why don't you take the utes back to the lines. I think the pork roast is open for business now. It's good tucker. And the music will be starting soon. You don't want to miss that.'

'No.'

'Course not.'

Still mumbling, the drivers got back into their utes and drove slowly away, making as little noise as their highly worked engines would allow. Except for the last. The belligerent youth gave one defiant rev of his engine just as he dropped the clutch and slipped away.

'They'll be back,' Nick said as he and Rod started following the vehicles towards the campsite.

'Probably.' Rod didn't seem too concerned. 'I'll get one of the constables to keep an eye open here. And I'd better make sure they don't leave the site and go looking for somewhere else to play. I doubt there's more than a handful of people here who are still legal to drive on a public road.'

'Well, there's you and me,' Nick joked.

'Yeah. I guess we're not having any fun.' Rod grinned and raised a hand in salute as he turned his steps towards the track that led to the entry gate.

Nick kept walking towards the main compound. They would be opening the gates to the stage area soon. He was supposed to check tickets as people came inside. And check for contraband in the form of food dye. He was wondering just how he was supposed to do that when he spotted Bec weaving her way through the crowd. His feet just stopped moving.

It wasn't as if he had never seen Bec in a skirt before. When they were at school, she had worn a uniform that had tormented his teenage dreams. She occasionally wore a skirt or dress at town functions. A wedding perhaps. Or a funeral. Nick had even noticed her wearing a skirt at the pub on one or two occasions when the weather was hot. But he had never seen her look like this.

She moved through the crowd like a goddess among lesser creatures. The dress clung to her body, revealing curves that would drive a saint to drink. The movement of her skirt revealed flashes of thigh that teased and enticed. Her hair floated around a luminous face, and when she smiled, the rest of the world faded to dull grey. Nick suddenly understood all those scenes in the old movies Bec had made him watch – the ones where the picture went all soft and fuzzy as the lovers approached from opposite sides of a sunlit field. Any moment now, he and Bec would start running towards each other in slow motion, arms open to embrace. The music would swell as their lips touched, hesitantly at first, then their bodies would entwine, they would sink towards the earth and . . .

She walked past just a few feet away, without even noticing him.

Unable to take his eyes off her, Nick turned to watch her. He knew where she was going. To whom she was going. Sure enough, Gordo appeared through the crowd. Bec raised a hand to catch his eye and walked up to him, flirting with every movement. Nick watched as she stopped in front of Gordo and twirled for his approval. He turned away before he saw any more. He didn't need that image to make him feel any worse than he did right now. He was beginning to think he had made a mistake. It was all very well for him to decide to wait until he had something to offer before he told Bec how he felt about her. But he was beginning to believe that he had waited too long. By the time he had made something of himself, she might no longer be there.

A queue had already formed at the gate when Nick declared the ballroom open. As well as looking for food dye, there was the not insignificant issue of the dress code. That meant shoes and shirts for everyone – and bow ties for the men.

'But man, I haven't got a bow tie!' The complaint came from a kid who looked barely seventeen. Nick wasn't going to argue about the legalities of the drink in the youth's hand, but on the subject of bow ties, he stood his ground.

'That's the rule. Maybe one of your mates can help?'

'But . . .'

'You know,' Nick said, 'it doesn't have to be a formal one like mine.' He touched the scrap of black fabric at his throat. He thought it looked ridiculous with his T-shirt, but Bec had insisted all the stewards wear one. 'There are lots of ways you could pass muster.'

'Yeah?'

'Here, Pete.' The youth's girlfriend untied the fabric sash around the waist of her frock. She flicked the end around the youth's neck, and deftly tied a bow. Then she looked up at Nick, a flirtatious smile on her face. 'Will that do?'

'You bet it will. Have fun.' Nick waved them through.

The lad standing next in the queue had been taking careful note of the preceding conversation. Holding up one hand to forestall Nick's comments, he pulled a plastic shopping bag from the pocket of his jacket. As Nick watched with interest, the youth tied a knot in the bag, leaving two ends protruding. These he pulled and twisted until he held something that vaguely resembled a plastic bow. Nick opened his mouth to speak, but the lad shook his head. He unbuttoned his shirt to reveal a leather thong around his neck. This he removed and threaded through the knot in the plastic bag. With some help from one of his companions, he retied the thong around his neck.

'Voila!' the youth said triumphantly. 'One bow tie. Designer original.'

Nick laughed with him, but before the youth continued into the compound, he laid one hand on his shoulder. 'Now, if you'll just hand over the dye.'

'Dye?' The kid's face was a picture of innocence. It was all Nick could do not to laugh out loud.

'Yep. The food dye that was in that bag before it became a bow tie.'

The youth's face fell. Sheepishly he dug into the pocket of his jacket and pulled out four small plastic bottles.

Nick held out his hand. Reluctantly, the youth handed the bottles over, and Nick added them to the growing pile of similar containers in the box at his feet. 'You have a good night.' He waved them through.

For the best part of an hour, Nick watched the faces of the revellers as they poured into the ballroom. They were mostly about his own age, but they seemed so much younger. So much more carefree. He wondered if any of them had ever felt the shattering blow of the bank taking away their home. Their work. Their inheritance. Nick didn't blame his father for what had happened. He wasn't alone in going under in that terrible drought. But it had changed everything for Nick. He was now dependent on some distant employer for his livelihood and his home. He was little more than an itinerant worker. He couldn't live like that much longer. He had thought of leaving once before, but then Bec had come home and fixed him to the Creek as if with red-hot rivets. Then things changed again. Gordo had driven into their lives in his flashy ute and taken her away. Now Nick had nothing left, only the too real memory of a lost dream. There was nothing he could offer Bec. No home. No future. He couldn't stay here and watch her choose someone else. He would finish what he had started and establish the bush fire brigade, but then . . .

A sudden roar from the direction of the stage brought Nick back to the present. The ball proper was about to begin.

'I'm going inside for a while,' he told the other steward.

'I'll be fine. Have fun!'

'Yeah, right.' Nick grinned ruefully. This wasn't about fun.

He edged his way through the crowd towards the stage. He could see Ed Rutherford making some sort of a speech. There was a girl on stage holding a large trophy, and Nick suddenly realised that this was the presentation of the Best Ute award. The noise around him was a bit too much for him to hear the announcement, but he recognised the figure leaping on to the stage. Gordo. He should have guessed. Gordo lifted the trophy high, enjoying the cheers for a few moments before dashing off stage. Nick didn't look to see. He knew Bec would be waiting in the wings to congratulate her man.

He edged his way a little closer to the stage as another loud roar announced the arrival of the band. He saw the band leader step to the microphone, a bottle of champagne in his hand.

'Welcome!' Steve cried as he started to shake the bottle. The crowd cheered in anticipation of what was to come. 'It's time to party . . . Are we all Up The Creek?'

The crowd hooted with laughter.

'Well then . . . here we go!'

As he shouted the last words, Steve twisted the champagne cork. It exploded from the bottle with a loud bang, sending a fountain of sparkling droplets over the heads of the audience. He kept shaking the bottle as the champagne foamed over his hands. In response, from among the audience there was an explosion of noise as fountains of red, green and yellow dye sprayed from people's mouths to cascade across the crowd. Nick grimaced as a splash of green stained his shirt. He obviously hadn't done such a good job of catching the contraband.

On stage, Steve had picked up his guitar, and a loud chord ripped though the night.

The ball had begun.

16

Behind the stage, the sound was almost unbearably loud. Hailey sat nervously strumming Steve's Martin guitar. He had given it to her to play while he used one of several that he kept on the bus. A low rumble of applause from the crowd grew to a thunderous clamour, drowning out the final bars of the first song. The cheering and clapping continued until the music started again. Hailey's stomach lurched. In a little while, she'd be on the stage in front of that crowd. Playing. She set the guitar aside. Her fingers were shaking too much to play. She clasped her hands tightly in her lap and sat for a few more minutes listening to the music. Listening to the sound of Steve singing. She got to her feet to move closer to the stage. Closer to Steve. He was very, very good. What on earth made her think she could play with him? She turned towards the gate as if to leave, but then turned back to the stage. Feeling restless, she kept moving, until she realised that she was pacing like a caged animal, desperate to escape. All she needed was someone to open the gate.

'Hailey!'

The shout made her look up. Steve was standing between the black curtains at the back of the stage.

'You're all right?' he asked, his voice barely

distinguishable above the sound of Blue's enthusiastic drum solo.

Unable to speak, she smiled and nodded.

'All right. Just three more songs, and then we'll bring you on stage. You'll be great!' He smiled at her, that wide, enthusiastic, loving smile that completed the jellification of her insides. With a nod, he vanished back on to the stage.

Three more songs? Hailey didn't think her nerves could hold out. If she had to wait too long, Steve would put his head through those curtains to find her gone. How she wished Bec was with her. Strong-willed, confident Bec who believed all things were possible. Bec who wouldn't let fear stop her once she set her mind to something. Not fear or even common sense. Where was she? Bec had promised to be here to help her. She was supposed to stop her from turning tail and bolting back to the safety of her house. Hailey was disappointed. She was even a little angry. She needed Bec! She should be here. Where the hell was she?

Hailey felt her stress levels rising. That wasn't good. She needed to calm down or she would never get up those steps on to the stage. Maybe it would help if she watched Steve perform. She walked along the back of the stage, past the piles of empty equipment cases, and slipped out through the stewards' gate. She was near the back of the crowd. All around her people were jumping up and down and singing. Most seemed to have a beer or a Bundy rum clutched in one hand and a person of the opposite sex in the other. The noise was almost deafening – a cacophony of music and voices. The whole area was moving like waves on an ocean. Hailey was being overwhelmed and was losing herself. She needed a life preserver to grasp.

Steve was standing at the front of the stage, his Fender electric guitar slung from his shoulder. His hands flew along the strings, as the notes from the guitar soared above the heads of the audience. Then he started singing, his voice almost a physical thing as it flowed out to meet the listening crowd. Hailey could feel the intensity of the song; feel the electricity Steve generated to bring several hundred people under the spell of the pulsing rhythm. It was mesmerising. *Steve* was mesmerising. He had the audience in the palm of his hand as they worshipped him with their bodies and their voices.

She could never do what he was doing. Not in a million years!

Panic surged through her and she turned as if to run. Her way was blocked by a large man in a shirt that was all the colours of the rainbow. She tried to push past him, but his hand reached out to hold her shoulder.

'Hailey?' The voice was loud and close to her ear.

She looked up sharply, into Nick's concerned face.

'Nick!' The word was a sigh of relief.

'Are you all right?' he asked her, shouting to be heard above the crowd.

'Yes, of course. I'm fine,' she answered hurriedly, even though his face told her that he didn't believe her for one instant.

'They are pretty good, aren't they?' Nick indicated the band with a nod.

'They sure are,' Hailey responded automatically as her eyes sought out Steve one more time.

'You'll be great too,' Nick reassured her.

Hailey wasn't so sure about that. 'What happened to your shirt?' she yelled, keen to change the subject.

'I wasn't very good at confiscating food dye.' Nick

grinned ruefully. 'Come on, we need to get you out of here before the same thing happens to you. You wouldn't want to go on stage looking like I do.'

Nick placed a strong, comforting arm around her shoulder, and guided her back through the stewards' gate to the sanctuary of the backstage area. Once there, they found the esky full of refreshments. Both ignored the beer and picked out cans of cola.

'Have you seen Bec?' Hailey asked, trying not to sound complaining. 'I was expecting she'd come back here and keep me company.'

'She was going to,' Nick replied. 'But the crowd out there is really thick. She decided she'd better head for the front of the stage. She sent me to make sure you were all right. And to tell you to look out for us.'

'She sent you . . .'

'Yes,' Nick said with a smile. 'She figured I was big enough to push my way back to the front.'

'I guess she's right.' Hailey hid her disappointment. She had expected Bec would be backstage with her. What Nick said made sense, but . . .

Another blast of enthusiastic shouting and applause from the crowd interrupted her thoughts. The backstage curtains parted, and Blue appeared, wiping the sweat from his tattooed brow.

'We are nearly ready for you,' he said as he descended the stairs in two leaps. 'There's this guitar piece, then Steve will introduce you. How are you feeling?'

'Nervous,' Hailey said quietly.

'Well don't be.' A thick tattooed arm circled her shoulders and almost squeezed the fear out of her. 'You are going to be great.' Blue reached into the esky, and downed a can of beer in about three gulps.

'I'd better get back,' Nick said. 'It's hard work

fighting my way through the crowd. Look for Bec and me right in the front. Good luck.' He kissed Hailey's cheek.

Hailey watched Nick walk back through the gate and vanish into the crowd.

It was almost her time. She took a long, deep breath to steady her nerves and reached for the beautiful guitar that Steve had loaned her.

The crowd at the bar was at least ten deep. Bec stood in the middle, being jostled by the people around her as they fought their way to the front. She supposed she should have gone around the back and slipped through the staff gate. But that wouldn't have been fair, really. She wasn't being staff right now. She was just being Bec. Trying to have some fun and trying to get a couple of Bundy rums before she died of thirst!

'Careful,' she said to the large man beside her as he stumbled and nearly knocked her over.

'Sorry, darling.' He tipped his Akubra in a most gentlemanly fashion, which brought a smile to her face.

He smiled back. He was about her own age, and dressed in jeans and a dinner jacket. His obligatory tie was made from what looked like a pair of jocks tied on with a piece of string. Through the haze of alcohol that surrounded him, he looked Bec up and down, and his smile got even wider.

'Well, hello.' He made another grab at the brim of his hat, and missed by several inches. 'I'm Jacko. Who are you, darling?'

Bec stifled a giggle. It must be the moonlight. Or the dress. She hadn't attracted this much male attention since . . . well, never. Of course, it might also be the vast quantities of Bundy at work. Whatever the reason, she was more than happy to take the compliments as they came.

'I'm Bec,' she said. 'I'm one of the organisers of this ball. And I hope you're having a good time.'

'You're the organiser? Well, that's just great. It's just great. You're just great . . .' He seemed to run out of things that could be described by the only adjective active in his sodden brain. 'Hey,' he said suddenly, 'you shouldn't be queuing for a Bundy. Guys, let the lady through. She's the boss of this bash. Come on, let her through.'

Ignoring Bec's protests, her new admirer bulldozed an opening in the crowd and she found herself leaning against the bar, with Bill Davies smiling down at her.

'Hey, Bill,' she said. 'I guess I don't have to ask if it's going all right at this end.'

'I guess you don't.' Bill's face said it all. The revellers would have long since used up their free drinks tickets. Now they were paying, and Bill was raking it in. 'I can see one hell of a fire engine at the end of all this.'

'I hope you're right.'

'So? Bundy?'

'Two, please.'

Bill turned to the bench behind the bar, where two local teenagers were pouring drinks that vanished as fast as they were filled. He deposited two plastic glasses in front of Bec. She held out two drinks tickets.

'Don't worry,' Bill said. 'I'm sure the bar can—'

'No way,' she protested. 'Just because I'm on the committee, you don't have to give me free drinks. Well, not this early in the night anyway.'

'Okay.' He took the tickets and turned to the next customer.

Bec held the drinks high and began fighting her way

back through the crowd. She emerged at the back with only a few splashes of drink on her clothes. She turned towards the place where she knew Gordo would be waiting. She had taken just a few steps when a familiar face appeared in front of her.

'Hey, Bec.'

The girl was in her late teens, dark-haired, pretty and not very smart. Bec had met her before. She was dating Gordo's friend Mutley. Her name was . . . was . . .

'Hi.' Bec smiled widely. 'It's good to see you again.'

'You too,' the girl giggled. 'Are you here with Gordo?'

'Sort of.' It would be far too hard to explain to the girl that she was one of the ball organisers.

The girl giggled again. 'Wow. You two must be really serious.'

Bec frowned. 'What do you mean?'

'Gordo's never taken the same girl to more than one ball.' Another giggle. 'But now you've been to *three* with him.'

Actually it was four, but that wasn't important. 'We're not . . .' Bec hesitated. Did she really want to try to explain to – whatever her name was? She was still trying to frame an answer when she spotted Nick pushing towards her through the crowd. He was tall enough for her to clearly see the look on his face.

'What's wrong?' she asked as soon as he reached her.

'What's wrong?' Nick sounded livid. 'Your best friend is about to do the scariest thing in her life – and you're at the bar!'

'Oh my God! Hailey!' Guilt crashed down on Bec. How could she have forgotten? 'What's the time? I didn't think she was on for ages yet.'

'I just left her backstage. She's a bundle of nerves and wondering where the hell you are.'

'Shit.'

'I lied for you. I said you were waiting for her in the front row. So you had better be there when she comes on stage.'

Bec thrust the drinks at the startled girl beside her. 'Give these to Gordo. Tell him I'm over by the stage. Or drink them yourself. I don't care.' She reached for Nick's hand. 'Come on.'

Pushing their way through the crowd, there was no chance to talk. Bec was glad of that. Whatever Nick was going to say to her, it was only a fraction of what she was saying to herself. How could she have let the time get away like that? Hailey was her best friend and needed her. She had to be there when she walked out on stage. Not just be there, she thought in despair as the crowd in front of her thickened into a solid wall of people. She had to be in the front row. She was never going to make it!

'Come on.' Nick took her by the shoulders and placed her behind him. 'Follow me.'

Bec grabbed hold of his belt and did just that. Slowly they moved forward. Bec marvelled at the ease with which Nick slipped through the crowd. His size helped, of course, but it wasn't just that. He didn't threaten or bully anyone. He just smiled, and people made way for him. He must have some sort of magic charm. Or was it his own charm that made people seem to like him the moment they laid eyes on him? Whatever it was, Bec followed in his wake gratefully.

On the stage, Steve was finishing a country music classic, but played with far more rock and roll than its writer ever intended. The crowd was jumping up and down, sweat streaming from every pore. Nick took advantage of the general movement to step forward the last few feet, and Bec found herself at the railing that protected the stage. She strained to see what was happening through a tiny gap between the black curtains that hid the rear of the stage. She thought she could see some movement there, perhaps a flash of sequinned silk that might be Hailey. Bec was almost quivering with tension, and she wasn't the one about to step in front of this rowdy bunch of half-tanked party animals. She glanced up at Nick. His anger seemed to have abated, and he dropped his arm around her shoulders to give her a quick hug.

'She'll be great,' he shouted into her ear.

Bec nodded. Of course she would.

On stage, the song reached its climax and the crowd went wild. Steve raised his guitar above his head to accept the applause, then waved his hands for silence. Gradually the crowd stilled.

'Thank you. Thank you,' he said. He waited for a new round of applause to die down. 'All right, you bachelors and spinsters . . . Are you all having a good time?'

Bec guessed the answering cheer could be heard for miles.

'Well the good time is about to get a whole lot better,' Steve yelled. 'She's beautiful, she's talented . . . and boy can she sing. Will you give a big B&S welcome to Farwell Creek's own Hailey Braxton!'

The crowd exploded as Hailey stepped on to the stage.

The noise was almost a physical blow. Hailey forced her mouth into a smile as she stepped forward into the spotlight. She looked out into the crowd, but could see nothing beyond the blinding lights. She could just sense a dark mass of sound and movement. If Bec was there,

Hailey could not see her. She felt panic reaching out to claim her. She turned, and there was Steve. His face was glowing with excitement and . . . dare she believe it might be pride? Or even love? He held out his hand, and without hesitation she stepped towards him. He took her hand in his, and, bowing, kissed her fingers.

The crowd cheered its appreciation of the gesture. As he lifted his head, his eyes met hers and she felt as if he had gifted her with his talent, with the magic of his music, and with his love. She was still a quivering mass of nerves. This was all so new and terrifying. But Steve was there with her. He was there for her.

Nodding his encouragement, Steve stepped back and played the opening bars of the song.

Hailey lifted her fingers to the strings and played the first few notes, realised as she did that her hands were still shaking. Steve played the opening riff again, and so did she. He nodded, and her hands stopped shaking. She was ready. Steve didn't take his eyes from her face as he started to sing the song they'd rehearsed together – a truck driver's cry of loneliness and long nights on the road . . .

> *'I started out from Sydney*
> *I was queuing for the lights*
> *Drove on to Katoomba*
> *Love those clear blue mountain nights.'*

His voice was as clear and strong as a curlew's cry. Hailey listened to the lyric, her lips moving soundless with the words. She could feel the whole band willing her their courage. And she could hear Steve's song calling to her heart. As her hands played the first notes of the next verse, she stepped to the microphone.

'On the long dark outback highway
Thirsting for a taste of home
Drink the hot dry air of freedom
Taste the endless hours alone.'

Steve smiled at her, and suddenly the whole world was at her feet. The crowd was with her. She could feel the energy flowing on to the stage, circling her and Steve and the rest of the band, lifting them to heights she had only ever dreamed of. Steve stepped across the stage to stand next to her, singing into the same microphone: *'How I long to rest there in your arms . . .'*

The song seemed to last only a moment, then it was gone and the crowd was cheering wildly. Hailey felt the tears pricking her eyes as she looked at Steve. His own eyes were none too dry. He took her hand and led her to the front of the stage as the cheering got even louder. When he leaned over to kiss her cheek, the crowd let out a shout that would have raised the roof – if they'd had one.

'Do you want some more?' Steve called to the crowd.

The answering roar almost blew Hailey off the stage.

'I can't hear you?' Steve yelled, miming deafness.

Hailey started to laugh.

'I want them to hear you all the way back to Brisbane,' Steve called. The resulting cheer almost lifted him off the stage. Nodding his satisfaction, he turned to the band – turned to Hailey – and started to play again.

Hailey recognised the song and smiled at him. It was her song. Steve was at her side singing with her: *'Down by the creek at the break of day . . .'*

She never, ever wanted it to end.

Hailey walked down the steps from the stage, but she didn't feel the metal under her feet. She couldn't hear the clamouring crowd behind her. She felt as if she was flying. Looking around the backstage compound, she wondered vaguely why the world still looked the same as it had half an hour ago, before she had walked through the black curtains and into the shining light. Surely there should be fireworks. Or bright new stars glinting in the sky. Why were there no angels in the treetops? Didn't the world know that everything had changed?

'Hailey!'

She turned as Steve flung himself down the stage steps. In a heartbeat he was with her, his arms around her. His lips were on her lips.

'That was the most amazing thing I've ever seen,' he breathed between kisses. '*You* were the most amazing thing I've ever seen.'

Her heart was so full she felt as if she might explode.

Steve hugged her again, and she winced as the guitar still slung around her shoulders bruised her skin. But that didn't matter. Nothing mattered but the music, the cheering of the crowd and Steve. Steve beside her.

Steve singing with her. Steve kissing her and holding her as if he would never let her go.

Slowly he pushed her away and stood back looking down at her.

'Wow!' he said, his face glowing with pride . . . and something else.

'Hailey!' Bec's voice finally intruded upon them. Hailey looked around to see her friend duck through the stewards' gate.

'That was AWESOME!' Bec cried as she enveloped Hailey in a bear hug.

'Yes, it was,' Nick agreed as he caught up with them.

'Hailey, I've got to get back on stage,' Steve said, 'or else that lot is going to riot.'

Hailey became aware that the sound in her ears was the roaring of the crowd, not the pounding of her heart.

'We'll do a few more songs, then take a break. You'll be here, won't you?'

Where else would she be? She nodded and Steve flashed her one more smile before leaping back up the steps. He disappeared between the curtains and on to the stage, and the crowd screamed their approval. The first guitar riff exploded a few seconds later. Hailey felt it tugging her back on to the stage, but it wasn't her time. Instead, she took Bec's hand and dragged her back towards the band's bus. Nick followed. Once the three of them were inside, the noise level dropped enough that they could talk.

'That really was awesome,' Bec said again, her face split by a grin so wide the top of her head should have fallen off. 'A star is born. Move over, Judy Garland.'

'I was so nervous,' Hailey said. 'My hands were shaking so much, I didn't think I'd be able to play a note.'

'You didn't look nervous,' Nick told her.

'Steve saved me,' Hailey said. 'I felt him with me. I didn't want to let him down.'

'And you didn't,' Nick said. 'He must be so proud of you.'

'It's really hard to see up there, with the lights,' Hailey continued. 'I just knew there were hundreds of people out there and I had to sing for them. At first I couldn't even see the two of you. After the first song, they turned the lights on the crowd and I saw you in the front row. I was so glad to see a friendly face.'

As she spoke, Hailey saw a glance pass between Nick and Bec, and Bec looked away. She didn't know what it meant, but it didn't matter. Nothing mattered but the way she felt.

'Your parents would be very proud of you right now,' Nick said quietly.

Hailey nodded; the lump in her throat made it impossible for her to speak.

Bec reached out to squeeze her hand, then grinned at her mischievously. 'And what about you and Steve together – like wow! The two of you were on fire.'

Hailey felt herself blushing.

'You were Bogie and Bacall. You were Rhett and Scarlett. You just sizzled.'

'Isn't he . . .' Hailey stopped. She couldn't find the right words for what was in her heart. She looked at Bec, and Bec nodded. She understood.

'I'm really happy for you,' she said softly.

'Are you going to play again tonight?' Nick asked.

'No. That was it.'

'Why don't you come with us?' Nick said. 'We've all worked so hard to make this night happen, it's time we had some fun. We've earned it. The three of us. Just like old times.'

Before she could answer, the commotion from outside signalled the end of another song. Hailey's eyes flew to the open door of the bus. Her heart was pounding with anticipation. Within seconds Steve was there, his handsome face glowing with sweat and exhilaration. Hailey wasn't conscious of moving. She was in his arms and his lips were on hers, and that was all she wanted.

The rest of the band materialised at the bus door and pushed their way in, adding their hugs and congratulations.

'We are on a break,' Steve said when he could get a word out. 'We've only got ten minutes. And in that time we need to find two more songs you can play with us.'

'Two more songs?' Hailey gasped.

'Yep!' Blue grinned. 'That was so good. The crowd wants more . . . and so do we.'

'But . . .'

'No buts, Hailey,' Steve said. 'You are an artist now. A performer just like the rest of us. And your fans await.'

'All right. All right.' Hailey held her hands up in mock surrender. 'I do want to play with you again. If you'll have me.' She said the last words quietly, afraid that what was happening wasn't real.

'Have you?' Blue bellowed. 'I, for one, want to get every song out of you that we can before you leave us for bigger and better things and forget all about us.'

'I will never forget you,' Hailey said, and impulsively threw her arms around the big man's neck in a hug. 'Never,' she whispered fiercely.

'I guess we'd better leave, then,' Bec said. 'You've got work to do.'

'You'll come back for the next set? Won't you?' Hailey asked.

'You bet.'

'We both will,' Nick told her. 'Nothing would make us miss it.'

Hailey thought she detected a tense note in the exchange, but Bec and Nick were gone before she could say anything. She felt a momentary flash of concern, but there were more important things to think about. Most important of all, Steve was asking her for some songs she would feel comfortable playing. She started to name a few, eager to play with him just one more time. Those moments up on the stage had felt so good. She had felt so alive. Singing with Steve was everything she had ever imagined and more. If this was to be her one night, she wanted to drink as deeply as she could. To taste as much as she could before the harsh light of dawn thrust reality back in her face. Before the big band bus took it away from her, for ever.

'Hailey?' Steve spoke gently in her ear.

'Sorry.' Hailey pulled her errant thoughts under control

'You looked like you were a million miles away,' he whispered.

'I was,' she admitted, smiling softly.

'Remember this night,' he said so quietly she could hardly hear him. All round them the other band members were talking about music, gulping back long cold drinks and tuning their instruments ready for the next set. But there was no one in the world but the two of them. 'The first night is pure magic. There will never be another night quite like this for you. Or for me.'

'It has been more than I could ever have dreamed,' said Hailey. 'As if I could ever forget it.'

'There are going to be a lot more nights for you,' Steve breathed. 'Hailey, I wanted you to sing with us tonight because you're good. Your music is good. But singing with you is about more than just the music.'

Hailey knew exactly what he meant. The spark between them was ignited by the music, but that was just the beginning. Their hearts took them the rest of the way. To some place where no one could ever go alone. A place where two souls were as one. Perfect harmony. Perfect joy. As Hailey looked into his face, she knew they were both thinking the same thoughts. Maybe there could be more than just this one night.

'Hailey, I think—'

'Sorry to break this up, but we haven't got much time.' Blue was at Steve's side. 'We need to work out Hailey's next set.'

Bec walked away from the bus, but she didn't want to go back to the crowded ballroom. She didn't want to be around people. She wanted a little peace and quiet. She walked towards the schoolyard. Nick followed her. The two of them leaned against the fence they had climbed under and over so many times during their lives.

'I'm sorry,' Bec said.

'I'm not the one you should apologise to,' Nick said.

Bec turned to look up into the familiar face. He was right, of course, but that only made her feel worse.

'Well then, thanks for what you did. I would have hated to let Hailey down. Tonight is so important to her. For so many reasons.'

Nick nodded. They stood in silence for a few moments. Bec knew Nick wasn't really angry with her. She was also beginning to understand that she was happier leaning on a fence with Nick than dancing at the ball with Gordo. That she was happier doing almost anything with Nick than with Gordo.

'Remember when we were kids,' she said. 'We used to sneak away from school and hide behind the church. We were determined to learn what life was all about. Cigarettes. Booze ...' She let the sentence trail off, unable to give voice to the images that were hanging so clearly in the air in front of her.

'I remember,' Nick said.

Bec thought she heard a catch in his voice. She waited for him to go on. She needed to hear him say how much those times had meant to him. How much she meant to him. When he didn't speak, she couldn't look at him any more. She turned to stare out into the night.

'We said we were going to get married when we grew up. And work your farm.' She tried to keep her voice light, but the memory sent such a pang of emotion through her that he must have felt it too. He had always known what she was thinking. What she was feeling.

'Everything changes, Bec,' he said. 'You went away. Dad lost the farm in the drought. Dreams die.'

Bec felt her heart shrivel a little. 'Everything is so different. Hailey's parents are gone. Mum and I fight all the time. There was the fire. Now this ball. Hailey and the band. Sometimes I just want everything to be like it was back then.'

For a very long time, Nick didn't speak. Bec didn't dare turn to look at him. She was too afraid of what she would see in his eyes.

'You can't go back, Bec,' he said at last. 'People move on. That is the way of the world. Wishing won't change it. You have to be prepared to accept changes.'

He was right, and she knew it. Whatever they might

have had in the past was gone. Maybe it really was time to move on.

'I guess I'd better go and find Gordo.' Bec straightened up. 'I'll drag him back to listen to Hailey play the next set. See you there?'

Without waiting for him to answer, she started to walk away, every fibre of her being hoping he would call after her. Ask her to stay with him.

He didn't.

Nick sank back on to the rail of the schoolyard fence and watched her walk away. He could not remember a time when he hadn't loved Bec O'Connell. As a kid, he had loved her as his best friend. He had loved her as a hormone-fuelled teenager, as a big brother, and as a man. He loved her still. Loved her enough to let her go. He closed his eyes, but that didn't block out the vision of her walking away from him, taking with her the very last splinter of his dreams.

She wanted everything to be as it had been back when they were teenagers. So did he. He wanted her to look at him again the way she had back then. He wanted the future they had planned together. Until tonight, against all common sense, a small spark of hope had still flickered inside him. Maybe they could make a future for themselves, despite all the barriers. But Bec wanted everything to be as it had been. It couldn't be, and that tiny glowing spark inside him began to dim.

He kicked his boot heel into the dry, dusty earth. The land. It was all about the land. The land gave and it took away. Or rather, the bank took away. The drought had left him nothing to offer Bec. The dream that they had both cherished had dried up and withered like the grass during those long hot months. She hadn't been here to watch the rich earth that they both loved turn to dust. She hadn't been here to watch the dams shrink to nothingness. Even the creek that gave the town its name had run dry. Bec hadn't been here as the cattle slowly starved. She hadn't seen his father's face as he'd shipped them off to sale, knowing he would almost give them away to save him the cost of a bullet to end their suffering.

Bec hadn't been here when Nick lost everything, including his future with her.

He hadn't given up right away. He had worked like there was no tomorrow, and saved every cent he could. That was why he was seldom in the pub these days. That was why he still drove the same battered old ute. He had taken tentative hold of a new dream; of buying some place that he could call his own. Some place that he and Bec could turn into that dream they had shared as children. But that was gone now too. Organising this ball had brought home to him the reality of his situation. He was no more or less than the other labourers. No more or less than Gordo. He could save every penny he earned for the rest of his life, and he would not be able to afford to buy a property like the one taken by the drought. He might be able to buy a small business, which would have suited him well enough. But in a place like Farwell Creek, there was one shop, the pub and the garage. Hailey owned the only other possible business with her feed store. There was nothing for Nick.

Bec had vanished through the gate into the crowd. It was better that way. He didn't like Gordo and he hoped she would get over him. But at least Gordo would take her where she might meet someone who was worthy of her. At least he would take her away from the Creek –

because Nick didn't want her to see his failure. He didn't want to have to live the rest of his life knowing she was near but knowing that he couldn't have her. That would be more than he could stand.

Slowly he levered himself off the fence rail. His dreaming was done. Reality had raised its ugly head, and it was time he stopped fooling himself. He would see this thing through, then look to the future. A future without Bec held little appeal, but that was the only future waiting for him. He'd find a life for himself without her. And if that meant he had to leave the Creek . . . so be it. He would.

18

When Hailey walked on stage the second time, the crowd greeted her with a roar that would have disturbed the sleep of cattle several miles away. She strode across the boards glowing with confidence and bowed. Steve lifted her hand and kissed her fingertips, as the audience screamed their approval. Then Hailey and Steve started to sing.

Bec was again in the front row, this time with Gordo at her side. She waved wildly as Hailey walked on stage, trying to catch her eye. Deep inside, she still felt guilty about last time. She looked for Nick's face in the crowd, but he was nowhere to be seen. She suspected he would be close by, but not so close he had to join her and Gordo. From the stage, Hailey flashed her a quick smile, but her main focus was the music. The band. And Steve. She had found her dream, even if it was just for one night. Bec was happy for her.

As the music swelled, the audience sang along with more enthusiasm than talent. Feet pounded the hard-packed earth in time to the beat of the music. Beer and rum were drunk and spilled in roughly equal quantities. Gordo's arms were around Bec as they both stamped and swayed in time to the music. Bec tried to lose herself in the moment, but she just didn't feel the same connection that she had felt earlier, when she and Nick had shared Hailey's music. Maybe it was just the jostling of the crowd, or the mood of the ball in full swing. Gordo's voice was loud in her ear as he sang along, but he didn't really share Bec's joy at her friend's success. How could he? He wasn't one of them. Not like Nick was.

Gordo suddenly ducked as a sudden spurt of dye burst from a reveller behind him. The dye splashed down on Bec. Grimacing, she wiped it away from her face with the back of her hand. Gordo was laughing, and she felt an irrational desire to yell at him. Until this moment, she had managed to dodge most of the dye. Still, she thought wryly, at least it was yellow. It would hardly show at all against her frock. Gordo, on the other hand, had a wide streak of blue on his shirt, and a patch of green in his hair. It was all part of the B&S experience, but not a part that Bec particularly liked.

Hailey's second set ended well after midnight. Although the band was still playing, a few people were staggering away from the stage, looking very much the worse for wear. Bec guessed that some wouldn't be on their feet much longer. A few were helped by friends who were slightly more stable. Bec was feeling ridiculously sober. During the day, she'd been too busy being a steward to even think about having fun. Her last attempt to buy a drink had been forestalled by Nick dragging her off to watch Hailey perform. In fact, in the midst of all this fun and revelry, she seemed to be the only one who was sober – and not having a ball.

'Gordo,' she yelled in his ear, 'I think my stewarding duties are well and truly done. I want a drink!'

'All right! Follow me.' Gordo turned to push his way

through the crowd. Bec grabbed hold of his waist and followed in his wake. Gordo was already quite drunk, and his course was a little erratic. As they reached the edge of the dance floor, where the crowd thinned, she moved next to him. His hand snaked around her waist and gyrating to the beat of the music they made their way towards the bar. The ballroom was ankle deep in rubbish. Beer cans and plastic glasses. Paper plates and paper napkins. Bec was very glad she was wearing boots.

The bar was packed six deep with people, as it had been all evening. Gordo left Bec at the edge and began to work his way to the front. Bec stood swaying to the music, watching the party around her. There was no doubt the B&S was a success. The committee would definitely make a profit. It could well be enough to buy that fire engine. She had achieved what she had set out to do. It hadn't been easy. She'd had more opposition than she'd expected. From townsfolk. From her mother. There had been unexpected help too, not the least of which had come from Gordo. Tomorrow the revellers would have their breakfast and all head back to their homes. Back to their big towns, their jobs, their lives. And she would stay.

Would she stay?

For the first time Bec realised she was seriously considering leaving. This time for good. When she had left for college, she had never thought it was permanent. Even accepting a job in the city had been a temporary thing. She was always coming home. But maybe Nick was right. Maybe you couldn't go back. And if there was no going back . . .

Gordo emerged from the crowd, a plastic glass in each hand. She took the offered drink and had a long swig of the dark, sweet liquid. The rum burned into her gut, leaving no room for any other feeling.

'Ah . . . a double. Just what a girl needed!' she declared.

'Have you eaten anything?' Gordo asked. 'Because it's just occurred to me that I'm hungry.'

As soon as he spoke, Bec felt her stomach rumble. She tried to remember when she had last eaten. Breakfast? 'What a great idea,' she said. 'I am ravenous.'

As they weaved through the crowd towards the all-night hog roast, Bec glanced over at the souvenir stand, and stopped dead in her tracks. The stand was still doing good business, although from the look of it the stock was running very low. Her mother was behind the counter, but that wasn't the surprise. The real shock was that Miss Mills was standing next to her, taking money from drunken customers.

Miss Mills?

Bec glanced at her watch again. It was after midnight. Hailey had told her that Miss Mills was rarely out of bed after ten thirty. Pumpkin time came early for her. Yet here she was, still up and apparently enjoying her role as saleswoman. Bec guessed that was proof, if any was needed, that things were changing at the Creek. If the schoolteacher could sell stubbie holders, then maybe there was hope for Bec too.

'Will this do?' While Bec had been staring at the souvenir stall, Gordo had procured food for the two of them – bread rolls overflowing with roasted pork and apple sauce. Bec took hers. She carefully balanced drink and roll in one hand, and removed the big chunk of crisp crackling that was sitting on the top of her meal.

'Don't you want that?' Gordo asked.

She shook her head. Solid fat just wasn't on her menu today.

'Don't waste it.'

Bec held it out. Gordo had a drink in one hand, his dinner in the other. He leaned forward and gently took the crackling in his lips. He raised his head and let it slip back into his mouth, before crunching down on it with a sigh of contentment. It was the work of just a few seconds to dispose of it.

'That was good,' he said, smacking his lips. 'Ah – wait a second.' He did a swift shuffle to get both drink and pork roll into one hand. With the other he took Bec's hand, and raised it to his mouth. Slowly and deliberately he closed his lips around each of her fingers, making a show of licking off the pork juice. Then he turned her hand over and ran the tip of his tongue over her palm in a way that had nothing whatsoever to do with the food. As he did, his eyes never left Bec's face. Bec understood what he was asking, and felt a tense twist in her gut. If it wasn't the same fire she had felt all those years ago with Nick, at least it was something. And something was better than nothing, wasn't it? She couldn't put Gordo off any longer. It was time for her to decide.

'Gordo! Bec!'

Bec recognised the voice, and sure enough, a few seconds later Gordo's friend Mutley appeared at their side, his girlfriend attached to his arm.

'I'm feeling hot,' Mutley said, grinning wildly as he stumbled forward. 'We are on fire!'

'My man!' Gordo slapped his friend on the back. 'Let's get to it.'

Bec hesitated. They had all been drinking. She knew

what they were planning, and wasn't thrilled with the idea. Maybe it would be better to stay in the ballroom. By the time the music was finished, they might all be too tired, or too drunk, to carry out their plan. They would just head for the tents.

And that, she realised, would bring her face to face with her problem. Gordo would want her to go with him to his secluded campsite. He would want . . . That was a decision she didn't want to face.

Maybe playing with the utes wasn't such a bad idea.

From her place behind the counter of the souvenir stall, Jean watched her daughter walk away, surrounded by her laughing friends. She shook her head slowly, hoping Bec wasn't making a terrible mistake.

No one knew better than she how easy it was to make a mistake. How easy it was to get things wrong, and spend years regretting it. Life as a single mother wasn't easy, but she had never, for one moment, regretted having Bec. What she regretted was the lie. The problem with lies was that once you started, it was impossible to stop. They grew and took on a life of their own. You told one person, but that wasn't the end of it. Someone else would hear the lie. They might tell one person, and that person would tell another. It wasn't long before the whole town knew the lie. Knew it and believed it. The lie took on a life of its own, until she almost believed it herself. But things changed. A year ago, Kevin and Barbara Braxton had died in a crash. Bec had come home. And suddenly, the lie was back. Only this time, it wasn't so easy to deal with. That was why she and Bec were not getting on so well these days. How could she tell her daughter she had been lying all these years? The fights were hard to live with, but it was easier to live with the fights than to break the silence of years. A lifetime's silence. Bec's lifetime.

'Mrs O'Connell?'

The voice dragged Jean out of her reverie. A young policeman was standing at the counter. It was the constable who had arrested Matt Johnson for being drunk in charge.

'Hello, Constable,' Jean resisted for a few seconds, then gave in to the impulse. 'Have you arrested any more horses this evening?'

'No, ma'am,' the young man said. He didn't blush, but Jean guessed he was very close to it. Well, she thought, this was one assignment he'd never forget. She imagined that in years to come he'd probably joke about it with his friends. At least she hoped he would. But not for a little while yet.

'What can I do for you?' she asked.

'I have a message, ma'am, from the sergeant. He wonders if you could spare him a few minutes.'

Of course she could. 'Where is he?'

'He's over near the old church, ma'am.'

'Fine. I'll go there now. Thank you, Constable.'

'Ma'am.'

Jean wished he wouldn't call her that, but she guessed that was her punishment for giving the lad such a hard time.

'Will you be all right on your own if I step away for a few minutes?' she asked Eudora Mills, who seemed to be enjoying her role as a souvenir saleswoman.

'Of course. I'll be perfectly fine,' Eudora said with a smile.

Jean slipped out the back of the tent, wondering at the change that had come over the Englishwoman. Perhaps at last she was settling in. She might even be beginning to think that Australia in general, and Farwell Creek in particular, was not the worst place in the world. She might even sign on for another year. Maybe it was the nice new cottage the department had built for her after the fire. Maybe it was the B&S. Perhaps the teacher was a secret party animal! Smiling at the incongruity of that thought, Jean crossed the school grounds and entered through the small gate into the churchyard. There was no sign of Rod. Puzzled, she walked to the far side of the church.

The police car was parked on the short grass. On the bonnet of the car, two candles flickered in glass dishes. The light glinted off the water drops running down the side of a silver ice bucket. The neck of a champagne bottle protruded from the ice, and two long-stemmed glasses stood waiting. There was also a plate of cheese and biscuits. Rod Tate was leaning against the side of the vehicle. His uniform was as smart as always, despite the long day. For once, he was hatless. He smiled as he saw her.

'Hello, Jean. I was a little afraid the constable wouldn't find you.'

'I don't think he would have dared,' Jean said, laughter bubbling behind her voice. 'What are you up to, Rod Tate?'

'Well, you did promise me a dance,' Rod said. 'And I thought this might be a better place than down there.' He nodded in the direction of the B&S site.

'But aren't you on duty?'

'I think I've earned a few minutes' break. Would you like a drink?'

Jean felt the tension of the day start to slip away. The sounds of the B&S were muted here, the lights and the people hidden from view behind the church. For the first time today, she didn't felt overwhelmed by outsiders.

'I think that is a fine idea,' she said.

Rod poured the champagne. His face looked very handsome in the candlelight as he handed her a glass. He raised it in salute. 'What shall we drink to?' he asked.

Jean searched for something appropriate, but all she could think of were tired, worn old phrases. She shook her head in bewilderment. 'I don't know.'

'To bachelors and spinsters,' Rod said quietly.

Jean laughed softly. 'Bachelors and spinsters.' The glasses chimed musically as they touched. The champagne was crisp and ice cold and tasted beautiful.

'I honestly can't remember when I last had champagne,' Jean said.

'In that case, it was far too long ago,' Rod replied. 'Now, about that dance?'

'I don't think I want to dance to that . . .' Jean waved a hand in the direction of the stage, from where they could still faintly hear the sound of a rock-and-roll beat.

'I know I don't,' Rod said. He reached through the open window of the police car and pulled out a large portable CD player. He hit a button and a few seconds later the swell of an orchestra playing filled the night, drowning out all sound from the ball. Jean recognised the music instantly.

' "Moon River",' she said softly. 'It's the theme from one of Bec's old movies. I really love this.'

'I know,' Rod said. He stepped towards her and held out his hand.

Jean placed her hand in his and allowed him to pull her gently to him. As the orchestra played, their feet began to move and their bodies to sway to the music. Jean was very aware of Rod so close to her. The warmth of him. The gentle strength of him. Their dance floor was the dry earth. Jean wore no glittering gown. No chandeliers lit their way. The ceiling was the midnight-blue sky, dotted with stars. Both of them were dust-stained and weary from a hard day's work. But the scent of the night was sweeter than perfume. The music was the sound of angels singing and magic flowed around them as they danced.

As the music faded, their feet stilled, but Rod did not let her go. Nor did Jean want him to. How many years was it since she had last felt a man's arms around her? And when had any man made her feel this good? Made her feel like a woman? Made her feel attractive and wanted? She leaned her head against his chest and breathed deeply, revelling in the musky scent of him, and the feel of his arms as they tightened around her. She knew that if she lifted her head, he would kiss her. If that happened, their comfortable relationship would change into something new. What a risk that was. Rod might not know it, but the enormity of her lie lay between them. Could there be something between her and Rod, despite that lie? Maybe . . . Slowly she lifted her head.

'Base calling Sergeant Tate. Sir, are you there?' The harsh sound of the radio cut through the still night air like a scythe. Reluctantly, Jean let her arms drop to her sides. Rod let her go, and returned to the car.

'What is it?' he said into the microphone.

'Sir, you're needed at the ute lines,' the tense voice crackled out of the machine. 'Immediately, sir. There's trouble.'

'I'm on my way.' Red looked up at her, shrugging in

apology. Jean was smiling her forgiveness when the radio sounded again.

'Sir, do you know where Mrs O'Connell might be?'

'Yes, I do. Why?'

'She needs to get here too. Her daughter's involved.'

Nick saw the flames from the stage gate. After watching Bec and Gordo leave, he had returned to his steward's duties. He had seen a few other people making their way back to the campsite and the ute lines. He guessed there would be some partying going on down there. If it involved Bec and Gordo, he really did not want to know what was happening. He wasn't prepared for what came next.

A sword of flame cut through the darkness. It flared for four or five seconds, then vanished as quickly as it had come, leaving nothing but a glowing after-image when he closed his eyes. He could hear nothing over the sound of the band and the cheering from the stage. He had almost convinced himself he was seeing things when another jet of flame suddenly burst to life.

'What the . . . ?'

'It's a flaming ute,' a voice said near him.

'I know it's a bloody ute,' Nick said. 'But what's going on?'

'No, man,' a dye-covered figure clutching a drink said, 'the utes are flaming. You know – exhaust flames. Whoosh – burn, man, burn.' The figure staggered off into the crowd.

Nick had a bad feeling about this. He decided he'd

better get down there. After the circle work incident earlier in the day, Rod had left one of his young constables on duty near the ute lines. Nick guessed that the kid might need some help.

The spurts of flame were coming faster now. Each one seemed to last a few seconds longer than the one before. He could hear the roar of the engines as the utes spewed out fire. In the back of his mind, Nick said a silent thank-you for the rain earlier in the week. Without that, the grass would have been tinder dry ... and by now the whole campsite might be burning. He wondered if that thought had even occurred to the idiots who were dancing in the light of the flaming utes, cheering their friends on to bigger and longer burns.

A particularly long jet of flame exploded in the darkness to his right. It seemed to go on and on. Nick stopped moving. In the light of the flames, he could see two figures beside the ute. He recognised them instantly. Bec and Gordo. Bec was gesticulating and waving her arms. Just as Nick realised that they were arguing, the flames began changing shape, spreading outwards and upwards. The cheering onlookers had suddenly fallen silent. Nick realised, as they had, that the vehicle was on fire.

'Get back, everyone!' he called as he broke into a run. 'Get those other cars out of there. Get them out fast!' Cars didn't explode easily. He knew that. But it was always possible. Even without an explosion, with one car burning, all the others in the same line were in danger.

Nick glanced around. A few tents had been erected near the cars. 'Is there anyone in those tents?' he yelled, but no one was listening.

He sprinted to the tents and quickly checked each

one. In the last, he found a young man already sleeping off a heavy night's drinking. Nick grabbed him by the ankles and pulled him feet first through the tent flap. Without even thinking, he dragged the kid upright, draped him over his shoulder and lifted him in the classic fireman's hold. He half ran until he was a safe distance from the burning car. He was lowering the still unconscious youth to the ground when he heard someone call.

'Look out, there's a gas bottle there!'

The two explosions came just seconds apart. Whether the car or the gas bottle exploded first, Nick never knew. A wave of heat hit him. He staggered back, tripping over the youth he'd just saved and falling heavily to the ground. The noise of the explosion was almost a physical assault. Nick rolled over and pushed himself to his knees. He felt as if he'd been hit with a battering ram, but he didn't think he was hurt. With his ears still ringing, he checked the youth lying next to him. The kid was as awake as his alcohol level would permit, which wasn't very. He looked confused, but not injured. As Nick staggered to his feet, he shook his head. His hearing began to return, and he was assaulted by the crackling roar of the fire, and the muffled cries and exclamations of those around him. The ute was now well ablaze. A few metres away, tents were also burning. No doubt the gas bottle had been there. All the other utes had escaped, driven out of danger in the few seconds before the explosion. The grass was on fire, but with no wind, it wasn't spreading very fast.

Up at the stage compound, the ball continued, the sound of the explosion masked by the band's amplifiers and speakers. People from other areas of the campsite were running towards the burning ute. Shaking his head to try to clear it, Nick knew he should get to the water truck he'd parked nearby. He needed it. As he started to move, he spotted the young constable on the other side of the fire. He made his way around to him.

'You should call Rod,' Nick said as soon as he was close.

'I have. The ambulance is on its way too. And Mrs O'Connell.'

'Mrs O'Connell?' The heavy hand of dread seized Nick. 'Why?'

The constable's eyes shifted. Nick followed his gaze.

Two people were lying on the ground a short distance from the burning ute. A man and a woman. Their clothes were ripped and stained. The man's face was black with soot. The woman was lying on her side, her face hidden from him. But he didn't need to see her face. He instantly recognised the pale yellow dress and the fringed red boots.

The police car crawled slowly over the rough track towards the ute lines. At least, to Jean it felt like it was crawling. She looked ahead and saw the glow of flames in the darkness.

'Oh God . . .'

'We'll be there in a second.' Rod's hand gripped her arm. 'We'll find out then what's happened.'

Jean bit her lip to stop from screaming with fear for her daughter. She wanted to grab the radio and call the constable to find out more. But if Rod hadn't called, there must be a good reason. She must not panic! She was out of the car the moment it stopped, pushing her way through the crowd of onlookers.

It was like a scene from hell.

Blackened and twisted metal that had once been a

ute was still burning. Another, smaller fire showed where several tents had also been destroyed, and flames were licking at the grass. The flickering light lit the shocked faces of a crowd who were rapidly sobering up. Not far from the burning car, Nick was on his knees, tending to someone on the ground. Someone wearing red boots.

'Bec?' Jean felt the earth drop out from underneath her. 'Bec!' The cry was almost a scream as she flung herself forward.

Under the grime and soot, Bec's face was deathly white and her eyes were closed. She was lying with one arm twisted in a most unnatural position.

'Bec.' Tears almost blinded Jean. She reached out to straighten her child's arm, but someone stopped her.

'Don't. I think it's broken. Best leave it until the ambulance gets here.'

Confused, she looked at the man next to her.

'Nick?'

'She'll be all right, Jean.' Nick's voice was a rock in the midst of the storm. 'I think she was too close to the ute when it exploded.'

'Exploded? What . . . ? Why . . . ?'

'It doesn't matter,' Nick's voice soothed. 'What matters is that she's going to be fine. The ambulance is on its way.'

Jean nodded, unable to speak. Carefully she reached out and brushed some of the hair away from Bec's face. She put her hand on top of her daughter's. Bec's eyes flickered open and she made a sound that was somewhere between a sob and a groan.

'It's all right,' Jean said, careful to keep her voice calm. 'You're going to be fine. The ambulance will be here in a moment.'

Bec's eyes moved away from Jean's face and looked at Nick. Her lips moved as if she was trying to say something, but the words never formed. Slowly her eyes closed again.

'Bec?' Jean said.

'It's probably better if she stays out for a while,' Nick said. 'When she does wake up, she's going to be in a lot of pain.' His voice broke on the last words.

'Jean, the ambulance is here. You need to let them help her.' Rod was at her side.

She moved away to let a man in uniform look at her daughter. He was carrying a torch. Bec looked so pale in the harsh light that Jean had to fight back her sobs.

'I need some help here,' the man said. 'Anyone have any training?'

Before anyone else could speak, Nick answered. 'I did some first aid as part of the fireman's course.'

'Good.' The ambulance officer nodded. 'I have to get her on to a spine board. I need to you cradle that arm. It's broken.'

Spine board? The words sent an icy shaft of terror through Jean.

'Just tell me what to do.' As Nick spoke, the second ambulance officer arrived, pushing a wheeled stretcher across the rough ground.

They placed a long, flat board on the ground behind Bec's still form. With one ambulance officer at her head and the second at her feet, they prepared to turn her on to her back. Nick was at her side, gently holding the broken arm. There was absolutely nothing Jean could do to help her daughter. Her hands crept to her mouth as tears blurred her vision.

'Hang on, Jean.' Rod's arm was around her shoulders.

'They know what they are doing. This will only take a second.'

It seemed to take an eternity. The ambulance officers began to fit a temporary cast to support Bec's arm.

It was only then that Jean noticed the second figure on the ground. Gordo was sitting up, his head in his hands. A friend helped him to his feet. He looked a bit dazed, but seemed unhurt. He stepped forward to watch as Bec was gently placed on the stretcher.

'What the hell happened?' he asked of the world in general.

'What happened?' With Bec now safely on the stretcher, Nick's attention had turned to Gordo. 'What happened was you nearly killed Bec.'

'We were just having some fun. Flame-throwing. You know. Something went wrong . . .'

'You're damn right it did.' Nick was nose to nose with Gordo now. 'You could have killed her, you stupid bastard.'

'Enough!' Rod stepped between them and put his hand on Nick's arm. 'Not now, Nick. Gordo, there's another ambulance crew still up at the stage. Can you get to them, or should I call them to come down here?'

'I'll go,' Gordo said. 'What about Bec?'

'She's none of your concern,' Nick broke in angrily. 'You've done more than enough.'

'She's going to Roma hospital.' Rod was still playing peacemaker.

Jean wished he wouldn't. If Nick wanted to have a go at Gordo, she was all in favour of letting him.

'Are you coming with us, ma'am?' the ambulance officer asked as they carefully slid the stretcher into the back of the ambulance.

'Of course I am.' Jean climbed into the back of the vehicle. Nick made as if to follow her.

'No, Nick.' Rod held him back. 'I need you here.'

'No way. My place is—'

'Your place is here. I need you to get that water truck, now. We've got to put this out. And I'm going to need your help with crowd control when the stage shuts. No one up there knows about this. I can't keep it secret, but we can keep it low key. There's still a B&S happening. We need you here.'

Jean looked at Nick's face. She could see how much he wanted to be with Bec. 'I'm with her, Nick,' she said. 'And we have to go now.'

Nick's face was a mask of pain as he slowly nodded. 'Let me know . . .'

'I will,' Jean assured him.

Nick stepped slowly back to stand beside Rod.

The ambulance officer climbed aboard, closing the doors behind him. A few seconds later, the vehicle began to move. Jean winced every time it hit a bump, imagining what that was doing to Bec's injured arm. After a few minutes, the bumps stopped. They had left the dirt track and were back on the proper sealed road. The ambulance gathered speed.

'If you could just move towards the back for a few minutes, please,' the ambulance officer said. 'I need to get her settled. It's a long run to Roma hospital.'

Jean nodded and made as much room for him as possible. She watched as he set up a drip. Bec showed no reaction as the needle slid into her arm, but Jean winced. The officer smiled reassuringly.

'I've made her as comfortable as possible,' he said. 'Are you all right?'

Jean nodded.

'Well, just let me know if you need anything. It'll take us a while to get there.'

Jean sat with her hands clasped between her knees to try to stop them shaking. She had never felt so totally helpless. She couldn't even hold her daughter's hand, for fear of hurting her. Bec would be all right, she told herself. The ambulance officers knew what they were doing. They would call ahead and doctors would be waiting to help as soon as they reached the hospital. Bec would be fine. But for a short time, Jean had been so afraid that . . . The thought was unbearable. Bec was all she had in the world. If she lost her, she would be totally alone. Terrible as that thought was, there was one thing that made it even worse. That Bec would never know the truth about her father. For a long time, Jean had been trying to find the right way to tell her. There was no right way. But Bec needed to know the truth. As the ambulance sped on through the night, Jean realised that as soon as possible, she would have to tell her daughter that she had been lying to her for her entire life.

20

Watching the ambulance drive away was the hardest thing Nick had ever had to do. Every atom of his being wanted to be with Bec. That was what loving someone was all about. You had to care for them. Be with them when they needed you. Bec needed him now . . . and he needed to be with her.

'She'll be fine.' Rod put a comforting hand on his shoulder. 'She's in good hands.'

Nick knew that, but the knowing did not make it any easier to watch her being taken away. A sound nearby made him turn around. Gordo was looking at the remains of his ute.

'What the hell happened?' Nick demanded.

'I don't know.' Gordo was shaking his head as if to clear it. 'We were just, you know, doing some burns.'

'Bloody stupid thing to do.' Nick stepped closer, his hands curling into fists. 'Haven't you ever heard of bushfires? That's just the sort of thing to start one.'

Gordo wasn't paying any attention. He was obviously struggling to remember the events of the past half-hour. 'I was just doing a real long burn. A good one. Then the ute . . .' It was almost a cry of despair.

The ute was still burning. The tyres were sending pungent black smoke wafting into the night sky. The interior was also still alight; the fine upholstery and carpets had given ample fuel to the fire.

'Oh God. My ute.'

The horror in Gordo's voice was the last straw. Nick grabbed him and spun him around. 'Your ute?' he snarled. 'What about Bec? She's hurt. Don't you even care that you've hurt her?'

'Hey, I didn't hurt her,' Gordo weakly tried to defend himself. 'It was an accident. There must have been something wrong with the flame-thrower.'

Nick was quivering with rage that would no longer be contained. He raised one fist, but before he could lash out, Rod's hand came down on his arm.

'Nick. This won't help her,' he said quietly.

'But it will make me feel a whole lot better,' Nick bit back between clenched teeth, but he lowered his fist.

'All right, I need a couple of you to help Gordo back to the compound,' Rod said to the assembled audience. 'People who are sober enough to get there without getting lost.'

'Yeah, sure, Sarge,' a couple of the men mumbled.

'The back-up ambulance crew will be near the stewards' gate. Take him there.'

'Sure.'

'And don't start telling wild tales about what happened. I don't want crowds coming down here to gawk.'

'Yes, sir.' Two men took Gordo by the arm and guided him away. Gordo was still too shaken to protest.

'Nick.'

Rod's voice called him back. Nick took a long, deep breath to steady himself. 'What do you need?'

'You've got that water truck here?'

'Yep.'

'Okay. Get it down here and put this fire out. The music will be over soon. Once the bar shuts, there are going to be a lot of people heading this way. I don't want this to become the star attraction.'

Maybe having something to do would distract him. Maybe helping Rod would erase the image of Bec lying on the ground, her lovely face white with suffering. Maybe fighting a fire would ease the terrible fear that had locked itself around his heart. And maybe the world would stop turning on its axis. 'I'll do it,' Nick said, because with Bec beyond his aid, putting out the fire was the only thing he could do.

'Fine,' Rod said, then turned to the crowd. 'All right. I need to talk to anyone who was here when this happened. Everyone else – the band's still playing. You should head back to the party. And don't start spreading stories. This was just a bit of an accident. Everyone is just fine.'

Nick walked swiftly to where he had parked the water truck. It was the work of just a few moments to get it started and drive to the burning remains of Gordo's ute. The old truck wasn't designed for fighting fires. It had no big hoses and no pressure pump, but it did have a supply of buckets and that would have to do. Nick found a few remaining onlookers who seemed sober enough. He gave them buckets and wet chaff bags and set them to work.

As they threw water on the ruins of Gordo's ute, and beat at the burning grass with the bags, Nick couldn't help but think of the last time they'd fought a fire like this. The destruction of the schoolteacher's cottage had started the chain of events that had brought them all to this place. Bec had been at his side as they fought that fire. How he wished she was at his side now. He could still see her face as they loaded her into that ambulance: pale and drawn under the layer of soot and grime. She was going to be all right. Telling himself that did not make it any easier to stay here, when he so desperately wanted to be with her. Not that his presence would save her one moment of pain, but it might ease his heartache. But Rod needed him to help keep the ball on track. This ball was Bec's project. Her dream of raising the money to buy a proper fire truck. The only way he could help her now was to make sure her dream wasn't destroyed by what had happened.

By the time the fire was out, Rod had finished talking to the witnesses. He placed a friendly hand on Nick's shoulder.

'Thanks, Chief Price,' he said with a rueful grin.

'When I agreed to take the job, I didn't think we'd be doing this again quite so soon,' Nick said.

At that moment, a thunderous cheer floated towards them from the direction of the stage. Rod looked at his watch.

'That must be the last song,' he said. 'They'll all be heading back to the campsite now. I need to stay here and keep an eye on things.'

Nick nodded. 'Do you still need me?' he said, hoping the answer would be no. Roma and the hospital and Bec were less than two hours' drive away.

'I'm afraid so,' Rod said. 'I'll need my constables here with me, and someone has to keep an eye on the compound. The bar will be open for a while longer. Once it shuts, everyone has to clear the compound. Then you need to lock the gates.'

Nick felt an incredible weariness settle on his shoulders. Would this night never end? He took a deep breath. 'All right,' he said.

'Word of what has happened is going to get around, but it's all over now, so it shouldn't cause any strife.'

'Has anyone told Hailey about Bec?' Nick asked.

'I doubt it. But she needs to know . . .' Rod let the words hang in the air.

'I'll tell her.' Nick didn't relish the task, but knew he was the right person to do it.

Rod nodded. 'I'll check how she is as soon as I can. The ambulance won't get to Roma for a while yet.'

Nick was surprised. It seemed like hours since it had pulled away. He nodded wearily.

'She's going to be fine, Nick,' Rod said. He dropped a friendly hand on Nick's shoulder. 'I appreciate that you stayed to help. I'll get word to you as soon as I hear anything.'

Nick nodded his thanks. Tired as he felt now, he still had a long night in front of him. He walked back to the main ball compound, passing crowds heading in the other direction. He knew Rod would have his hands full at the campsite. He wasn't looking forward to the job he faced. The crowds were still fairly thick around the bar, as people stacked up with last drinks before Bill Davies called time. There were enough stewards keeping an eye on things for a few minutes, so Nick let himself through the backstage gate.

A major celebration was under way and Hailey was the centre of attention. From just inside the gate, Nick watched as the band and the stage crew raised their glasses to toast her. Steve's arm was around her shoulders and every few seconds she looked up at him, her face glowing with joy. Nick hadn't seen her this happy for such a long time. Since before her parents died. On second thoughts, he had never, ever seen her this happy. How could he take that away from her? He would tell her about Bec's accident later. There was nothing she could do to help now. Of course, she would be pretty pissed at him for keeping the news from her, but he'd rather face that than know he'd spoiled her big night. Slowly he backed out through the gate before she saw him.

Hailey was walking on air. She had a drink in her hand, but she didn't need it. Pure happiness enclosed her like bubbles in a glass of champagne. Every time she looked up at Steve, he felt that his heart was going to explode. She was radiant. Her second appearance on stage had been even better than the first. Without the almost paralysing fear of the first time, she had been mesmerising. She and the Kelly Gang had played the songs they'd rehearsed during the break, but that wasn't enough. It wasn't enough for Steve and the band, it wasn't enough for the crowd, and it certainly wasn't enough for Hailey. She stayed on stage, joining the band for a succession of popular songs and crowd-pleasers. After the last song, Steve had held her hand tightly as they bowed to the thunderous applause. He was still holding her hand.

'Here's to Hailey.' Blue lifted his beer can for the third or fourth time. 'Not only can she play and sing – she brings some much-needed sex appeal to this band!'

A cheer of agreement was followed by a clanking of beer cans.

'Thanks, guys,' Hailey said. 'Thanks for letting me play with you. This has been the best night of my life.'

Which gave rise to another rousing cheer.

One of the stage hands suddenly appeared with a box of rolls from the hog roast stand. 'Anybody hungry?' he called.

Steve grinned at Hailey. 'Have you eaten at all today?'

'No,' she admitted with a shake of her head. 'Far too nervous.'

'Well then.' Steve let go of her briefly to retrieve two rolls overflowing with pork and dripping with apple sauce.

They moved away from the rest of the crew to eat. The rolls, washed down with cold beer, tasted better than anything Steve had eaten for a long time.

'So, how did it feel?' he asked when they had finished and licked the overflowing apple sauce off their fingers.

'Amazing. Terrifying. Exhilarating,' Hailey said. 'At some point I'll run out of adjectives.'

Steve chuckled. 'Nothing beats the first time on stage.'

'Thank you,' Hailey said. 'It was all because of you. I'll never forget tonight. And I'll never forget you.'

'I should hope not.' Steve looked around. 'It's a bit crowded here. Let's go somewhere we can talk.' He held out his hand and Hailey took it.

Once they'd left the compound, it was Hailey who led the way. They avoided the main campsite and the ute lines, walking into the tree line near the fence. Away from the lights of the ball ground, they had only moonlight to guide them, but Hailey knew exactly where she was going. In silence they walked on until they reached the top of the small rise. A fallen tree provided a comfortable seat, from where they had a clear view back towards the lights of the ball ground and the town beyond it. For a few minutes they sat in silence, just enjoying the view. Steve was so very aware of Hailey sitting close to him, still glowing from her triumph. He longed to take her in his arms. But not yet. They had something important to talk about.

'Hailey,' he said, hardly knowing quite how to begin. 'I'm planning to leave the band.'

'What?' She turned to look at him, her eyes wide with surprise. 'Why would you leave the band?'

'I want to work on some solo projects. I want to take my music in a different direction. I've enjoyed doing the balls, but that's not where I want to be for ever.'

'Have you told the guys?'

'Yes. They understand. We are spending the next couple of weeks recording an album. I'll do some promo gigs with them for that, but the new material I write won't be for the band.'

Hailey fell silent as she gazed out over the flickering lights. The faint noises from the ball site were carried to them on the gentle breeze.

'You know, the band will need a new singer and songwriter. That could be you,' Steve said.

Slowly Hailey turned towards him. He studied her face, trying to read her feelings.

'You were great down there. You had the crowd eating out of your hand. Blue and the guys would be thrilled to have you singing with them. You could write for them too.'

Still she didn't answer. Steve found himself racing on. 'The band is based in Toowoomba, so you'd need to move closer to there.'

Her face froze as he said that. 'Leave the Creek?' she said in a small voice. 'You mean sell the house?'

'You'll need a bit of a stake when you get started,' Steve said. 'But I'm sure you'd soon settle in. You'd be on the road a lot, but that's the way it is with musicians . . .' His voice trailed off.

At last she spoke. 'But you wouldn't be there.'

The words sent a spark of hope through him. 'Well,' he said slowly, 'there is one other option. You could come with me.'

'With you?' He hardly heard the words, they were spoken so softly.

'With me.' Steve reached out to take her by the shoulders. He looked down into her beautiful face. 'Hailey, we are so great together. We could write and play together. I've got a producer in Sydney who is willing to give me a shot, and I know he'd love your stuff. There's no guarantee we'd make it. It'll be tough, but we could try. And we'd be together.'

He still couldn't read her face, and he felt just a tiny touch of panic.

'I want you to have a chance to be all you can be,' he said. 'But I've got an ulterior motive.' He tried to make it a joke, but he couldn't. This wasn't a joke. This was probably the most important moment of his life.

'It's not just about the music,' he confessed. 'In fact, I am beginning to realise that music isn't even the most important thing. It's about you and me. I know we barely know each other, but you touch me in a way no one else ever has. I feel as if some missing part of me has come home. I just want to be with you.'

She didn't answer.

'I guess I'm trying to say that I think I'm falling in love with you.' As he spoke the words, Steve understood that they were the simple truth. He just hadn't known it before. He watched the emotions play across Hailey's face. He saw surprise and elation, then she hesitated.

'Steve, I . . .'

He was suddenly afraid of what she might say. He couldn't bear to hear the words. He pulled her to him and kissed her. Her lips were soft and warm and she wrapped her arms around him. As she pulled him even closer, her lips seeking his with a kind of desperation, Steve had a terrible feeling that his dreams were slipping away.

21

Bec had joined the cast of *ER*. She must have. She
was lying in a strange bed, feeling fuzzy and
looking up at the white ceiling. She must be in a
hospital, because she couldn't remember getting here.
Any minute now George Clooney would slowly lean into
her field of vision, his handsome face a picture of
concern. He'd be wearing a steta ... steth ... thingy
around his neck. He'd smile that lovely cheeky smile
and tell her that she was going to be all right. He had
removed the tumour and saved her life. And then she'd
fall in love.

Bec sighed.

An out-of-focus figure crossed into her line of vision,
looking down at her with a worried expression.

'Bec?'

'George,' she murmured.

'Bec? Are you awake?'

That didn't sound a bit like George Clooney. Bec
forced herself to concentrate. The face came into focus.

'Mum?'

There were tears in Jean's eyes, and Bec wondered if
she had done something to upset her mother again.

'Hi.' Jean's voice was shaky. 'How are you feeling?'

Bec wasn't altogether sure. 'Where's George?'

Her mother looked up at someone on the other side of the bed.

'That would be the drugs wearing off,' said a voice that also was not George Clooney.

If the drugs were wearing off, Bec wanted some more. It felt like she was waking up, and she really didn't want to do that.

'Here, Bec.' Her mother was holding a glass of water.

Why did people always do that? Bec wondered. She didn't want water, she wanted George Clooney back. She drank some water anyway. It was cold and tasted wonderful. She was definitely waking up now, and it hurt.

'Where am I?' That was what they always said in the movies, so it had to be the right line.

'You're in Roma hospital,' her mother said.

Bec was suddenly aware of two things. Her mother was holding her hand, and the other arm hurt like hell. She tried to move and then decided that was a really bad idea. Instead she tried to focus on the room. Her mother was sitting on the edge of her bed. On the other side of the bed was the person she assumed was a doctor. The white coat was a hint. Unfortunately, he looked more like George Lucas than George Clooney.

'What happened?' It was always the next line in the script.

'There was a fire. At the B&S.'

Fire? Bec frowned. What fire? Then images began flooding into her mind. Images that were most definitely not from any movie. She gasped. 'Gordo's ute. It caught fire.'

'It exploded,' Jean said.

'Gordo?'

'He seemed all right when we left,' Jean said. 'There was no need to bring him to the hospital.'

Bec nodded, slowly. It hurt a bit less if she did it slowly. 'I remember the fire. The guys were all playing with their flame-throwers. I tried to stop them, but they wouldn't listen. Gordo wouldn't listen. They got a bit carried away. I don't remember an explosion.'

'I think there was a gas bottle involved,' Jean said. 'And the ute.'

'You were knocked out,' the doctor offered. 'Thrown about a bit, from the look of it. Your arm is broken.'

Bec noticed the cast for the first time.

'Don't worry,' the doctor added. 'It's a good clean break. It should heal just fine. The arm will be as good as new.'

'When can she come home?' Jean enquired.

'Later today. I want to keep an eye on her for a few more hours.'

That was good news. Bec had decided that George Clooney was unlikely to appear. That being the case, she wanted to go home. In the meantime, it wouldn't hurt just to close her eyes for a few minutes.

When she opened her eyes again, there he was, bending over her bed. His handsome face really was creased with concern. In fact, his eyes shone with something that might have been tears.

'Hi,' she whispered.

'Hi,' said Nick.

'You were supposed to be George Clooney.' Bec was rewarded with the ghost of a smile.

'Sorry.'

'That's all right. It would be just my luck to run into George Clooney when I couldn't do anything about it.' She moved her broken arm cautiously.

Nick was the one who winced. 'The doctor says you're going to be fine.'

'He also said I could go home soon.'

'I know. That's why I'm here. I figured you could use a lift.'

Using her good arm, Bec carefully pushed herself upright. She was wearing one of those revolting hospital gowns, and it was probably open at the back. She decided she might stay in bed for a while longer.

'What time is it?'

'Two o'clock Sunday afternoon.'

Bec collected her muzzy thoughts. 'The ball? I missed the last part.'

'It was a huge success,' Nick told her. 'Hailey was a star. She sends her love, by the way.'

'You told her I was here?'

'Before I left to come and get you.'

'Where's Gordo?'

Nick started to frown. 'When I left, he was still doing paperwork with Rod. His friend is driving him home. He knows you're here. Perhaps he'll drop by on the way.'

Bec felt let down. She had expected Gordo to be here when she woke up. Surely she meant more to him than his ute . . . Then she remembered. Before the fire, they'd been fighting. Bec thought what they were doing was dangerous. But Gordo had been drunk. He and his mates were egging each other on. It was a side of him she hadn't seen before, and she hadn't liked it one little bit. She supposed some good came from almost everything. The fire had stopped her from making a stupid mistake with Gordo.

'If I'm allowed to go home, I'll be gone before he gets here.' Far from distressed at that idea, Bec was really quite relieved. She had a feeling she was well and truly over Gordo. She wondered if Nick heard the relief in her voice. If he did, he said nothing.

Jean returned at that moment. She smiled when she saw that Bec was awake, then gave her a brief and careful hug. Bec could see that she had been crying. Before she could say anything, the doctor arrived. After a short and not too painful examination, he decided Bec could go home. He armed her with packets of pain-killers and told her to come back in a couple of weeks.

Bec was put into a wheelchair for the journey to the front door. At first she protested that she was well enough to walk, but after a few minutes, she decided that it hadn't been such a bad idea after all. She wasn't feeling all that good. Nick brought the car around, and Bec noticed with great joy that it wasn't his beaten-up old ute, but rather a big, comfortable Mercedes.

'Isn't that your boss's car?' she asked.

'It is,' Nick said as he opened the door. 'But as he's in America, he'll never know.'

With relief, Bec settled into the big, comfortable bucket seat. Nick helped her to recline it until she was comfortable. Her mother sat in the back as Nick guided them carefully out on to the road back to Farwell Creek. Bec guessed she must have slept for much of the journey. Before she knew it, they were pulling up outside the post office. She eased herself gently out of the car.

'Do you need a hand?' Nick asked.

'No. I'll be fine,' she said. She really was feeling better. In fact, she was awake enough now to notice . . . 'Nick, you look terrible. How much sleep did you get last night?'

Nick didn't answer.

'You haven't been to bed yet, have you?'

He shrugged. 'Rod needed me last night, so I stayed. Once the campsite started to clear this morning, I came straight here.'

He said it so simply. As if it was inconceivable that he would have done anything else. Bec suddenly realised that for Nick, it was. He would always put her welfare ahead of his own. Which meant . . . She shook her fuzzy head slowly. She was too tired, too full of drugs and in too much pain to continue that thought with any chance of it making sense. Instead, she kissed Nick on the cheek. 'Thanks. Now go home and get some sleep. You look dead on your feet.'

Nick grinned ruefully. 'Well, I had to stay awake while I was driving.' With one last long look at her, as if to reassure himself that she was all right, he turned to get back into the car.

Slowly Bec made her way inside the house. It felt good to be here. Whatever restlessness she might have been feeling over the past few weeks, it was gone now. All she wanted was the comfort of home.

'You should lie down,' Jean said. 'Do you want something to drink? Probably not coffee, but I could get you some cold water. Or if you like, I can run over to the Ryans' store and get something else. Some juice . . .'

'Mum, stop fussing.' Bec said. 'I'll be fine.'

'Well, do you want to watch a movie or something?'

'What I really want,' Bec said, 'is a wash and some clean clothes.' She was still wearing her ball dress. It was stained and ripped in places, and smelled of smoke. She was desperate to get comfortable. 'I promise I won't drown in the bathtub.'

As the bathroom door closed behind Bec, Jean dropped into one of the big armchairs in the living room. She was utterly exhausted and emotionally drained. Last night had been the longest of her life. Last night? No. This morning. The accident had happened well after midnight. The journey to Roma hospital had been interminable, sitting in the back of the ambulance, unable even to hold Bec's hand. Then the wait while the doctors tended her arm. Jean knew she had dozed in the chair in Bec's hospital room as she waited for her to wake up, but she felt as if she hadn't slept for days. Her nerves were jangling, and her emotions were raw. She desperately needed to sleep, but she didn't dare close her eyes while Bec was in the bathroom. Her daughter would not drown in the bath, but Jean had to be ready in case she was needed.

The knock on the front door felt like a hammer blow to her exhausted body. Slowly Jean got to her feet, almost hoping it would be Gordo. She had a few things she wanted to say to that man – none of them very pleasant.

Hailey was standing on the top step.

'We just got home,' Jean said before Hailey could ask. 'Bec's fine. She's just having a bath.'

Hailey looked startled. 'Oh.' Her face fell.

'Come on in.' Jean stepped back, but to her surprise the girl stayed where she was.

'No. I . . . I just wanted to . . .'

Slowly, Jean began to realise that Hailey looked upset. Her eyes were red from crying, and she was clasping and unclasping her hands in distress.

'Hailey? Is everything all right?' Jean asked.

'Yes. Yes. I was just worried about Bec,' Hailey said quickly.

'She'll be fine,' Jean said, realising as she did that she almost believed it herself now. 'Come on in. She'll be pleased to see you. I think she's sick of me fussing over her already.'

Hailey didn't return the smile. 'No. She probably

needs to sleep. I . . . I just wanted to see how she was. Tell her not to worry. I'll talk to her tomorrow.'

'Are you sure?'

But Hailey had already turned and was walking down the stairs. Jean returned to the living room, wondering what had upset Hailey so much. Surely it wasn't just Bec's accident. It must be something to do with that singer she was involved with. That damned ball! She had known right from the start it was a bad idea. Her steps took her not to her comfortable chair, but to the bookshelf. As she had done so many times in the past when she was troubled, she took a photo album from the shelf. Sitting down, she put it on the coffee table. It fell open at a much-used page. She looked down at the photo. It was more than a decade old. Bec and Hailey weren't yet teenagers. The photo had been taken one weekend, when the O'Connells and the Braxtons were picnicking down by the old swimming hole. The girls were laughing as they clambered all over Kevin Braxton. His handsome face shone with happiness and pride. To one side of the photo sat Jean. Alone and slightly apart, as she had always been. It wasn't Kevin's fault that she felt alone. Nor was it Barb Braxton's fault. They had always made the O'Connells very welcome in their home. Bec had almost been part of the family. Jean had always been apart, because that was the way it had to be.

She felt the sadness almost overwhelm her. She was too tired and too overwrought to really notice that tears were streaming down her face. Her life wasn't supposed to have been like this. It just wasn't fair! She started to sob quietly.

'Mum!' Bec was standing in the doorway.

Jean wiped the tears from her face and looked at her

daughter. Bec was much cleaner now. She had managed to dress herself in shorts and a tank top. She looked awake, unhurt and so much like her father it sent a shaft of pain straight to Jean's heart.

'Mum, it's all right. There's nothing to cry about. I'm fine.' Bec came to sit by her. 'It's only a broken arm. I survived last time. Remember?'

Jean did remember. Bec had broken her arm when she was eight. She and Hailey had been playing in the Braxtons' store. They had climbed to the top of a massive stack of hay bales. Bec had slipped and fallen. Kevin Braxton had taken her to hospital.

'It's not that,' Jean said, her voice small and shaky.

'Then what is it?' Bec asked.

Jean shook her head, unable for a few seconds to speak. She took a long, deep breath. It was time. If she didn't do this now, she never would. 'I've got something to tell you,' she said.

'What?'

'It's about your father.'

Bec looked surprised, but said nothing, waiting for her mother to continue.

'I should have told you this a long time ago,' Jean said. 'But somehow it was never the right time. Then last night . . . sitting in the hospital . . .'

'What's this all about, Mum?'

Jean sighed. She wiped the last remaining tears from her cheeks and looked her daughter squarely in the face. 'It's time I told you the truth.'

'The truth about what? My father?'

'Yes.'

Silence filled the room for a few moments, as Jean mustered her courage. She had no idea what this revelation would do to her relationship with her daughter, but having come this far, she could not turn back.

'I lied to you when I told you about your father.' Jean forced the words out.

'You know, I sort of guessed you had,' Bec said. 'I figured that you probably hadn't been married. But that's okay, Mum. I know it was difficult at the time, but it doesn't matter to me.'

'You guessed . . .' Jean looked down at her hands, clasped in her lap. If only it was that simple. 'That's not it,' she said.

'Then what?'

'You're right about one thing. O'Connell is my maiden name. I have never been married. There was no Ken O'Connell. I made him up.'

'You made him up? Why?'

'When I came here to live, it seemed the best thing to do. To pretend I was married and he had left us. I thought it would make things easier for you too.'

Jean waited for the question that had to come next.

'If there's no Ken O'Connell, who is my father?'

Jean looked at her daughter's face, trying to read the emotions there. Trying to predict what would happen when she learned the truth. Slowly she reached out for the photo album. She pushed it towards Bec.

Frowning, Bec glanced down at the photo taken all those years ago down by the creek. 'I don't understand,' she said.

Jean gathered herself for the storm. 'Kevin Braxton.'

'Hailey's father?'

Jean nodded. 'Hailey's father is also your father.'

B ec hadn't heard that right. She couldn't have. Her mother could not have said that Kevin Braxton was her father.

'Is this supposed to be a joke?' she asked, her voice hard. 'Because it's not funny.'

'I know this must be a shock,' Jean's voice continued. 'I wanted to tell you when you came home last year. After Kevin and Barb were killed. But . . .'

Kevin Braxton? The name echoed through Bec's head, along with a thousand images of the man she had always called Uncle Kevin. 'Kevin Braxton was my father?'

Her mother looked up at her again. There were tears in her eyes, but beyond the tears, Bec could see pain and guilt that stretched back for years.

'Yes.'

That one simple word made Bec realise that her mother was telling the truth. She looked at the woman who suddenly seemed like a stranger to her.

'Kevin Braxton was my father.'

Bec wondered how many times she would have to say it, to think it, before it ceased being a shock. She reached for the photo album and stared down at the picture. She looked at Kevin's face – her father's face –

and then at herself and Hailey. The resemblance was there for anyone to see. As she stared down at the image, another, shocking thought struck her.

'You had an affair with Kevin Braxton?' She saw her mother flinch at the anger in her voice.

'It wasn't like that.'

'Wasn't it?' Bec asked. 'Then what was it like? Tell me.'

'You know I grew up near Charleville. When I was at school, we sometimes had sports events with the other schools in the region. I used to see Kevin then. He was a couple of years older than me. He was so handsome . . .' Jean's voice tailed off with the memory.

Bec looked at the photograph again. Her mother was telling the truth about that, at least. Uncle Kevin . . . her father . . . had been a handsome man.

'I had a crush on him at school, but he didn't even know my name. A couple of years after I left school, I went to a bush dance. We didn't call them B&S balls back then, but they were pretty much the same. Anyway, Kevin was there. We both got drunk . . . and . . . well . . .' Jean's voice trailed off.

'And where was Hailey's mother?'

'Kevin and Barb hadn't even met then. That happened a couple of weeks later, when her father was sent to manage the bank at Roma. It was pretty much love at first sight.' Bec heard a touch of bitterness in her mother's voice, but she was incapable of feeling sorry for her.

'And what about you?'

'When I knew I was pregnant, I went looking for Kevin, meaning to tell him. But he and Barb had just gotten engaged. I went away again without even talking to him.'

Bec shook her head. There was too much to take in.

She glanced across at her mother. Jean was looking intently at her, trying to judge her reaction. Bec dropped her eyes back to the table. Right now, she just could not bear to look her mother in the face. Her father smiled back at her from the photograph.

'Did you ever tell him?' she asked.

'No.'

Bec got to her feet. She was dimly aware that her broken arm was hurting, but she couldn't stand still. She felt as if her whole world was shifting around her. All these years – her whole life – she hadn't been who she thought she was. She was . . . Well, she no longer knew who she was.

'Why the hell did you come here to live?' she demanded. 'You could have just gone away.'

'When you were just a baby, the job at the post office opened up. It was the perfect job for a single mother. And I thought . . .'

'You thought that maybe you could get him back?'

'Bec, I don't know what I thought.' Jean's voice quivered. 'I loved him. You might find that hard to believe, but I really did love him.'

'He didn't guess?'

'I don't know if he even remembered that night. If he did, he never gave any sign of it.' Jean's voice broke. 'By the time we arrived here, he was married. He had a new baby.'

'Hailey?'

Jean nodded.

'Why didn't you just go away again?'

'I wanted the two of you to know each other. I thought you both deserved that. And I guess I thought that maybe, one day, at the right time . . . But that time never came.'

'And all these years . . .' Bec's voice trailed off as memories crowded into her mind. She could hear Kevin laughing as he watched her and Hailey at play. He had scolded them both when they skipped school to go down to the creek and swim. She remembered crying in his arms when she fell and skinned her knee. In so very many ways, he had treated her like a daughter.

'Then the accident . . .' Jean's voice broke and she stopped speaking.

Bec's mind also went back to that dreadful day when the Braxtons had been killed. She had still been living in the city when her mother called to tell her. She remembered Jean sobbing over the phone. Now she was beginning to realise that it was more than just grief for a friend and neighbour. If her mother had truly loved Kevin . . . Bec had raced home to be with Hailey, without realising that her own father had died that day.

'Why the hell didn't you tell me then?' She fought to stop herself screaming the question.

'God knows I wanted to.' Tears slid down Jean's cheeks. 'I tried, but I couldn't. I had just lost the only man I ever loved, but I couldn't let anyone see how I was feeling, least of all you. I didn't want the truth to get out like that. Everyone was comforting Hailey, but I was grieving too.'

'Don't try and make me feel sorry for you.' Bec spat the words out. 'You don't deserve that. If you knew how much I envied Hailey when we were kids. To have a father like him. I wanted him to be my father. I sometimes pretended he was. And now you tell me . . .' She couldn't get the words out. Her anger was making her shake.

'Bec, I'm so sorry. He did love you. Even without knowing that he was your father, he did love you like his own.'

'No he didn't, Mum. He couldn't. You didn't let either of us have that.' She couldn't stay in the room a moment longer.

'I only did what I thought was right.'

Bec ignored her mother's voice. She found some shoes near the back door and slipped them on. Then she was outside, gulping deep breaths of air as she fought to control her emotions. She had to get away. Her first instinct was to turn to Hailey. She and Bec had always been there for each other. Whenever one had a problem, the other was ready with comfort or advice or just a hug. If ever she had needed her best friend, it was today. Except . . . Hailey wasn't her best friend. Hailey was her half-sister. The realisation crashed down on Bec like a clap of thunder. Her half-sister! All these years, they had been as close as sisters. That was a laugh! They *were* sisters. Bec wasn't sure how she felt about that. She wasn't sure how she felt about anything. She couldn't go to Hailey. Not now. There was only one other place she could possibly go.

Her mother's car was parked in the driveway. The keys were in the ignition. Rod had constantly warned Jean about this habit, but today Bec was glad of it. There was no way she could walk back inside that house. It wasn't easy to get into the car with her left arm in a sling, but she managed. Thankful that the car was an automatic, she started the engine. With some painful twisting and reaching, she managed to slip the car into reverse. Carefully she backed out of the driveway. Praying that neither her mother nor Rod Tate would appear, she struggled to get the car into drive. When at last she succeeded, she pressed down on the accelerator. She would have to be careful, driving with a broken arm. But she didn't have far to go.

It didn't take long to get there. She pulled up outside the house that was as familiar to her as her own. She was about to get out of the car, but stopped. He wouldn't be there. Nick's parents still lived in this house, but Nick had left two years ago, when the bank took the farm. He'd moved into a small stockman's cottage a short distance away, near the cattle yards. When he'd told her, Bec hadn't really understood why he didn't want to live as a tenant in the house that used to be his family home. After all, the house hadn't changed. It was still the same. Now she was beginning to understand. Something might seem the same. Might look the same. But it was the underlying truth that really mattered. She re-started the car and turned the wheel toward the stockyards.

When she reached the stockman's cottage, Bec turned off the car engine with a sigh of relief. Her arm was killing her. But that didn't matter. All that mattered was reaching Nick,

She tapped on the front door, but there was no answer. He had to be here, she thought. He had been too tired after the night's events to work. He must be asleep. The door wasn't locked. She opened it and walked through into the small living room.

'Nick?'

There was no answer.

'Nick? Are you there?' She spoke a little more loudly this time, but still there was no reply. Although she'd never been to this cottage before, it wasn't very big. There were only two doors leading from the living room. Both were open. One led to the kitchen, which she could see was empty. The other led to a short hallway, with a bathroom visible at the far end and two other doors, one to each side. Both were open. She stepped hesitantly down the hallway.

Nick was sound asleep, lying on top of the double bed. He must have been asleep on his feet when he entered the room. He had removed his boots and his jeans, but exhaustion appeared to have caught up with him as he was unbuttoning his shirt. He lay on his side, his shirt hanging open. He was also wearing red jocks and a pair of black socks. Bec felt a warm flush through her entire body as she looked at him. This was Nick, who had driven through the night to be with her at the hospital. The same Nick she had kissed when she was just eleven. The Nick she had got drunk with, and fought a fire with. This was the Nick who would always look after her. He was the one thing in her life that was solid and unchanging. And he would never, never lie to her.

She felt the tears coming, and this time she didn't try to hold them back. Slowly she crossed the room. All she wanted was to lie down next to him. She wouldn't wake him, but if, in his sleep, he was to hold her, that would be all right too. She sat down carefully on the edge of the bed and kicked off her shoes. It was hard to lie down with her arm in a cast, but she managed it without waking Nick. Tears were pouring down her face now. She moved closer to him, seeking the comfort of his warm, strong body and the love she knew he felt for her.

Nick stirred in his sleep. Bec took the opportunity to move a little closer. His arm dropped gently across her waist. That felt good. The last teardrops ran down her cheek as she closed her eyes.

In the depths of slumber, Nick dreamed that Bec was calling him. He couldn't see her, but he knew from the sound of her voice that she needed him. He wanted to go to her, but he couldn't move. Something was holding him back. He tried to call out to her, but he couldn't speak. If he didn't get to her, she would be lost for ever. His hands moved as he reached out, hoping to find her in the darkness.

Nick came awake very slowly. He didn't open his eyes, but clung to the last few moments of peace. His inner clock told him it was early morning. The combination of physical and emotional exhaustion had flattened him for more than twelve hours. He felt well rested. That was strange, given the nature of his dreams. More than rested; he felt . . . restored. As if the bruises, both visible and invisible, had faded as he slept. Perhaps some of those dreams hadn't been so bad. He felt as if he was not alone. He could almost hear the slow sound of someone breathing; feel the warmth of another human presence, as if there was someone lying beside him in his bed. He opened his eyes. There *was* someone beside him. Bec! She was curled up in her sleep, her back nestled against his chest. Her body lay against his. She was only wearing shorts and a tiny top, and her skin was warm where it touched him. His arm was around her waist, and with just the gentlest of movements, he could lean forward to run his lips over the bare skin of her shoulder. He would wake her gently, and when she opened those big bright eyes, she would look at him the way she had when then were teenagers. Then they would . . .

What was he thinking? With an effort, Nick dragged his thoughts back under control. Not when Bec's broken arm was in a plaster cast. And besides – his sleepy brain sprang to full wakefulness – what was she doing in his bed in the first place? He raised himself on one arm and gently moved away from her sleeping body. She whimpered slightly as he did, and he wondered if it was because her arm hurt, or because even in her sleep she felt him pulling away from her. Slowly he eased himself out of the bed, and stood looking down at her. She was beautiful when she slept, but he could see that her eyes were puffy from crying, and small lines of tension or pain creased her forehead. Something was very wrong in Bec's world – something that hurt a lot more than her broken arm.

'Nick?' Her voice was so soft he could barely hear it.

He lowered himself gently on to the side of the bed. Bec rolled on to her back and looked up at him. Her eyes were still a little misty from sleep.

'What's wrong?' Nick asked.

She opened her mouth to speak, but no words came out. The tears welled up in her eyes. In all the years he'd known Bec, he had never seen her like this. He reached out to her, and she came to him like a hurt child. He gathered her up in his arms and held her as she started to sob. She cried as if her heart was breaking. Nick's mind raced, wondering what could have caused her so much pain. If that bastard Gordo had done this, Nick would tear him apart. He held her until her sobs started to ease. Gradually her shoulders stopped shaking, but he didn't let her go. At last she began to speak, her voice rough with emotion.

Nick listened to her words with a growing sense of shock. Bec's mother and Hailey's father? It was almost too much to take in. He didn't doubt for a minute that it was true. Jean had kept her secret well, but now that he knew the truth, he realised that it had been obvious all these years. The two girls were so alike. How many times had they joked that they could be sisters? Should be sisters. Well, they were. After a very long time, Bec stopped speaking. She was still in his arms, her face buried in his chest.

At last she drew back and looked up at him. 'I don't know who I am any more.' It was a cry straight from her wounded heart.

'I do,' he said. 'You're Bec. The same Bec you've always been. The Bec I know and love.'

She smiled at him, a thin smile. As she did, the look in her eyes changed. She leaned towards him, her face lifted to his in invitation. Nick felt every fibre in his body respond to her. She needed reassurance. She needed someone to tell her they loved her. She wanted to feel good about herself. She wanted him.

Nick reached out to gently wipe the last tear from her cheek. He was so very aware of her warm bare flesh against his. Her lips were so close, he could feel her breath. He could almost hear the pounding of her heart. He could feel her need, and he did the only thing he could do.

Slowly and gently, he moved away from her. He let his arms slide away from her shoulders, and reached for her hands. He saw the hurt flash in her eyes, before she dropped them to look down at their clasped hands. That flash cut Nick like a knife, but he knew he was doing the right thing. To make love to Bec now would only give her one more cause for anguish in the days ahead. She didn't need that.

'You know what you have to do, don't you?' he said.

'Can't I just stay here?' she asked in a very small voice.

'You can stay as long as you like, but at some point you will have to go home.'

'I know.'

'And you are going to have to talk to Hailey.'

'I know that too.'

He nodded. 'In the meantime, I think you could use

some breakfast. Do you think you can handle my cooking?'

He was rewarded with a small smile and a nod.

'All right. The bathroom's that way.'

While Bec disappeared into the bathroom, Nick dressed and busied himself in the kitchen. He was still trying to absorb what Bec had told him. If it was this hard for him to take in, how much harder must it be for her? He thought about his reaction when the bank had foreclosed on his father's property. He had struggled to cope with losing his home and family legacy. But he still had his family. He still knew who he was. Bec had lost the rock on which she had stood for her entire life. Nick was amazed that she was coping as well as she was.

When she appeared in the kitchen, she was looking a lot less tense. She was also wearing one of Nick's T-shirts. It was several sizes too big, and she looked small and lost. She had devised a sling for her cast out of one of his shirts. She smiled at him so bravely that Nick wanted nothing more than to take her in his arms again and tell the whole world to leave them both alone. He wanted to build a wall around the two of them, so that no one could ever hurt Bec or come between them again. But he could no more do that than he could take away the pain she was feeling. All he could do at this moment was be her friend.

Coffee was a good starting point. As they drank, he fed Bec scrambled eggs on toast. She scoffed that down like she hadn't eaten in days. Which, he realised, wasn't that far from the truth.

'By the way,' he said as they ate, 'how did you get here last night?'

'I drove.'

'What? With one arm in a cast?' Nick was horrified.

'Mum's car is an automatic,' Bec said, as if was the most natural thing in the world to drive with one arm.

Nick shook his head. 'When you're ready to go back, I'll drive. You're a big enough danger on the road with two good arms.' It was a pretty weak attempt at a joke, but they both smiled anyway.

When she had finished, Bec sighed deeply. 'Thanks,' she said. They both knew she wasn't talking about the breakfast.

'You're very welcome.'

'I guess I should go back to the Creek now.'

'All right. I'll drop you at the post office.'

'No. I don't think I'm ready to be around Mum yet. I need to talk to Hailey.'

'What are you going to tell her?'

She didn't answer for a long time. 'Everything, I guess. She has to know.'

23

The Martin guitar seemed to gleam in the morning light that streamed through the kitchen window. It sat on the table, the polished wood inviting her fingers to stroke it. Hailey reached out slowly, but stopped when her fingers were just a hair's breadth from the wood. She pulled her hand back and stared at the guitar. It truly was a beautiful thing to look at, and when it was played, it sounded sweeter than a chorus of angels. She had always dreamed of owning a guitar that fine. With such a guitar, she would have sung all the songs that filled her heart. But not now. She would never play the Martin again. She would never sing those songs. Her heart was enclosed in ice. It hurt so badly, but what made it even worse was knowing that her own cowardice had made it so.

She wasn't crying. She had no tears left. Her eyes were red with too many tears already shed. She'd made her decision. Now she just had to live with it. She knew she would feel this sadness and regret for the rest of her life. The guitar still lay where Steve had left it on Sunday. She would never forget the look on his face as he put it on the table and turned away from her. The disappointment. The hurt. The sadness that she had brought upon them both. If only she could have given him a different answer. It should have been so easy to follow her heart. It sounded so simple. Sell the house and the store. Take the money and go with Steve. Travel with him. Play with him. Live with him and love him. It was everything she wanted and more than she had ever dared dream. But when the time came, she just couldn't do it.

'I'm so sorry.' The words echoed around the empty house.

Hailey didn't know how long she had been sitting there when someone knocked on the kitchen door.

'Go away,' she whispered, but it was too late, the door was already opening.

Bec took two steps into the room, and then stopped. 'Hailey?'

Hailey wiped her hand over her tear-streaked face. 'Hi.' She didn't even try to hide the sadness in her voice.

'God, Hailey.' Bec crossed the room in a few strides. She crouched down and wrapped her arms around her. 'I guess Mum's been here.'

'Your mother? No.' Hailey wondered what on earth Bec was talking about.

'Then what . . . ?' Bec sat down on the chair next to her and looked at the guitar. 'This has something to do with Steve?'

Hailey nodded dumbly.

'He's gone?'

She nodded again.

'What happened?'

'Oh Bec,' Hailey said. 'He wanted me to go with him. He said he loved me. He said we could be together. Play together.'

'And?'

'And I said no.' The words were a whisper.

'Why, Hailey? Maybe it's too soon to say you love him. But there is something between you. Something special. Anyone can see that.'

'I do love him.' How it hurt to say the words. 'But I was too afraid to say yes.'

'Why?'

'Because I'm the biggest coward in the world,' Hailey said, realising that she did have more tears to shed. 'Too scared to leave this house and everything in it.'

Bec didn't say anything.

'It's all I've got left.' Now that the words had started, Hailey couldn't stop them. 'Sometimes I have trouble remembering them. I can remember Mum singing as she cooked, but I can't remember the sound of her voice. I remember working with Dad at the store. We laughed together a lot, but I can't hear his laugh in my head any more. They've only been gone a year, Bec, but I'm losing them. And there isn't anyone else.'

The tears were pouring down her face now. 'I love him. I want to go with him. But everything I am is here, and I'm afraid that if I go, I'll lose myself. It would be different if I had some other family somewhere. But I don't. So I said no. I'm staying.'

She said the last words firmly, as if by doing so she would convince herself. Slowly she got to her feet and picked up the guitar, then carried it carefully out of the kitchen and through to what had been her parents' bedroom. It was empty now that Miss Mills had moved back into her own cottage. The familiar things had been restored to their positions, but for once Hailey did not stop to feel the memories the room evoked. She laid the guitar gently on the bed and, stepping back, pulled the door firmly shut on the guitar, and on her memories and dreams. She turned around to see Bec standing in the living room. She was staring at the sideboard, and the collection of photographs on it, with the strangest look on her face. Hailey went to stand beside her. In the centre of the sideboard was a photo her mother had taken years before. Down by the old waterhole. Bec and Hailey and her father. They all looked so happy together.

'Haven't you got a copy of that one too?' she asked.

Bec nodded.

Hailey glanced over at her, and suddenly realised that Bec was standing there wearing an oversized T-shirt, her arm in a sling.

'God, Bec. I'm sorry. I've been so caught up in my own misery, I forgot that you . . . How's the arm?'

'It's all right.' Bec seemed unconcerned by her injury. She was far more interested in the photo.

'Why are you here this early? I would have expected you to sleep in today. I wasn't expecting you at the store.' In fact Hailey wasn't even sure if she expected herself at the store today.

'Nick just dropped me off.'

'Nick?'

'Yes. I spent the night at his place.'

Hailey's eyebrows shot up in surprise. 'You and Nick . . .'

She saw Bec close her eyes as if in pain. Was it the arm, she wondered, or something else?

'Look, I've got an idea.' Bec turned to her suddenly. 'I need to get out of this one-horse town for a few hours. I guess you probably do too. Let's just go.'

'Go where?'

'Anywhere.' Bec looked once more at the photo. 'How about there? The waterhole. We could take some food. Talk. Just . . . have some time to ourselves.'

Hailey hesitated. She wanted to be alone in her

misery. Didn't she? Maybe Bec was right. Maybe some girl time was just what she needed. What they both needed.

'Fine,' she said. 'I can pack some supplies while you go home and change.'

'Ah . . . do you mind if I borrow something from you?'

Hailey could read between the lines on that one. Bec was fighting with her mother again. And this time it sounded serious. What a pair they were, her and Bec. So alike in so many ways. Not for the first time in her life, Hailey was glad to have her friend by her side.

'Take whatever you need,' she said.

Fifteen minutes later they were in Hailey's car and heading out of town. For a short time they drove along the main road, and Hailey felt as if her load was getting lighter with every mile. Then they turned off on to a dirt track. The old ute bounced about with every corrugation in the track.

'I hope this isn't hurting that arm,' Hailey said.

'Don't worry about me,' Bec said with a grin. 'I'm feeling better all the time.'

The creek that gave their town its name wasn't very wide or deep for most of its length. But in this place, it swept in a broad curve. In the good years, when rain was plentiful, the rushing water had cut a deep hole against the bank. Even when the creek was low, there was still enough water here for kids to swim. Only once had they known it to be dry. That had been during the terrible drought two years ago. Tall gum trees lined the creek, casting a welcome shade on hot days. There was a stretch of bank that almost qualified as a beach. The real beach was hundreds of kilometres away, and the town had no swimming pool, so this was their only option. On hot days, it got a bit crowded. But today Bec and Hailey had the place to themselves. They set up in the shade of a big gum tree. Hailey spread an old blanket on the ground. They had a thermos of coffee, and a water bag full of cool, clear water. Hailey had made some sandwiches and thrown in some biscuits.

It was very quiet by the creek. The water flowed noiselessly between its banks. Occasionally they heard the chortle of a kookaburra or the distant cry of a crow, but that was all that came to disturb the peace that was unique to this place. Lying on her back, staring up at the treetops and the brilliant blue sky above, Hailey felt the peace surround her. It didn't lessen the pain in her heart, but somehow being here with Bec made it just a little easier to bear.

'Hailey,' Bec was the first to speak, 'when Steve asked you to go with him . . . would your answer have been different if your parents were still alive?'

'Yes.' It hurt, but it was the truth.

'You said that it might be different if you had some other family.'

'It probably would,' she said. 'But that's not the point.'

'Yes it is.'

Hailey sat up and turned to look at Bec. 'I don't get it.'

Bec lifted herself on one elbow. She didn't meet Hailey's eyes, but stared out over the water as she said, 'If you knew you had a relative somewhere, someone who shared your memories, someone who would always welcome you home, would you go with Steve?'

The question seemed very important to Bec. Hailey didn't understand why, but she took a few minutes to think. 'Yes,' she said slowly. 'Family is special. Family is what makes a person who they really are. If I was going to risk everything, I would need an anchor. Farwell Creek is all I have. If I had family, places and things wouldn't matter. But I don't. Not any more.'

'Yes you do.' Bec spoke so softly, Hailey thought she had misheard.

'What do you mean?'

Bec was still looking at the creek. She picked up a small stone and tossed it into the water. They both watched the ripples spread.

'I spent last night at Nick's place, because I had . . . I guess you'd call it a fight with Mum.'

Hailey nodded. She'd already figured that out.

'She told me she's been lying to me all these years. Lying about my father.'

Hailey's mouth fell open. 'That . . . that must have been really hard to hear.'

'She told me she had never been married.'

Hailey nodded thoughtfully. 'But you had already guessed that. Years ago,' she said.

'I know. But there's more. She said Ken O'Connell just didn't exist. She made him up when she moved to the Creek.'

Hailey blinked. That was a shock.

'She says she did it to make life easier for me,' Bec continued.

'I guess she was trying to make life easier for both of you,' Hailey said. Her own woes faded as she realised how hard her friend was struggling to come to terms with the revelation. 'Did she tell you who your father really is?'

'Yes.' Bec let the word hang.

Hailey wanted to ask, but she didn't. Bec would tell her when she was ready.

At last Bec took her eyes from the river. She turned

to look at Hailey, and reached out to take her hands. 'Hailey. You do have still have family. You have me.'

Hailey didn't understand. 'We've always been like sisters—' she started to say.

'No,' Bec interrupted her. 'We *are* sisters.'

Hailey's breath caught in her throat. 'I don't understand.'

'We are sisters. Or rather, half-sisters. Your father was also my father.'

Hailey heard the words, but she couldn't grasp the meaning. 'My father . . .'

Bec was squeezing her hands so tight that it hurt. 'Mum told me last night.'

'My father . . . and your mother?' The implications began to dawn on Hailey. 'No.' She tried to pull her hands away, but Bec held them too tightly. 'Dad would never have done that to Mum. Never!'

'No. No. It wasn't like that,' Bec said. 'I'm a few months older than you, remember. It happened before your father and mother even met.'

Hailey shook her head. 'No. That can't be right.' If she said it often enough, it might make this horrible conversation stop.

'It is, Hailey.' Bec spoke with a blunt finality. 'I had trouble believing it too. But now . . .'

Hailey looked Bec squarely in the face; a face so similar to hers, with eyes that were a mirror image of her own. It was impossible to believe, but with a flash of insight, she realised that Bec was telling the truth.

'Tell me everything,' she said.

It didn't take long. When Bec had finished, Hailey slowly got to her feet. She walked away down to the edge of the water, and stood there for a long time. Her eyes were red with tears. Her head was spinning. It was all too much to grasp. She knew, deep down, that her father had done nothing wrong, but it was so hard to come to terms with the thought of him with Jean in that way. Even if they had been drunk. It was still an image that just did not seem right. Even if it had happened before her parents met, it still felt like he had betrayed her mother. She stared unseeing across the water, remembering all the good times they had spent at this waterhole.

'You know, I sometimes used to pretend that your dad was also my father.' Bec had come up behind her. 'I used to think you were so lucky to have such a great dad. Especially when I didn't even know what mine looked like. I always wished he could be mine too.'

That brought a faint smile to Hailey's lips. 'He did love you,' she said. 'He told me that he thought of you as another daughter.'

'If only he'd known.'

Hailey heard the regret and longing in Bec's voice. In her sister's voice. Her sister! She turned to face the person she had always considered her best friend. She looked at Bec's tear-stained face, and knew that she wasn't alone in her pain. 'We are sisters.' Speaking the words out loud made it suddenly real.

Bec nodded.

'I have a sister!' Joy surged through Hailey. She wrapped her arms around Bec, and felt her sister's arms tighten around her in a hug that threatened to break her ribs.

'Sister!'

They were both crying, but this time, it wasn't a bad thing.

'This is going to take some getting used to,' Hailey said when the tears stopped.

'It is,' Bec agreed.

'What about your mother . . . and you. How . . . ?'

'It wasn't good. I yelled at her and left.'

'At some point you are going to have to talk to her again,' Hailey said. 'You have to make up with her.'

'I know. I'm just not ready to do that yet. And what about you? How are you going to feel when you see her?'

That was an added issue Hailey hadn't even considered.

Bec went back to their blanket under the big gum tree. But before she could sit down, she suddenly spun around, her face alight.

'*Thelma and Louise!*' she said.

'What?'

'Hailey, let's go away. The two of us. We could just get in the car and drive. Go somewhere. Anywhere. Just like Thelma and Louise – only better. Because we are sisters!' The last word came out as a shout.

'But what about . . .' Hailey stopped. She had been thinking about the feed store. But wasn't she the one who'd said family mattered more than places and things. And that was what Bec was. She was family. 'Let's go,' she said.

24

The mess was nearly all gone. Jean leaned on the schoolyard fence and looked out across the B&S site. The stage had been dismantled and taken on to its next destination. The power generators were also gone. The schoolkids had done an emu parade earlier today. At any other time, Jean would have smiled to see them, heads bobbing up and down as they picked up the litter – so like the great flightless bird the exercise was named after. But not today. Nothing would bring a smile to her face today. Now the volunteers were pulling down the fences around the stewards' compound. By tomorrow, the cattle would be back and there would be little to show for the ball, except, of course, for the dark patch of charred ground where Gordo's ute had burned. The ute was gone now too, taken away to the scrap heap. There was nothing else to do with it. Jean shook her head. When Bec had proposed the ball to raise funds for their fire brigade, no one had thought that it would turn out the way it had. She had always been afraid of what changes the ball might bring. Now she knew. If only she knew where Bec was. And Hailey. They must be together, but Jean had no idea where they had gone or when they would be coming back. If they came back. No, she wouldn't let herself think that. They would come back. They had to.

A tall figure detached itself from the group of workers and made its way towards her.

'Hello, Nick.'

'Have you heard from Bec?'

She shook her head. 'I was hoping you might have heard something.'

'No.'

When both Bec and Hailey had vanished two days ago, Nick had been the first person Jean had called. She knew now that Bec had spent one night with Nick. She knew that Bec had told him the truth and she also knew that Nick had kept that truth secret. Even now she saw no judgement in his face. Only concern for her daughter.

'Are you all right?' he asked. Jean was touched that he should also be worried about her. But that was just who Nick was.

Jean nodded. She didn't trust herself to speak. She patted Nick on the shoulder and walked away. She didn't want to go home. The house was so empty without Bec. But she didn't want to be too far from the phone, in case the girls rang. She would just pick up a couple of things from the shop, then she'd watch some television while she waited for the phone to ring. It wasn't until she walked into the shop and saw Anne Ryan's face that she realised her mistake. Anne's face lit up when she saw her. Then she adopted a look of solicitous commiseration that was as false as it was annoying.

'Jean, dear.' She would have patted her hand, had Jean not kept it firmly at her side. 'Have you heard from them yet?'

'No.' Jean didn't want to have this conversation. 'I just dropped in for some milk, thanks, Anne.'

'Of course.' She made no move to fetch the milk. 'I see Hailey's feed store was still closed today. I guess the girls must be together.'

'I guess so,' Jean said. 'Now, my milk . . .'

'Unless, of course, Hailey went off with that musician fellow. He was at her place on Sunday.' Anne nodded knowingly. 'And no one has seen her since.'

Jean fought down an overwhelming urge to slap her. The woman was the personification of all the reasons Jean had lied about having a husband. She guessed every small community had someone like Anne Ryan. It wasn't just that the woman liked to gossip. In small towns everyone gossiped. But Anne was the only one who took pleasure in the hurt that gossip could cause.

'I'll just take the milk, thanks, Anne.'

'Yes, of course.' Reluctantly Anne turned to get some milk from the big refrigerator that took up the area behind the counter. 'I noticed Nick driving your car on Monday,' she added with a raised eyebrow. 'I was wondering how he had come to have it. I do hope—'

'Anne Ryan.' The voice cut through the shopkeeper's words like a knife. 'You ought to be ashamed of yourself!' Eudora Mills stepped through the door, a shopping bag in one hand. 'That's none of your business.'

Jean blinked in surprise.

'Well!' Anne tried to defend herself. 'I was just concerned . . .'

'If you are going to be concerned like that, be careful that you don't get yourself caught out. There might be some who could become "concerned" over members of *your* family. I'm sure you wouldn't want that.'

The words hung in the air between the teacher and

the shopkeeper as the silence stretched uncomfortably.

'Really!' Anne breathed the word so low, Jean hardly heard her. She took the money that Jean had put on the counter, and handed over the milk.

'And I'll have the same,' Eudora said.

The transaction was completed in silence.

'Shall we?' Eudora asked Jean, and they left the store together.

'That woman,' the schoolteacher exploded as soon as they were out of the shop. 'She has such a vicious tongue.'

'What on earth did you mean – things about her family?' Jean's curiosity got the better of her.

'Well, really.' Eudora looked quite put out. 'I hope you don't think I'm the sort of person to indulge in malicious gossip.'

'No. No. Of course not,' Jean hastened to reassure her.

Eudora looked at her, and seemed to soften. 'I'm sure your daughter will come back soon,' she said. 'Girls will be girls. Why, when I was young, I once ran away with a friend. A female friend, of course,' she added quickly. 'But I came back.' The teacher patted her comfortingly on the arm and walked back towards her cottage, leaving a slightly stunned Jean standing outside her own gate.

After putting the milk away, Jean wandered around the house for a few minutes. She checked the answering machine on her phone. Nothing. The waiting was driving her crazy. She slipped out through the kitchen door and walked next door to the police residence.

'Come in, Jean,' Rod called in response to her knock.

'How did you know it was me?' she asked as she joined him in his kitchen.

'The post office shut about forty minutes ago. I figured you'd drop by.' Rod was pouring water into a big teapot.

Jean took some mugs out of the cupboard, thinking as she did that she was almost as at home here as she was in her own kitchen.

'Before you ask,' Rod said as they settled on either side of his kitchen table, 'I've been checking. There are no police reports that could be the girls.'

'Well, at least I know they haven't had an accident.'

'They will be fine,' Rod said. 'And they will come home, when they are ready.' He reached out to place his hand over hers. Jean looked down. Rod's hand was large and strong, the skin weathered and brown. A hand with strength. Like the man himself. She found a surprising comfort in his touch.

'You haven't asked me why they left,' she said.

'I figure you'll tell me when you are ready.'

There was a world of compassion and understanding in his gentle smile. Jean realised that it was time he knew the truth. Rod was a good friend. He might have been more, but for the lie that had lain heavy on her heart for so many years.

She gathered herself. 'On Sunday, after we got back from the hospital, I told Bec the truth about who her father was.'

'I see.' Neither his eyes nor his voice showed any trace of condemnation or curiosity, or any pressure for her to go on.

If she wanted to, she could end the conversation there. He would never ask her for more than she was willing to give. Maybe that was why she wanted to tell him everything.

'She knows now that her father was Kevin Braxton.'

She watched his face as she spoke. There was no sign of surprise. 'You knew?' she said.

'I suspected,' Rod said.

'How?'

'I saw the way you used to look at him, when you thought no one was watching. I saw the way you grieved when he died. The two girls are so much alike. It wasn't that hard to figure it out.'

'No one else did.'

'I'm a policeman. I'm supposed to see things other people don't. And besides, I had more reason than most to notice.'

'You never said anything.'

'Jean, it wasn't any of my business. Whatever happened was a long time ago.'

'I know I was wrong to lie to her all these years, but I was just trying to protect her,' she said. 'I wanted to tell her after Kevin died, but I couldn't bring myself to do it. I guess that's one of the reasons we fought so much when she came home. I was feeling so guilty . . . Then, at the ball, I thought I was going to lose her too.'

'I guess she didn't take it well?'

'She's angry at me, Rod. Very, very angry. And who can blame her? I've been lying to her for her entire life. She had every right to hate me for it.'

Jean felt tears pricking her eyes again. Rod put his arm around her and hugged her.

'She doesn't hate you,' he said.

'She ran away.'

'She was upset. She had a lot to think about. My guess is that the two of them have taken off to talk this through. Just the two of them. They'll be back.'

'I guess so,' Jean said. 'But how am I going to face

Bec again? How am I going to face Hailey? They both have every reason to despise me.'

'No they don't. It's going to take some time, but both girls love you. You'll get through this.'

Jean laid her head against Rod's shoulder and felt a little of the despair lift from her heart. The burden was easier to carry when you shared it with someone who cared.

Rod's voice was gentle when he spoke again. 'I just hope you won't spend the rest of your life punishing yourself for whatever mistakes you think you made all those years ago.'

Jean took a slow, deep breath. Maybe he was right. The secret was bound to get around now. Soon the whole town would know. It might be awkward for a time, but at least the lying was over. If only Bec would come back . . . If only Bec would forgive her . . .

'I'll tell you what.' Rod pulled a large clean handkerchief out of his pocket and passed it to her. 'Instead of spending the evening rattling around the house by yourself, why don't you have dinner here with me? I can rustle up a steak or something.'

'No thanks.' She had said the words so often, they were out before she had a chance to think. She saw the smile on Rod's face falter just a little. 'I want to be home, just in case Bec calls,' she hurried on. 'Why don't you come to my place? I do a pretty good steak too.'

The sign at the crossroads was very clear. They could take the road to the east, towards Toowoomba and beyond that Brisbane and the coast. They could go further west, through Charleville, maybe even as far as Birdsville and the desert beyond. Or they could go south. Home.

'What do you think?' Bec asked.

'At some point I have to go back and reopen the store,' Hailey said with a smile.

'I know. And I am going to have to go back and tell Mum that it's all right. That I sort of understand.'

'It doesn't have to be today.'

'No.' Bec grinned. 'It doesn't.'

They were parked by the side of the road, drinking warm water from a bottle that they'd bought at a petrol station a few hours ago. The day they left Farwell Creek, they had driven north up the Great Inland Way to Carnarvon, buying whatever they needed on the way. Because of Bec's broken arm, Hailey had done all the driving. It hadn't bothered her. If anything, she found it therapeutic. They had rented a cabin in the national park, and talked and walked and talked some more. They had dangled their feet in the waterholes, fed crumbs to the rainbow lorikeets and admired the scenery. They had talked about their father. About Hailey's mother, and about Jean. They had laughed and cried over shared memories. Now the talking was done. They had been friends all their lives. Now they had discovered each other as sisters, and it felt good. But there were some things still to resolve.

'It might not work out,' Hailey said as she sat with her hands on the wheel, looking out at the road sign. They both knew what she was talking about.

'It might not. But you'll never know if you don't give it a go.'

Her sister was right, of course. Hailey felt a tug at her heartstrings. She turned the ignition key, slipped the car into gear and moved out into the roadway. At the crossroads, she turned east.

'Let's try that again.' The voice in his headphones dripped frustration. Steve knew just how the sound guy felt. The session was not going well. Steve had been screwing up all day. He was distracted. Playing badly. And as for his singing ... his voice had about as much emotion as a rock.

'I'm sorry,' he said.

'Hey, man, it's cool.' Blue was as laid-back as always.

Steve felt a warm affection for the band. They'd travelled a lot of miles and sung a lot of songs together. They understood.

'Do you want to go again from the top?' the sound guy asked.

'Sure.'

This was Steve's last Kelly Gang album, and he wanted to get it right. It was the least he could do for the guys, before he deserted them. They'd be fine. They'd find another singer and keep playing the balls. They understood that Steve had the talent to go solo, and they wished him luck. The trouble was, he didn't want to go solo. He wanted Hailey with him. In his music. In his bed. In every part of his life.

'Steve?' The sound man kept coming back.

'Yeah.' Steve dragged his thoughts back into the studio.

He settled his guitar around his shoulders. The guitar was new, and he wasn't really comfortable with it. Not like he had been with his beloved Martin. He didn't regret leaving the Martin with Hailey. He couldn't have played it any more. Not with the memories it would bring back. He was having enough trouble fighting those memories without the guitar to remind him. He could still see the way her fingers caressed the strings. Still hear the music she coaxed from it. He could close his eyes and see the way her eyes sparkled as she played. He could see those lovely lips shining as she sang with all the passion she held in her heart. The lips, so soft and warm and tasting of . . .

'Steve?'

'I'm ready,' he said, although he wasn't.

This time he made it through the entire song without making an error, but it wasn't very good. No one said it, but everyone knew it. Steve slipped the guitar from around his neck.

'Do you mind if we take a break?' he said to Blue and the others. 'I just need to get my head together. Then we can have another go.'

'Sure, mate.' Blue patted his shoulder. 'It's lunchtime anyway. Let's go down the pub. We can grab a steak and a beer.'

'No thanks,' Steve said. 'I'm not hungry. You guys go ahead.'

Blue nodded and the band left, taking the sound man with them. Steve was alone in the recording studio, surrounded by the musical instruments and electronic accessories of the job he loved. He thought about going to the kitchen for coffee, but just couldn't be bothered.

He sat down on a stool and picked up an acoustic guitar. His fingers started strumming a chord progression. It was Hailey's bird song. The first one he had ever heard her sing. He softly hummed a couple of lines. He could almost hear her sweet voice singing with him. His fingers faltered. The song hurt too much. He changed his grip on the guitar, and played a couple of notes. Soft, sad notes. He tried another note, then another. Gradually a melody emerged. He played it again, hearing his own longing in the music. Well, he was a songwriter. Weren't songwriters supposed to be inspired by their own emotions? He played the melody softly again. This would be a lovely slow ballad. It just needed words. Words that told of a desperate yearning for something so very precious. Something he had fought for, but lost.

'It's supposed to be just down this street,' Bec said as Hailey drove slowly through the row of almost identical warehouses. 'They must be here. There can't be more than one recording studio.'

Hailey's eyes searched the street. Steve was here somewhere. He had to be. He'd said he would be, if she changed her mind and wanted to be with him. But maybe his plans had changed. Maybe he'd given up on her and gone away. Maybe she'd never find him. Never be able to tell him what a terrible mistake she'd made. What if she never saw him again?

'Hey. Isn't that the drummer?' Bec pointed to a group of men walking up the road. In the lead was a huge man covered with tattoos. Hailey swung the ute off the road and jumped out.

'Hi, Blue,' she said uncertainly.

'Hailey!' The cry of welcome was swiftly followed by a bone-crushing hug. 'You've got no idea how pleased we are to see you,' Blue said when the chorus of greetings was over.

'I sort of guessed,' Hailey said. She had been touched by the band's welcome. It was good to see them again. But where was Steve?

'It's been a dreadful session so far.' Blue didn't mince words. The rest of the group muttered dark agreement. 'But now that you're here, things are going to get better.'

'Steve . . .'

'. . . has been a total waste of space all week,' Blue finished for her. 'But you're here now. That'll fix him.'

Hailey wasn't so sure. 'Where is he?'

'Still at the studio.' Blue pointed. 'We're on a break. Lunch. There's a pub just up here that does a great steak.'

'Do you mind if I join you?' Bec asked.

Hailey looked at her friend in surprise. What was she thinking? They were supposed to be in this together. Whatever happened to Thelma and Louise?

Bec dropped an arm around Hailey's shoulders. 'Go on,' she whispered. 'Go find him. I'll keep this lot out of your hair for a while.' Her arm tightened in a quick hug, then she gathered up the band and they all headed off, leaving Hailey standing by the side of the road.

She turned and began walking in the direction Blue had indicated. The studio wasn't an impressive building. It was long and low and didn't seem to have many windows. The front door wasn't locked. Hailey hesitated before she pushed it open. It was all very well for Blue to say that things would get better now she was here. He had only seen the good times. The triumph on the night of the ball, filled with joy and music and laughter. Hailey and Steve singing as one person. He hadn't seen those dreadful moments when she had told Steve she could never leave the Creek. Hadn't seen the terrible hurt in Steve's eyes, nor heard the long arguments all through the night that had failed to change her mind. Only Hailey had seen the pain in Steve's eyes as he laid the Martin guitar on her table and walked out the door. Now, she was racked with uncertainty. After so much hurt, how could Steve want her back? How could he ever trust her again? For one long moment, she almost turned around and ran, back to the safety of Farwell Creek and the shelter of her home. Almost. She took a long, deep breath. She was a different person now. She wasn't alone in the world any more. She had a sister. Someone who would stand by her whatever happened. She could take a risk. She had a chance for something very, very special with Steve. Something she had barely dared dream about. She would not run away this time. She pushed the door open and walked inside.

The reception area of the studio was empty. Perhaps they didn't have a receptionist, or maybe she was also on lunch. A single door led from the reception area, and Hailey just walked through. A long corridor stretched in front of her, with doors opening to each side. One of them must lead to the recording studio, if that was where Steve was. She guessed she would just have to try every door until she found the right one. Then she noticed the red light. Of course, a studio would have a sign to warn people not to enter when recording was in progress. It wasn't lit now. Maybe that was a sign too.

She heard the music as she pushed the door open. A single guitar was playing a slow, sad melody that tugged her heartstrings. Each note seemed to weep as it wafted through the air. It was beautiful. She stepped through the door into the sound booth. She was surrounded by recording equipment, which at any other time would have been a source of endless fascination to the musician inside her. But at this moment, she was simply a woman. She looked through the open door from the booth on to the studio floor. Steve was sitting on a stool, his eyes closed as he listened to the music of his guitar. Then he started singing.

> 'Tell me Cinderella,
> Why won't you try the slipper?
> It lies there at your feet; yet you turn away.
> You were Sleeping Beauty
> And I woke you with a kiss,
> But my dream is not your fairy tale.'

Tears sprang from Hailey's eyes as she listened. She stepped to the open door, drawn towards the song and the man who was singing it. The music was indescribably beautiful. The man was everything she had ever wanted. After just a few lines, Steve's voice trailed away. He ran a hand over his face, as if to wipe away a tear. Then he opened his eyes and looked straight at her.

For a long time neither of them spoke.

'That was beautiful,' Hailey said at last.

'It was about you.'

Hailey nodded. The space between the two of them seemed almost to vibrate with feeling. She wanted to run to him, to throw her arms around him and never let him go. But she couldn't. Not yet. She didn't deserve him.

'Why are you here?' he asked at last, as he set the guitar down on its stand. His voice sounded wary. Defensive. Hailey was suddenly very afraid that it was too late for her. Too late for them.

'I came to tell you something.'

'What?' He remained sitting on the stool, his hands clasped in his lap.

'I said I couldn't come with you because I am alone in the world. Because the house is all I have of my family, and I can't walk away from it.'

'I remember every word.' There was a world of pain in his voice.

'Well, I was wrong. On two counts.'

His eyes were on her face, willing her to go on.

'I do have family. I have a sister I didn't know about.' She paused, waiting for him to speak. When he didn't, she kept talking. 'But that's not the most important thing. I know now that I will never be all alone in a world that has you in it. My family is my past. But you are my future. If you still want me.'

'If I . . .' Steve's voice broke as in one swift movement he crossed the gap between them. He stopped in front of her and took her face in his hands. 'If I still want you?' he said with amazement in his voice. Then he kissed her. He kissed her lips and her face and her eyes. He swept her hair back from her forehead and kissed that too. Then he held her so tight she thought she would die. If she did, she would die happy.

At last he let her go. He held her away from him, and looked into her face as if trying to burn the moment into his memory. Then a small frown creased his face.

'You've got a sister?'

'Yes.' Hailey laughed, a light, joyous laugh. 'You'll never believe it. It's Bec.'

'What?' She laughed anew at the shock on his face. 'Bec's your sister? How . . . ? When . . . ?'

'It's a long, long story,' Hailey said.

'Well, as I have no intention of ever letting you leave

me again, I guess we've got all the time in the world for you to tell me,' Steve said as he kissed her again. He took a lot of time to do it, and when he stopped, Hailey felt as if the whole world was glowing.

'I've got a good idea,' Steve said as he took a long, calming breath. 'The guys have gone for lunch. We could slip away now, and they'd never know. I don't think I could play this afternoon. At least – I don't want to play with them . . .' His eyes sparkled as he ran the tip of his finger down her cheek, to caress the warm skin of her throat. Hailey's insides turned to mush.

'They know I'm here,' she said.

'Well in that case, they won't even think about disturbing us.'

Hailey lifted one hand to touch his beloved face and knew then that she was home – because a building wasn't home: love was home. Unable to quell the passion flooding through her, she stood on her toes and kissed him again. He pulled her close and moulded her body to his, drawing warmth and strength and love from him. 'Oh yes,' she whispered.

'Guys, stop talking for a second.' Bec lifted a hand. 'Shut up!'

The band was shocked into silence. The voice on the television was suddenly very clear.

'. . . front nearly a hundred kilometres long. Volunteer firefighters from all over the region have been battling the blaze now for three days, without respite.'

Bec stared at the screen. The video had been taken from an aircraft. It showed a line of fire marching across the land, leaving a huge black scar in its wake.

'Whoa,' someone said.

Bec waved a hand for silence, her eyes glued to the screen as the news report continued.

'We've just learned that a group of firefighters have become trapped in the fire. Rescue efforts are now under way.'

Bec's hand flew to her mouth.

'Where's that?' Blue asked.

'South of Roma,' Bec said quietly. 'Home.'

She pushed back from the table, and pulled her phone out of her pocket. Without a second thought, she scrolled down the menu and hit the call button.

Nick's phone rang unanswered.

'Damn.' Bec hesitated a few seconds. This wasn't what she'd planned. But she had to know. She dialled again.

'Hello.' Her mother answered on the first ring.

'Mum . . .'

'Bec, thank God you called.' Jean's voice quivered with emotion. 'Are you all right? You and Hailey? We've been—'

'Mum,' Bec cut her off sharply, 'I just heard about the fire. I can't raise Nick.'

There was a moment's silence at the end of the line. 'He's out there,' Jean said. 'Left yesterday morning.'

'Mum, according to the news, there are firefighters trapped.'

'I don't know, Bec,' Jean replied. 'And I've got no way of finding out. Rod isn't here. They've closed the highway to stop people driving into the middle of it.'

Bec shut her eyes for an instant, but that just allowed her fear to grow.

'I'm coming back, Mum. But we're in Toowoomba. It's going to take a few hours for us to get there.'

'You're coming home . . .' Jean sounded close to tears. 'Oh Bec, I'm so sorry about everything.'

Bec realised then that her mother wasn't thinking about the fire. Her concerns were far more personal.

'Mum, it's all right,' she said gently. 'It really is. Hailey and I . . . you and I. We've got some things to talk about, but it is okay. Honestly. But first I have to find Nick.'

The early afternoon sun was just a faint glow through the drifting grey veil that obscured the sky. In a haze of exhaustion, Nick staggered back into the firefighters' camp. Smoke wafted between the trees, through the large open-sided canvas tent where the battle against the bushfire was being controlled. Weary men sat on the ground, trying to catch a few minutes' rest before they had to head back into the fray. Nick dropped his helmet and jacket on to the ground next to a forty-four-gallon water drum. A thin film of soot floated on top of the water, but he didn't care. He plunged his head and shoulders into the drum. The water was warm, but it felt wonderful. He kept his face under for as long as he could, then flung his head up, sucking in long draughts of air. Smoke filled his lungs, and he fell to his knees coughing. That hadn't been very smart.

'Are you all right?' another firefighter asked as he too headed for the water drum.

Still coughing, Nick nodded. Of course, a lot depended on your definition of all right. He was bone weary, every muscle screaming at him to just stop and lie down. His hands were covered with blisters. His body was caked with sweat and soot. His eyes and lungs were stinging with the smoke and his throat was raw.

But compared to some of the other men, he was all right. He'd been fighting this blaze for two days with just a few minutes' rest snatched when he could. Some of them had been here for longer. Just a few hours ago, they had reached some men who had been trapped behind the fire. They'd been taken to hospital, but the latest word was that they would all be fine.

Nick didn't know the names of most of the men he was with, but that didn't matter. They'd come from all over, travelling for hours to join the team. Some were landowners. Some were itinerant workers. Some were townies. They all shared a common goal – to beat the fire before it took too much away from them. Nick understood about fighting for something – or someone – that you loved. He'd learned that lesson on the night of the B&S ball. All it took was an explosion or two for him to figure it out. He'd do something about it, too, when this was done, but right now, he was far too tired to think about anything except getting a few minutes' rest.

Picking up his helmet, he walked slowly past the green military-style tent. A big map lay on a table, the outline of the fire marked clearly in red. It looked even bigger than last time he had passed this way. Senior officers were gathered around the map, trying to decide their next move. Every few minutes, the radio crackled with news of the latest outbreaks. So far the fire had claimed stock and property, but no lives. One of the officers gave him a nod as he walked past, acknowledging the work he had already done, and warning of more to come. Nick left them to their plans, and walked slowly over to the refreshments van. He reached for a bottle of water and drank it down in long gulps. He looked at the food boxes, but found only one sandwich and an orange. They must be expecting more food soon, he thought. The track back to the main road was safe, so supplies could get through. He ate the last remaining sandwich without even tasting it. He might be able to get a few minutes' rest before he went back out again. He spotted an almost comfortable-looking piece of ground at the base of a nearby gum tree. That would do just fine. He was about to close his eyes when he saw the ute drive into camp. That would be more food, he thought. He wondered briefly if he was hungry enough to get back on to his feet. He decided he wasn't. Someone got out of the ute. They had a plaster cast on one arm, and Nick wondered vaguely if another firefighter had been injured. His eyes flew open again and he leaped to his feet. Bec!

'Where have you been these last few days?' he shouted at her as he almost ran towards her. 'And what the hell are you doing here?'

'Nick! Thank God you're all right.' She dashed towards him and flung her arms around his neck, giving him a solid clout with the cast.

'Ouch,' he said.

'Sorry.' She slowly disentangled herself. 'I heard about the trapped firefighters. No one knew if you were one of them. I was worried.'

'So you walked into the middle of a bushfire with a broken arm?'

'But I—'

'Hailey. Steve.' Nick turned to Bec's companions. 'You both should have known better. You should have stopped her. She's in no fit state to be here.'

'Did you really think we could stop her?' Hailey said.

Nick sighed. She was right, of course, but that was no excuse. Bec shouldn't be here; in fact, none of them should. Didn't they know how dangerous it was? He had no idea what had happened during the past few days, or why Steve was with the girls, but now wasn't the time to ask. He looked at Bec and opened his mouth to speak.

'We brought the food supplies in,' Bec said before he could say anything. 'I came via the fire station in Roma. They needed transport for the food. I'm a trained firefighter, you know, just like you. Even with a broken arm.'

She stood in front of him defiantly, and Nick could have hugged her. This was the Bec he knew, jumping in the deep end for all the right reasons. Her energy and determination were a real shot in the arm when he most needed it. But she still shouldn't be here. It was too dangerous.

'All right. I'll help you unload the food. Then the three of you should get the hell out of here. We've all got enough on our plates without worrying about you too.'

'No way,' Bec said. 'I'm not leaving—'

Before she could continue, a loud shout brought all movement in the clearing to a halt. The commander waved to bring everyone closer.

'I know most of you have only just come in,' he said, 'but I need some men right now along the western firebreak in Sector Alpha. We have to hold it at that firebreak. There's a change in the weather coming. Maybe even a storm. If that happens, we might just have it beaten. I need all the hands I can get. Right now.'

All around him, men responded to the call, wearily lifting themselves from their resting places. Nick heaved a heavy sigh and placed his helmet back on his head.

'No, Nick. You can't. You're dead on your feet,' Bec said in a pleading voice, clutching his arm.

Her concern for him was written all over her face.

That look alone would make him stay, if he could. He leaned down and kissed her on the cheek.

'Could you use an extra hand?' Steve asked.

'You're not trained.' Nick shook his head. 'It's dangerous out there.'

'I can follow orders. And I'm fresh. He said he needed every hand he could get.'

Nick looked at Steve. He barely knew him, but if he was Hailey's choice, then he must be all right.

'Okay. Thanks. Stay close to me and do exactly what I tell you.' Nick clasped Steve's hand for a second, aware as he did that Hailey looked like she was about to cry.

'Bec,' he said, 'can you take over the radios? That would give us an extra man.'

Bec nodded.

'Good.' Nick reached out one hand to brush a piece of hair from her face. 'Try not to get into any trouble until I get back. Got it?'

Bec nodded. Nick almost smiled. He had never seen her look so subdued.

'Let's go,' the senior officer called. Nick grabbed a helmet and jacket from the back of a nearby truck. He was showing Steve how to put them on as they started walking down the firebreak into the swirling smoke.

'Damn this stupid arm,' Bec said as she watched Nick disappear. 'I should be out there too. I trained for it.'

'There's nothing you can do about it,' Hailey said weakly.

Bec walked over to the army tent. Only four men remained; the rest had vanished into the smoke. Bec looked around for the incident commander.

'I can take over communications,' she said. 'I'm trained.'

The officer looked her up and down. He noted the cast on her arm, but didn't seem concerned. Maybe he was just too desperate for help. 'You can operate the radios?'

'Yes, sir.'

The commander nodded. 'All right. Take over. Dave, they can use all the men they can get out there. You head out.'

The indicated officer left at a run.

Bec took her place at the communications desk. She checked that the equipment was the same as she'd been taught to use all those weeks ago at the Roma training sessions. She hadn't thought to use the knowledge this soon.

'This is Sector Alpha. Mick calling base. We've reached the firebreak.' The voice over the radio was tinny and scratchy.

'Roger, Mick. Hearing you loud and clear.'

The commander came to take the microphone from her hand. 'Mick, how's it looking?'

'It's a bit hard to see. The wind has died down, so the fire isn't travelling very fast. It won't reach this point for a while yet.'

Bec felt a surge of relief.

'When's this change coming?'

'The bureau says wind should start turning west in the next hour. That should turn the fire back on itself. I'm sending another team in from the other side of the firebreak. From Sector Bravo.'

'Roger that.' The radio fell silent.

The commander gave Bec an encouraging nod, then moved away to talk to his men. Hailey was distributing food and water to the officers, but it didn't take long. Then there was nothing more either of them could do but sit and stare at the radio, willing it to make a sound.

'Sector Alpha calling. Mick to base.'

'Base receiving you.'

'Any more word on that wind change?'

'Negative.' Bec shook her head as she spoke. 'The front has just about reached us. We could use a tanker up here if you've got one spare.'

'Roger that. I'll get back to you.'

Bec raised her eyes to the commander. He looked one last time at his map, then shook his head.

Bec took a deep breath. 'Base to Mick. There's no tanker available. Sorry.'

'Roger, base.' The radio fell silent again.

Bec wanted to ask what was going on. To make sure Nick was all right. She glanced over at Hailey and saw the same fear in her eyes for Steve. But she couldn't ask. Unnecessary questions just hindered the operation. They could put people in danger. There was nothing they could do but wait. And wonder. And worry.

Just when she thought she was going to explode with tension, Bec felt the slightest touch of a breeze on her face. She turned to face the way it had come. Was she imagining it? No! There it was again. The soft caress of air against her cheek. The wind was changing direction. She touched Hailey's shoulder. Her friend – her sister – looked up.

'The wind,' Bec said. 'It's changing.'

They weren't the only ones to notice. The fire officers were on their feet, looking at the map in front of them, not that there was any information there they hadn't already seen a hundred times.

'It's about time!' The commander's voice held a note of satisfaction.

If praying and hoping could change the wind, then it was working. The breeze was noticeably stronger now.

Relief washed through Bec. It wasn't over yet. Not by a long shot. But at last the tide was turning in their direction.

'Bec?' Hailey asked quietly. 'Why haven't we heard from them?'

'It'll be a while yet,' she told her. 'But I think everything's going to be all right. All we have to do is hope this wind holds.'

Not only did it hold; it got fresher with every passing minute. Bec scanned the sky and saw . . .

'Rain? It's going to rain?'

The fire officers saw them too, the dark storm clouds racing towards them, driven by the rising wind. The world seemed to hold its breath as the towering thunderheads drew ever closer. Then, with a deafening clap of thunder, the storm broke. The first heavy drops of rain hit the canvas roof of the tent. They were so very few, Bec felt as though she could hear each individual one strike the canvas. Then a few more fell. They came faster and faster. She looked out at the clearing. The first raindrops vanished the instant they hit the ground, absorbed into the dusty dry earth. But another followed. Then another. Dark patches began to form as the rain got heavier.

Laughing, Bec stepped from beneath the tent and raised her face to the sky. The water fell on to her skin, cool and clean to wash away the streaks of smoke and grime. She opened her mouth, trying to catch the sweet drops on her tongue. Hailey was beside her, laughing as she too lifted her face to the rain. Bec spread her arms wide, welcoming the life-saving water. Hailey spun around, jumping up and down as the rain soaked into her clothes and skin. They hugged each other.

'Sector Alpha calling base. Mick calling base.' The tinny

voice from the radio dragged them both back into the tent. The first officers clustered around as Bec answered.

'Base receiving you.'

'It's looking good,' the voice said. 'I'm sending everybody back there.'

Another loud clap of thunder almost, but not quite, drowned out the cheers from the small group in the tent.

'Roger that,' Bec said when the noise died down. 'We'll see you shortly.'

Shortly took for ever. Bec and Hailey stood under the cover of the tent, watching the rain falling in sheets. Even they could tell this was enough to douse the fire. The emergency was past, but they would not be happy until the firefighters returned.

The first vehicle into the clearing was a tanker truck. It disgorged a group of tired, wet men. Hailey and Bec ran out to greet them, but Steve and Nick were not among them. Next came a ute, with another load of firefighters. Still no Nick. Still no Steve. The exhausted men raised their arms to welcome the rain as they divested themselves of their jackets and helmets before seeking out food and rest.

Just when Bec felt she couldn't stand it any more, a group of men appeared at the edge of the clearing. They had walked, because there wasn't enough room on the trucks to take them.

'Nick!' Oblivious of the rain, or the watching men, Bec raced across the clearing. Nick opened his arms and she ran into them. His arms folded around her, and she felt a great weight lift from her heart. For a few seconds she simply buried her face in his chest, ignoring the smell of the soaking jacket, ignoring the soot and the rain. She just needed to be sure that he really was there. He really was safe. At last she lifted her face to his. He wasn't smiling. He wasn't laughing. His face was taut as he looked down at her. Slowly, his dark eyes softened and his lips moved in what could almost be a grin. Then he kissed her. He kissed her like she had never been kissed before. A kiss of love and passion and such desire that her legs began to tremble. She raised her good arm to his neck and pulled herself so close she could almost be a part of him as she kissed him back. The rain fell on them. It wasn't like waves crashing on a beach. It wasn't like any movie scene ever shot. It was better, because it was real.

The kiss had not lasted long enough when Bec felt Nick pull away. Reluctantly she let him go. Beside them, oblivious to the whole world, Steve and Hailey were locked in an embrace of their own.

'You shouldn't be out here in the rain,' Nick said close to Bec's ear. 'Your cast is getting wet.'

'It doesn't matter,' she said, waving it above her head. 'I don't care.'

'Well I do care.' With that simple declaration, Nick picked her up and carried her back to the shelter of the tent. Bec let herself relax into his arms. Around them, the other firefighters burst into cheers and laughter as Nick lowered her gently to the ground and kissed her again.

Bec didn't get it. She just did *not* get it. She stood in front of the feed store, looking up at the sign with her father's name on it. The two weeks since the bush-fire had passed in a whirlwind. So much had changed – and almost none of it in the way she had hoped.

Sometime today the store's new owners would arrive in town. Hailey would hand over the keys and leave with Steve. Bec had expected it would take weeks, months even, for Hailey to sell the store. But it hadn't worked out that way. Bec had mixed feelings about leaving the store. She'd hung around here since she was a kid. She'd played here with Hailey. Worked here with Hailey. Spent a lot of time here with her father, even if neither of them had known about the relationship. She had discovered that the store meant more to her than she'd known. But it was too late now to do anything about that.

Hailey hadn't told her anything about the new owners, but Bec guessed that she would be out of a job once they took over. She would have exactly nothing! She walked down the side of the store. The concrete slab outside the door was devoid of dead rodents. Even Cat, it seemed, was not himself. Maybe he was missing Nick. He would be the only one, because Bec wasn't missing him at all. Not one little bit!

She heaved a heavy sigh and unlocked the door. Hailey would be over later when the new owners arrived, but for the past two weeks she had been so busy preparing for her departure that she hadn't spent much time actually in the store. Bec had been left with all the work. Not that she begrudged Hailey her happiness. She was glad her sister had Steve. At least one of them had realised their dream. She wondered again about the conversation between her mother and Hailey. The two had talked, alone, for one entire evening, after banishing Steve and Bec to the pub. Neither had ever discussed what had passed between them, but Hailey seemed to have made her peace with Jean.

Bec shook her head and walked through into the office, where paperwork awaited. That was about all she had been doing lately. Her broken arm had made working in the store difficult. She'd relied on Hailey for some of the physical labour. Other townsfolk had helped out from time to time . . . with one notable exception. Not that she wanted Nick's help, but he should have offered.

Cat had taken over her office chair, and with some satisfaction, she pushed him off. He mewed in protest, and glared up at her. Feeling guilty, she poured some milk into his saucer. She rubbed a hand over the outside of the cast, wishing she could reach inside it and scratch the places where her skin itched. She was in a particularly foul mood today. It wasn't Cat's fault. It was Nick's fault.

Bec hadn't seen Nick since they arrived home in the wake of the bushfire. The four of them had driven back from Roma in the rain. Hailey and Steve had immediately vanished to her place. Bec hadn't needed to guess why. Their happiness surrounded them like a fuzzy pink glow, and they wanted nothing more or less than to be together. Alone. Lucky them. Bec had hoped for something similar with Nick. That kiss in the rain had finally resolved things between them. She knew now that the torch she had been carrying all these years was still as hot as the bushfire they had fought. Nick hadn't said anything, but his kiss had told her all she needed to know. The rest of the story was set. The happy-ever-after was right there, within her grasp. Except Nick didn't seem to see it. When he'd dropped her at her front door, he had kissed her gently on the lips, just enough to make her toes curl with delight, then stepped back. Then he had told her to go and make peace with her mother, and had walked away.

She hadn't seen him since. Two weeks and not so much as a phone call. Didn't he know that wasn't how it was supposed to end? She had made him watch enough old movies. He must know how the final scene went.

'Bec!'

'In here, Mum.'

Jean walked through the door, a plastic food container in her hand. 'I brought you some lunch.'

'Thanks, Mum.' Bec watch as Jean put it in the fridge.

She had made her peace with her mother. It was a fragile peace. Each tended to be on their best behaviour around the other. But it was getting better, and Bec had no doubt everything between them would be fine. At least now they weren't fighting. Her mother no longer burst into tears for no apparent reason. Bec had come to understand that Jean had done nothing wrong in her relationship with Hailey's father. In preserving her secret, she had probably done the best she could by

Hailey's entire family. Her sin had been not telling her daughter the truth. But even that had been for a good reason. Or what Jean had thought was a good reason. Who was Bec to say if she had been right or wrong?

'Is the arm bothering you?' Jean asked.

Bec nodded. 'How did you guess?'

'You get cranky when it hurts,' Jean said. 'Still, the doctor says it's doing fine. It won't be long until you're as good as new.'

That was all very well for the doctor; he didn't have to live with the terrible itching under the cast. Nor did he have to be dependent on others. Bec sighed. She really was in a terrible mood.

'The whole town is very excited about the new fire engine,' Jean said. 'I imagine there'll be quite a turnout when it arrives.'

That was the other big event scheduled for today. The money from the B&S had already been put to good use. Of course, the fire engine was being brought to town by the chief fire officer – otherwise known as Nick Price. The whole town would be on hand to welcome him and his prize. Well, good. That would make it easy for Bec to avoid him. The last thing she wanted to do was talk to him, especially in front of the whole town. She felt a pricking at the back of her eyes and knew that when she did see him, tears wouldn't be all that far away. She hated this new tendency to cry. Her mother blamed the broken arm and the painkillers. Bec blamed Nick. If he hadn't vanished like that, her emotions would not be teetering on the edge all the time. If he'd just call . . .

The phone chose that moment to ring. Bec reached for it, fighting back the little flash of hope that it might be Nick. It wasn't, of course. She forced herself to concentrate on the conversation with the sales rep.

When she handed over her keys to the store, no one was going to say she had shirked her duties.

The day seemed to last for ever. A constant stream of people dropped in to find out when the fire engine was expected, as if Bec was supposed to know. She was forced to admit that that wasn't such a ridiculous idea. After all, she was the fire brigade secretary. Nick should have told her. She hated having to confess that he hadn't. A lot of people also asked about her plans when the new store owners arrived. She had no answer for that either, and the questions only served to make a bad mood even worse. The visitors usually left at that point. Most went to the pub. If Nick didn't get back soon, his audience would be very much the worse for wear when they emerged to cheer him home.

Matt Johnson was among the last to arrive. His old brown horse sauntered down the street, Matt swaying easily to its stride. He raised a hand in greeting as he guided it towards the stable behind the pub. Standing in the open doorway of the store, Bec made a mental note to tell the new owners about Matt's horse when they got here. She hoped they'd fit in here. A town like the Creek needed the right sort of people to make it work. No one knew that better than her, now that she was facing the prospect of having no reason to stay.

That was the thought she had been fighting all day. When the new owners arrived, she would be out of a job. There were no others to be had in the Creek. She couldn't live off her mother. Besides, Jean and Rod Tate seemed to be getting close. She didn't want to be the third wheel. Her mother deserved some fun and happiness. If Bec stayed, the boredom would drive her crazy. She had come home to the creek when Hailey's parents were killed because Hailey needed her. No one needed her now. Not Hailey. Not her mother. And certainly not Nick. If there was any reason for her to stay, she couldn't see it.

Bec saw the fire truck coming when it was still half a kilometre away. You couldn't mistake it. There was a large tank on the truck bed, obviously to hold water. There were metal storage boxes along each side, and the roof of the cab was fitted with not only spotlights, but also a red light, which began flashing as Nick drove slowly past the pub. He hit the horn a couple of times, and people seemed to come from everywhere. Smiling broadly, he parked the truck between the pub and the feed store, and stepped down from the cab. He was wearing a shiny new firefighter's helmet.

'But . . . it's yellow,' Matt Johnson said. 'I thought fire trucks were red.'

'Not this one,' said Nick.

'Very nice!' Eudora Mills had appeared at the edge of the crowd. 'Of course, it would have been nicer if we'd had this before my cottage burned down.' She smiled as she said it, and a ripple of laughter ran through the crowd. Bec raised an eyebrow in surprise. Who would have guessed that Miss Mills had a sense of humour?

Bec stood back as people crowded around the fire engine. There were murmurs of praise and pleasure and many, many words of congratulation. Jean and Rod appeared from the direction of the police station. Hailey and Steve emerged and joined the crowd, who were patting Nick on the back, as if it had all been his idea and his work that had brought this shiny new toy to town. Bec avoided looking at Nick, but she watched out of the corner of her eye as he accepted the crowd's praise. He caught her looking, and grinned at her. She looked quickly away, but not before her heart had done some callisthenics. He looked so good in that silly hat. He was brimming with confidence and self-assurance.

'I think that at this point,' Ed Rutherford materialised beside Nick, 'we should have a little celebration. I would break a bottle of champagne over its noble bumper, but that seems such a terrible waste of champagne.' More laughter. 'So instead I propose we retire to the pub, and raise a glass to toast the Farwell Creek Bush Fire Brigade.'

That suggestion was greeted with the loudest cheer so far.

'Eudora, would you do us the honour perhaps of making the first toast?' Ed held out his arm in invitation.

'Well . . .' The teacher hesitated. 'Yes. I think that would be very appropriate. Thank you.'

Ignoring the raised eyebrows and surprised looks all around her, Eudora placed her hand on Ed's arm and allowed herself to be escorted to the pub. The crowd followed.

'Bec – are you coming?' Jean asked. 'This is your baby.'

'Soon,' Bec mumbled. 'I should wait a while longer, in case the new owners turn up.'

Jean grinned in the strangest way. She shared a conspiratorial look with Hailey, who was standing next to her. 'Then we'll see you in a minute,' she said. She let Rod lead her away.

Hailey grinned widely at Bec, and taking Steve's hand, she too headed for the pub. There was something going on that Bec didn't know about. She didn't have any time to think . . . because now she was alone with Nick.

'I guess I'd better park this somewhere safe,' Nick said, climbing back into the cab of the fire truck. Bec stood back as he drove it into the laneway beside the feed store and parked in a clear space near the back fence.

Bec followed on foot. She was beginning to think her bad mood was going to help her through this meeting. She could start out mad. 'I guess that will do for now,' she said abruptly. 'But the new owners might not want it there, and they are due to arrive any minute now.'

'I don't think that's going to be a problem,' Nick said confidently.

That was the last straw for Bec. Her frayed nerves could not take any more. 'Well, Nick, I'm glad you feel that way, because you can just wait here for them to arrive. I've had enough. I'm going home.'

'There's nothing to wait for,' Nick said.

The words stopped her in her tracks. 'What do you mean?'

'You don't have to wait any longer for the new owner.' He was grinning like a Cheshire cat.

'What are you talking about?'

'Let me show you.'

Bec watched as Nick started to detach something from the back of the truck. She hadn't noticed it before, but it looked like someone had strapped a large sheet of wood or metal alongside the water tank. Nick struggled with it for a few seconds. There was no way Bec was going to offer to help. Even if she'd had two good arms, he didn't deserve help. He placed his load carefully on the ground, and stepped back.

Farwell Creek Farm and Feed Supplies, the sign said in cheerful red letters. *N. & R. Price, props.*

'What . . .' Bec stared at the sign. Slowly the implication began to sink in. 'You?'

Nick looked very pleased with himself. 'Me.'

'You bought Hailey's store?'

'I did.'

'And you didn't tell me?' Bec's voice rose in anger.

'I didn't want to tell you until it was all set. It's taken a while to organise. I had to get a loan. And Hailey wanted to get the deal done quickly, so there were lawyers and so forth.'

'That's what you've been doing these past two weeks?'

'Yeah. And avoiding you. I didn't want you to know until I was certain it was going to work out.'

Those damn tears were back. Just as she had predicted. 'But I didn't know why you were avoiding me. I thought that you didn't . . . that you regretted what happened. At the bushfire,' she added, in case he had forgotten.

'Regret it?' He looked shocked. 'Why would I regret something that I have been wanting for ever?'

'But . . . ' Bec struggled to keep her cool. 'Ever since I came back, you have been . . . Well . . . That's why I went out with Gordo. I thought you didn't want me.'

'Didn't want you?' Nick suddenly laughed.

'It's not funny.' Bec took a swipe at him with her good arm.

Nick grabbed her and pulled her close. He held her in the circle of his arms, and looked down at her, his face suddenly serious.

'Bec, I always wanted you. You and me on the farm. We talked about it when we were kids . . . and I meant it. When you went to live in the city,' he said quietly, 'I was afraid you'd meet someone there. That you would forget the promises we made when we were kids.'

'No girl ever forgets a proposal,' Bec said softly. 'We were going to marry and live happily ever after.'

'Yes – but on the farm. When we lost the farm in the drought, I couldn't fulfil my promise to you any more.'

'It didn't matter.' There were tears on her cheeks now.

'It did to me.' Nick gently wiped them away. 'I had to have something to offer you.'

'All I ever wanted was you. That was enough.'

'It wasn't enough. Not for me. I had to give you more.' Nick took his arms from around her and stepped back. 'So . . . what do you think?'

Bec was laughing now as the tears continued to run down her cheeks. 'You bought Hailey's store. I'm really happy for you.'

Nick started to laugh. 'You really are having a bad day, Rebecca.'

He never called her Rebecca. She started to frown, then she looked at the sign again.

N. & R. Price.

When she finally dragged her eyes away, Nick was standing close beside her.

'I want our kids to grow up like we did – as part of this community.'

'Kids . . .' Bec's heart was singing, but she forced a stern look on to her face. 'Kids? Haven't you left something out?'

Nick put his arms around her. Careful not to hurt her broken arm, he pulled her close to him. He looked down at her and met her stern gaze with a gentle smile. 'You mean the part where I tell you that I love you, Bec O'Connell. I have loved you since I was about five years old. I will spend the rest of my life loving you.'

'That's better. And . . . ' Bec tried to joke, but the pounding of her heart was too much.

'And will you marry me?'

She said yes. At least, she must have said yes, because he was kissing her in such a way as to drive all other thoughts from her mind. Except for one thought – that she was finally home.

little black dress

brings you fantastic new books like these
every month - find out more at
www.littleblackdressbooks.com

Why not link up with other devoted Little Black
Dress fans on our Facebook group? Simply type
Little Black Dress Books into Facebook to join up.

And if you want to be the first
to hear the latest news on all things
Little Black Dress, just send the details below to
littleblackdressmarketing@headline.co.uk
and we'll sign you up to our lovely email
newsletter (and we promise that we won't share
your information with anybody else!).*

Name: _____

Email Address: _____

Date of Birth: _____

Region/Country: _____

What's your favourite Little Black Dress book?
_____

How many Little Black Dress books have you read?_____

*You can be removed from the mailing list at any time

Pick up a *little black dress* – it's a girl thing.

978 0 7553 4715 5

THE FARMER NEEDS A WIFE
Janet Gover
PBO £5.99

Rural romances become all the rage when editor Helen Woodley starts a new magazine column profiling Australia's lovelorn farmers. But a lot of people (and Helen herself) are about to find out that the course of true love ain't ever smooth . . .

It's not all haystacks and pitchforks, ladies – get ready for a scorching outback read!

HIDE YOUR EYES
Alison Gaylin
PBO £5.99

Samantha Leiffer's in big trouble: the chest she saw a sinister man dumping into the Hudson river contained a dead body, meaning she's now a witness in a murder case. It's just as well hot, hard-line detective John Krull is by her side . . .

978 0 7553 4802 2

'Alison Gaylin is my new must-read' Harlen Coben

You can buy any of these other
Little Black Dress titles from your
bookshop or *direct from the publisher*.

FREE P&P AND UK DELIVERY
(Overseas and Ireland £3.50 per book)

The Love Boat	Kate Lace	£5.99
Trick or Treat	Sally Anne Morris	£5.99
Tug of Love	Allie Spencer	£5.99
Sunnyside Blues	Mary Carter	£5.99
Heartless	Alison Gaylin	£5.99
A Hollywood Affair	Lucy Broadbent	£5.99
I Do, I Do, I Do	Samantha Scott-Jeffries	£5.99
Perfect Image	Marisa Heath	£5.99
Girl From Mars	Julie Cohen	£5.99
True Love and Other Disasters	Rachel Gibson	£5.99
The Hen Night Prophecies: The One That Got Away	Jessica Fox	£5.99
You Kill Me	Alison Gaylin	£5.99
The Fidelity Project	Susan Conley	£5.99
Leopard Rock	Tarras Wilding	£5.99
Smart Casual	Niamh Shaw	£5.99
See Jane Score	Rachel Gibson	£5.99
Animal Instincts	Nell Dixon	£5.99
It Should Have Been Me	Phillipa Ashley	£5.99
Dogs and Goddesses	Jennifer Crusie, Anne Stuart, Lani Diane Rich	£5.99
Sugar and Spice	Jules Stanbridge	£5.99

TO ORDER SIMPLY CALL THIS NUMBER

01235 400 414

or visit our website: www.headline.co.uk

Prices and availability subject to change without notice.